The book is set in the Interregnum, the period of Parliamentarian and military rule between 1649-1660.

Charlotte A. Hutt was born in Switzerland. She came to England to learn the language. Charlotte married in England where she has lived and worked for many years. She has two children and four grandchildren and lives in Suffolk, where she has completed a BA with the Open University.

Also by Charlotte A. Hutt

Rosalind Mayhew's Maxims
Bright Swan (Short Stories)
A Very Peculiar Talent
A Quarter Turn Of The Screw

BASHIBA'S TALE

(SANCTUARY)

By Charlotte A Hutt

 **New Generation Publishing**

Prologue

The children became bored waiting for the witch in the graveyard and started to play *Sanctuary*, like Aggy used to when she had been little.

'Home. Safe. You can't touch me,' Jenny yelled with the others, crouching down and touching her little bit of earth when she was chased by the child who was *It*.

But now the children fell silent letting the procession of adults pass, the adults who were about to try the Maid Agatha, no longer a child but a lovely young woman, for witchcraft in the church.

Aggy walked tall and erect, fiddling with her amazing red hair and adjusting her white bodice in an uninterested fashion. She looked as if she knew she was the most beautiful maid ever born in the village. Didn't she realise she was thought of as *It* as she was being led into the church by Squire de Breville, followed by the Parson and John Cooper, who was writing a record of the trial, and all able-bodied men in the village?

The trial was a farce.

It took about as long as swatting the blow fly which had winged its way into the church before the ancient wooden doors were shut against the afternoon's airless heat.

Squire de Breville led the trial.

Old Eli, in charge of the spell needle, and the men who had taken her into custody were sworn in as jurors.

So was John Cooper, who was about to keep a record and who was a relative of the accused.

None would be able to give evidence now.

Stuttering Jim and his mangy dog which never left his side, and Sidney, a great lad who was wanting, made up the rest of the jury.

There it was, but Squire was awesome when

crossed. The fat vein on his forehead was already throbbing and nobody dared point out the jury was short of men as everybody had enough of bad luck, which had come to the village threefold.

The old witch-elm by the pond, packed with rooks keeping a cackling guard over the village, sprouted no new greenery in the spring. It stood rook-stacked and desolate like a giant witch's broom, and then the wells ran low.

God sent the rain, and the devil kept it away in this unnatural summer. Empty bellies would follow a ruined harvest. The sun burned brown ridges through the barley, and polecats died within their stink in the open.

Stomach cramps came next, and then the Parson's wife found the witch out.

The maid Agatha, a servant at the parsonage, had been caught in the very act.

The charges laid against her by Squire were that of being a witch. She had conjured up spells to bring sickness on the Parson's wife by the manifestation of needles in her broth, and these spells were also used to bring evil and sickness onto the village by causing a drought.

'Handle yourself right, child, and then it will come out just for us all,' her father prayed silently.

His heart sank when he looked at her, so fresh, so lovely, so untouched by the heat, as she smiled her pearly smile at him. It enforced an impression that nothing could touch her.

Parson Wilcox gave his evidence first.

He was sworn in, and Squire said to carry on, they all knew who he was and what he did for a living.

'Agatha cleaned the house and washed the linen,' he said. 'She prepared the noonday broth, and it was as harmless as mother's milk when she placed it on the table.'

After they had helped themselves to the broth, he had said Grace.

'The Mistress's condition makes her agitated at times. She's new to the village, and she has no older woman she can turn to.'

'Is this relevant?' Squire asked.

'Do you want my evidence or not?' the Parson thundered, indicating he had authority in God's house.

Squire mopped his brow and waved him on with an impatient hand.

Parson said he was used to his wife's irrational moods. He paused briefly to swipe at a fly buzzing around his head.

'When the Mistress ran from the table I carried on eating for a while. Then I went upstairs to comfort her, but she wasn't there. When I came downstairs, I saw Agatha being bundled off by two men. You, Squire, were in the yard, but nobody furnished an explanation.'

Then he had seen his wife, who was bleeding from the mouth. She said it was caused by needles manifesting themselves in her soup. When he looked into her dish, he found it awash with needles.

'How did they get there?' he asked faintly, and Squire said sharply that was for the jury to decide.

'The Mistress does her sewing in the bedroom, and she had been engaged in tasks other than that upstairs, and she had never touched the broth as it was Agatha's task.'

Parson Wilcox removed his hat, swore he had told the truth, and the fly settled next to Squire's hammer.

Parson's wife said she had just lifted her spoon to her mouth when she had seen Agatha looking at her with her queer violet eyes. All of a sudden Agatha was bathed in a golden glow, and her hair seemed to be aflame.

T'was a sign from God, for I did not swallow. I

looked for the cause of the sharp pain suddenly in my mouth, and found it to be a needle. I ran away and found Eli, who fetched you, Squire, and your men.'

A long sigh swayed through the church, and finally Agatha was called.

'You've heard it all, and it's all lies,' she said. 'Do I have to go over it?'

Squire said it might be advantageous.

'It might be wot?'

'Just do it! Did you put needles into your Mistress's broth?'

'Hardly.'

'Did you put a spell on her?'

'I did not.'

'Did you wish evil on her?'

Agatha tossed her head, and her hair flew around her head like sparkling fire.

'I often wished the old harridan would drop dead and the well would run low.'

A deep silence, and Agatha realised her case needed restating.

'There's too much cleaning and washing, and I might have spit into her broth.'

She paused.

'I might have put a touch, just a touch, of hemlock into her soup, just to make her feel poorly and take to her bed. I mean, she is still here.'

Long intakes of breath; witches were drawn to hemlock.

Aggy looked around her.

'You folks ought to know this trial is all fixed.'

Uproar.

Squire used his order-keeping hammer three times, and the irritating fly would miss the grand display of the witch. It clung tighter to the tool than the mist which would shortly cloud memories.

'When her poison failed to work she resorted to trickery,' said Squire.

Aggy's father wept quietly into his hat.

He started to say his daughter was too stupid to differentiate between hemlock and cow parsley, but he was shouted down.

An examination revealed a witch mark on his daughter. A little whispering devil sitting on her shoulder had left his sucking mark under her shoulder blade. It was in the shape of a moon, and nobody was surprised when the spell-needle failed to draw blood.

'Put her to the test,' cried the Squire.

'I object,' cried the Parson, but he was overruled.

When at last the doors of the church were flung open, the children held hands.

One of them, a little girl, freed herself and ran towards her mother, hiding in her skirts.

'Oh! Jenny is unlucky,' the others whispered, watching her, slack-jawed; Jenny had broken the ring.

They scattered and hid behind the gravestones, secretly watching the ritual display of the witch before they joined the procession winding its way through the village. Raising clouds of dust, it was led by Parson and Squire, followed by the girl who tried to adjust her steps to those of the two men pinning her arms behind her back.

More and more villagers adhered to the procession, like bees to a hive, as they rolled through the village. The girl remained silent as she passed her cottage. She saw her cat nailed to her cottage door, her Ma moving her lips and wringing her hands.

Aggy looked back, queerly twisted between her two captors, her eyes staring and wide open and her red hair streaming loose down her back, her white bodice torn.

She never said a word. Then she saw her Pa on his knees, flailing the ground with his hands raising the dust.

Of a sudden there was a shriek. Aggy's Ma ran after them. She fought her way through the throng and threw her arms around Parson's neck, knocking his hat to the ground.

'Save her, Parson, save her,' she screamed, turning and looking at Aggy, 'save her sweet soul.'

The procession moved on as the woman slunk back to her cottage. She turned around once when she heard Aggy's screams, who had seen the pond. T'was proof of her guilt. Witches couldn't abide water, it was as hot as hellfire to them, some had melted in it.

The sun was yellow fire.

Aggy offered no resistance. Just before four men swung her over the pond, she said that *He* would be sorry, his life would be a living hell from now on.

She didn't scream it, shout it or hiss it, nor was it aimed at anybody in particular which was all the more disturbing. Who exactly was being cursed?

Most villagers chanted the count as she was flung into the stinking, stagnant water disturbing the hovering cover of gnats.

After the count of sixty the muddy island of water amidst the chickweed-covered pool remained undisturbed. They chanted the count again, and again until she rose up in the pond, her skirt billowing.

A mighty cheer went up which disturbed the rooks nesting in the witch-elm, filling the air with beating wings.

Aggy had drowned, she was guilty. Some of the men saw to her burial in the fields, some went about their jobs, and Parson Wilcox followed Squire de Breville to the Manor after it was done.

The Squire knew what the Parson wanted, but the record of the trial had been burnt, Squire said.

Parson Wilcox took off his hat.

10

'But I will have nought to show the Rector,' he said.

'T'was nought,' said Squire, and it was a very poor record John Cooper had kept, he had better forget it.

'She fell into the pond,' he added, 'stupid girl as she was, and lest we forget, she was a poisoner. She was spared a public hanging amongst strangers.'

He went indoors and slammed the door in Parson's face.

The women sat in their cottages. Some put their aprons over their heads as they rocked to and fro and wept and remembered a girl growing up amongst them, and some examined their children to see if something was amiss with them.

Lightning rent the sky and split the old elm in two, and still the rains failed. The sky above hung heavy with blood-purple clouds edged with gold, laced with lightning. A mighty gust of wind and they would float away and spread their load someplace else.

Pray God that doesn't happen, the villagers wanted to say, but their actions had been tainted and excluded God, so they drove Agatha's parents out of their cottage and onto the road. When they set fire to the witch's homestead a few drops of rain fell. After it burned down, it rained heavily and everybody slept well in the sweet, cooling air.

It rained for three days. The fourth day was a Sunday and they all went to Church.

Squire de Breville sat in the front pew with his beautiful daughter, the Lady Eloise, who was dressed all in green silk.

Parson's wife sat in the pew behind, wearing a spotless white fichue over her Puritan black dress, a sprig of rosemary for remembrance on her prayer book.

Parson Wilcox was absent. He had a fever, and the Rector, summoned to give sorely needed comfort to this congregation, preached a sermon about God's infinite goodness and mercy, the one he invariably preached when called upon.

He reminded his flock that Parson Wilcox was ordained by God as his Minister on this Earth and in particular that his living was in this parish and that the tithe was due come Michaelmas.

The villagers sang, *'Now thank we all our God'* with great gusto and willingly enough.

They didn't grumble about the tithe as they normally did, but they thought the Rector, who got a part of every vicar's tithe, could have left off pleading for his cut just the once. But there it was, the two sure things in life were, as always, death and taxes.

Before the Reformation, pilgrims to Our Lady's Shrine at Walsingham had broken their journey and worshipped at Saint Agnes in the village of Ninewells.

Walsingham had been razed to the ground, and the Virgin and the Babe Jesus had been taken from the church-niche of Saint Agnes's church and smashed into non-existence by the Reformation's iconoclastic horde.

They had left them Saint Agnes with her glorious reds and blues in the stained-glass window though. The patron saint of pure and innocent young girls, she was carrying a lamb.

The cottagers didn't dwell on the sacrifice pictured above them, of Saint Agnes eternally looking across to the broken body of Jesus in the opposite window, the sacrifice continued in the strip underneath with Abraham's knife at Isaac's throat, the unsuspecting sheep looking on comfortably from the bushes.

Sacrifice had become an unspeakable deed now that the hard, unyielding ground had water welling from every crack, overflowing water, an abundance of water.

It was the thought that putting one of their own to death might be repeated which reverberated like distant thunder in their minds. Could it happen again, they wondered, and could it be one of their own kin who would be *'It'* next time round?

A small girl was sitting in church waiting for Saint Agnes's light to shine on her. It happened sometimes when a shaft of sunlight struck the stained-glass window, but it didn't happen today. It was raining. The church was crowded with people huddled in their wet coats and shawls.

When Jenny looked up, she saw that Saint Agnes was weeping.

Chapter 1

From the outside there seemed to be no better place than the Parsonage.

Not large like the manor house with its two wings looming up on either side like two guard-dogs, it was just a gabled house with pretty little leaded windows glimpsed through the sprawling branches of an old, slanting willow, with white butterflies zig-zagging drunkenly across the lavender-lined path in high summer.

Sometimes Jenny felt uncomfortable in the Parsonage, but never in the mornings, when she rose with the sun. She liked this time of day, when the sun slowly edged over the horizon colouring the sky, and she liked being up and about before everybody else.

The whole world belonged to her then, and to Sidney who did the rough work in the grounds. At twenty seven he was a great lumbering lad ten years older than she was. He was a bit simple, but she could mother him like her brother Adam, although without any of Adam's lip.

She hastily collected the eggs from the coop before Sidney got his great paws on them; he liked a raw egg or two. When he lumbered to the back door with the wood and the kindling, she saw to the fire under the cooking pot.

It was nice and orderly, and Jenny liked it that way.

Sidney always ate alone in the kitchen, partial to the cold, left-over porridge from the breakfast. He ate great quantities of it as it was the one area the Mistress never investigated, mean as she was with food.

Most mornings Jenny's great black dog, Stray, came to the door, making sure she had survived the night, and although she begged the great black beast to relieve himself some other place than Parson's yard, it made no difference.

The Mistress disliked having the dog around. It paid to keep the Mistress on an even keel and she wasn't kept on it when the dog did his business here when he had the whole countryside to choose from.

Jenny's spirits always began to sag when the creaking stairs announced that the Mistress was about to descend into her day, but at times the Mistress left off clearing her throat, her disapproving looks softened and she let Jenny bake the sourbread loaves. At times she relented and let Jenny tend the kitchen garden, although the pleasures of these pursuits were always tempered by the thought that the cleaning would have to be done later, although washing the linen got her out of the house if nothing else.

There was no comfort here, Jenny thought, because there was no underlying care for people, not like at home.

She missed Ma and Pa, and Adam. She immersed her scrubbing brush in the pail of water and then she stopped.

A black pair of lace-up boots was planted squarely by the bucket and Jenny knew full well that these boots were filled to the brim with Parson's wife, whose misery covered everything like a creeping fen-fog.

Parson's wife waved a white cloth at Jenny like she always did, and Jenny knew full well what she would say before she said it, and moved her lips to the words.

'Set to, set to. Mind you do that floor properly, child. This chamber is square, not round, and when it's done, I intend to examine all the corners with this white kerchief.'

The harsh, unfriendly voice disturbed her even though she had expected it.

'Are you betrothed or walking out?' she asked and

Jenny shook her head.

That was a new one, she thought, although her Pa said many times that at her age her Ma was running after Jenny and looking after the old folks.

'Looks don't last. Has no young man shown any interest in a pretty girl like you?'

'No,' Jenny said, 'only Sidney, and he's wanting. Well, not exactly wanting, he's more like a brother.'

Then she thought she ought to explain this lack of interest shown to her by the village lads.

'They don't like me because I have a certain reputation.'

'A cer..tain repuu..ta..tion?!'

The Mistress's voice had risen with every syllable until it stuck to the oak beams.

'I see the lads off and tell 'em to keep their great paws to themselves, and now I have a certain reputation as being stuck-up, uppity, above myself. It's not because I think I'm better or anything like that, but because what the others call *larking about* seems a silly sort of a game to me.'

'There's not much choice in a village,' Parson's wife said in a more normal voice and Jenny replied tartly that was precisely why she wasn't walking out yet.

'I'm not fussed, there's plenty of time yet.'

'Not as much as you might think. You can't afford to be choosy in a small place,' Parson's wife advised her. 'It isn't a pleasant thing to be an elderly spinster of the parish,' she added grimly.

The Mistress turned away, and as she reached the door she turned back and asked Jenny a couple of peculiar questions.

'Have you ever been pursued against your will?'

'Pursued? By whom?'

'Did you hear aught last night?' Jenny was asked silkily, as if it was some kind of an afterthought, and

Jenny realised their talk before had been a conversation into which the Mistress hadn't been able to weave these particular strands.

Last night she had thought she dreamt of a fire and she had heard whispering voices, and so she said uneasily that she had not heard or seen anything. A dream was only a dream, after all.

After the Mistress departed silently, Jenny minded her peace. The woman was near her time, that could account for all manner of things.

Chapter 2

Two babes of Parson Wilcox and his wife had been born dead, and the villagers had been sorry for their heartbreak. For Parson more so than his wife; she was not from the village for a start and she didn't enjoy village life.

She kept herself to herself.

Fast approaching the end of her child-bearing years, just as the perceived village wisdom had it that there would be no more apples falling from that particular tree, she had upped and got herself with child once more.

Jenny got on with the floor, remembering what she was here for. Not for day-dreaming, but to earn a shilling or two to complete the rent-money for Ma and Pa come Michaelmas, and maybe there would be a goose for their Michaelmas feast this year.

They bartered a great deal at home. Ma had no oven but she made butter in exchange for bread. But no amount of bartering produced the coins for the rent. Pa grew and sold the barley he grew on his strip of land and helped out at the Manor. Keeping a roof over their heads was an eternal worry now that Squire had decreed that taking a rent-debt over into another year, even by a few coins, would nullify the agreement.

'In other words, Jenny,' her Pa had said, 'we'll be out on our ear if we don't pay up,' and her Ma said if Jenny was sensible she wouldn't be dismissed.

The Civil War had passed by the village and it had never touched some, all bar one family when their Joushua had gone as a pikeman for King Charles' army, and Pa had lost his small herd of cows overnight when the army had been near.

The Civil War had been the cause of the hole they

found themselves in now. It had taken an age just to get the one cow, and so much land had been enclosed, which had been King Charles's big idea, they had to walk far afield to find common land and collect their wood.

Some had done well for themselves though. Farmer Morrow for one. T'was rumoured that he was wealthier than Squire de Breville himself.

His son had been sent to the Inns of Court in London for his learning.

'Come back as a lawyer, Young Morrow has. He's learned how to be crooked in a legal fashion,' her Pa, who had crossed swords with him in the past, had said.

The law, the rules of the land, was conducted in Latin, a dead language which only other lawyers and university folk were familiar with.

'Only two universities in the whole of England, Oxford and Cambridge; that'll tell you how rare learning is.'

Even Pa himself had been taught to read and write by the Parson's wife afore this one, but not Latin. Women were just the same as the poor and lacked access to the seats of learning, even Pa would be hard-pushed not to sign his own death-warrant in Latin.

Right enough, Young Morrow had come back as a lawyer in silk breeches which set off his bandy legs a treat.

'Silk-breeches,' the children had called out, throwing stones through the arch once they had got used to his finery, and he had never said a word. One time though he had got off his horse to chase them, and he wasn't best pleased.

He put one of 'em on his horse, screaming, and rode him miles away from the village and left him there. A boy of no more than five.

The teasing stopped after that.

After two days, Silk-breeches let on where he had taken the boy; he had had to really when he had seen all the able-bodied men advancing with hoes and sickles, looking any which way but at him.

He had been mighty glad when he had found the child unharmed. Hungry, of course, and talking in tongues with fear.

Now it was rumoured that Silk-breeches, a coarse, tall man with pale eyes set wide apart in a swarthy face, wanted to wed Squire's beautiful, delicate daughter, the Lady Eloise, and that Squire himself was for the match.

There seemed to be some truth in it. Since his return from London, Young Morrow clung to the Manor tighter than a bad smell.

Squire was the county sheriff collecting taxes from the shire of Cambridge. Squire was also impoverished, so the saying went.

The Manor had been his country seat, but now it was his only seat. T'was rumoured he had lost his other houses through gambling.

Jenny's Pa often said he wished he was that impoverished that he had only one seat to his name, he was often hard pushed to find a seat for his old breeches.

Squire's first wife had died after three years of marriage, although 'committed suicide' might perhaps be a more accurate description according to Pa, seeing as how she had been dangling from the Manor's Great Gallery.

She had gone riding despite being eight months with child and she had lost the de Breville heir. All the same she had been well-liked, lively, kind, unlike the Lady Margot who came after her.

Lady Margot had been German, haughty, handsome, high-born and high-falluting. What's more, she had also failed to produce a male heir to carry on the old name of de Breville, and Eloise, their only daughter had been awesomely spoilt. Even more so after her mother had died of some long drawn-out illness.

The village gossip ran round in Jenny's head when she came back into the present. She shivered as the sun's sudden rays illuminated a dark afternoon sky, and she suddenly recalled last night clearly.

She had woken up and seen small flames. After a while she had realised it was Parson's face illuminated by a flickering candle held aloft.

He had taken a sudden tumble down the steep steps leading to Jenny's gabled room in a whirl of nightshirt and severe language, landing neatly at his wife's feet.

'The child had the night horrors,' he had whispered to his wife.

'Likely.'

'T'is my bounden duty to look after one in my care,' he had insisted and Parson's wife said likely it was.

Likely, Jenny had thought, and she had been as unconvinced as Parson's wife.

'When will you ever learn,' the Mistress had hissed of a sudden. 'All the things I have condoned in the past for the sake of a new beginning betwixt us and now....'

'Hush,' Parson had said, 'think on the listeners. Think on,' and, recalling it now, Jenny shuddered.

The attic space was cramped and offered no hiding-place. A curtain made a small space for her clothes, the bed under the roof-slope was narrow, and the bolt keeping the half-stable doors together had been broken.

The more she thought about it, the greater her unease became, but oftentimes the Parson talked to her when the Mistress was not about and she always enjoyed these lively encounters.

If an opportunity arose tomorrow, she would ask the

21

Parson what was amiss with him.

Sensible was always best, she decided. If she left in the middle of the week, her Ma might think she had misbehaved and had been dismissed, and she couldn't bear that. She would wait until Sunday.

After the service, she would walk home with Ma and Pa and Adam and she would ask her Pa for some way to fasten the doors from the inside. Then her mind turned to unravelling the meaning of *sensible*. Did it mean behaving well, or did it mean listening to her senses which told her that something was terribly wrong in this house?

Chapter 3

Finally it was Sunday.

When Jenny told her Ma and Pa of her unease, of the awful silences, the pair of 'em taking a turn in the garden silently and keeping an exact same distance from each other with their elbows tucked in so that they wouldn't touch, her Pa said that Jenny was at the Parsonage to work, not to busy herself ear-wigging.

'It must be vexing being spied on by you,' he said, 'leave 'em in peace.'

Ma had agreed.

'You know full well what happens when folks are cooped up together the livelong day. No matter how fond of 'em you are, there are times when you wish they would draw breath some place else, but t'is a private affair which bides no onlookers.'

Pa said no good would come of it.

Why didn't they have sensible children like other folks? Neither Jenny nor young Adam had the sense they were born with. Jenny didn't realise when she was well off in the Parsonage earning money, and as for young Adam, who had snared a rabbit on Squire's land practically in full view of the Manor, now Adam, he was bound to come to a bad end.

'I'm not proud of it,' Adam said, putting on a baby-voice, as if that made it any better. When Jenny ruffled his hair and asked him if he didn't think he was getting too old for baby-tricks he kicked her in the shins and said just because she had been away she didn't know it all now.

They had made it up and Jenny listened to his music. Adam was a wizard on the flute, and she promised to ask the Mistress if she would give Adam instructions on her spinet.

Pa wasn't against it. The Parson's wife afore this one had taught him the letters.

'She can only say aye or nay,' he said.

'Don't be bold, Jenny, it isn't becoming, and take heart, nothing is for always,' her Ma said before Jenny left that Sunday, knowing full well that she had passed her own spirited ways onto the girl. 'Sensible is always best, bear it in mind and then you won't be dismissed.'

Jenny ran back to the Parsonage in the late afternoon, earlier than she need have done to get into the Mistress's good books. She stared at the Parsonage's side-door for a long, long time. The roses rambling around the door were still tight buds waiting for sunshine to open them up and whilst Jenny was waiting for some courage to go into the house, she rehearsed the conversation that would ensue.

The Mistress was bound to ask how her family fared.

'I hope you're well and I'm back again, Mistress,' she announced finally when she went into the house.

'I can see that, and you're late.'

'Well no, I'm not late, not really. I'm not meant to be here until nightfall. That was the arrangement. You might recall it, Mistress. '

'In that case it would appear that you are early.'

The secret of good time-keeping appeared to be exact time-keeping, and Jenny thought to herself that she would be sensible from now on if it killed her. This meant that she would have to rearrange her face from its present scowl to something resembling winsomeness. She had to ask for a favour, a promise was a promise, although her Pa had been wrong, the Mistress didn't say aye or nay to her request, she didn't have to.

'Your brother Adam? Playing my spinet?'

The Mistress wrinkled her nose in her effort to

recall exactly which filthy urchin Adam might be. Her tone suggested that cottagers weren't likely to know the meaning of music, and very possibly didn't have souls. The spinet was a piece of furniture to Jenny and her ilk, to be polished and admired, and it wasn't to be mentioned ever again.

When Parson took Jenny to one side and explained that the spinet was very personal to the Mistress, Jenny felt smaller than ever. At home there had been some disagreements, but never like this. Here everybody was watching everybody else and people moved slowly and silently and carefully as if they were afraid that some animal might suddenly pounce, as Parson's wife was watching Parson and Jenny was watching Parson's wife.

Jenny stopped scrubbing the floor next day for a moment and looked at her white hands. The Mistress had made up a salve for her when they had turned red and sore and she had been unable to twist the fine thread she had spun. Their colour always made her think of Aggy's hair floating to the surface of the stagnant pond.

Jenny had been little, hiding in her Ma's skirts when cousin Aggy had been drowned. It was a dreadful time, a time when her Ma wasn't able to cope. When her Ma couldn't cope, nobody else could, and her Pa had said as they were Aggy's kin it would be an ill omen if they didn't go along to the testing.

Jenny couldn't connect the stinking pond-water with the sweet rain that fell later from the sky, nor the part cousin Aggy had played in it.

'Was there aught amiss with Aggy apart from a temper?' she asked her Ma.

Ma said no. Aggy had been spoilt on account of her beauty, and she wasn't overbright, that was all.

'If you had been allowed into the church at the trial,

you could have stopped it, couldn't you?' Jenny said, but her Ma didn't say anything and buried her face in her hands.

Chapter 4

Jenny's mother worried about her girl at the Parsonage.

The girl was like her in many ways, hard-working but not given to blind acceptance of what should or should not be questioned, a view shared by Parson's wife who thought of it as obstinate.

The girl was that, and also headstrong. Jenny couldn't understand why she couldn't work during the day and then go home and sleep there. And then she had grumbled about her cramped attic chamber, reached by a steep ladder housed behind a cupboard door in the kitchen.

'If Edith managed so can you.'

Edith had been a fair size, willing but thick as a wall, the Mistress had thought. It had taken an age to teach her to clean the stairs from the top, to sweep a floor before washing it, to put roasting beef into a hot oven to seal the juices and to break an egg into a cup before sliding it into a pan before frying to keep the yolk intact. Spinning the flax had seemed entirely beyond her.

When finally she had been able to tell her left hand from her right foot and she had got the hang of it, the girl had the gall to get wed.

She had to admit that Jenny had known all of this and more, but was she a child though, was she getting on sixteen, seventeen? She was not walking out, she had said, and there was such an open, child-like look of innocence about her it was hard to tell her age. She would have to find out how old the girl was, she thought, but softly, softly. She must have been quite, quite mad to have another young girl in the house, a cousin of Agatha at that, but she had been convinced that Agatha had been a singular moment of summer madness.

Her error had been brought home to her vividly when she heard the stairs creaking the night before, she had cursed her carelessness, she had caught him in the very act of climbing to the attic slope, and of course Jenny had lied to her, she had made out she had been asleep and had heard nothing of their early morning set-to.

The girl was covering up for the Parson and she intended to prove it this very day, whereas Jenny's day started with good intentions. The Parson did talk to her, but he merely liked the company of a cheerful sort like Jenny.

Sidney was walking around Jenny with a lot of sighing and her dog, Stray, had limped in late. It looked like he had been in a fight.

She put a bit of old hessian on the back-door step and told him to lie down and warm himself when the sun came out properly, then she saw to Sidney. He was sitting on the bench under the old crab-apple, the bee-tree as Adam called it on account of the many bees swarming in it in late spring.

'I don't mean to make you cry any,' said Sidney, 'only Pa said I would not have nought to do with you after the Mistress had a talk with him and I can't touch aught what's little. I hurt it. Like that kitten. I loved it but it died when I didn't let go of it.'

It was the longest speech of Sidney's life. It not only amazed Jenny but also himself that he had this unexpected gift for speech-making. It quite cheered him up.

So it did Jenny, who said she didn't mind Sidney as a friend, the Mistress would have to mind her business. When she ran down the path and into the house, he trotted beside her, beaming down at her as usual.

The Parson, who had been disturbed by the cramped

28

condition of their maid's chamber, was feeling out of sorts.

He had never troubled himself to look at the attic space before, but he had been restless in the night, writing up his diary in the parlour as was his wont, when he had heard a muffled cry from above.

He had opened the cupboard-door in the kitchen and climbed the narrow steps with his candle. It seemed an unkindly way to house girls, but the three small, unused bedrooms could only be accessed through the huge master- bedroom.

It might be wise to alter the house with a landing, but he couldn't say anything to the Mistress now; a thin line of meanness ran right through her in her present state. He was unclear as to its cause. He thought vaguely that it was the nesting instinct which made her focus entirely on herself.

'I have a mind to saddle the pony and...'

'Horse,' she said.

'Pony. Its span is less than fifteen hands.' He drew a deep breath. 'And see Joshua this morning, Mistress,' he continued. 'He's in a sore state of health and didn't attend church last Sunday. And his family is laid low, so they say.'

He might take Jenny. She had a pleasant way with her, and she had worked wonders with Sidney. Her pretty face might bring some cheer into the cottages where people had given up hope. Women dying before their time, worn out with continual childbirth or dying in its throes, men in ill-health passing away and leaving families without a breadwinner and without a roof over their heads. Men drunk and terrorising their families, leaving women and children with bruised limbs and faces and a dead spirit.

It happened when hope had fled, and sometimes it was all too easy to give in.

It needed strong people like Margret and John Cooper, Jenny's parents, to hope for a better life, ambushed as they had been just when the end of the road to being a yeoman farmer had been within their sight, their herd taken to feed the army.

He would make sure the Mistress paid Jenny well at Michaelmas.

He had hoped that a wife would take on some of the nearer cottages in his spread-out parish like his mother before she had passed on, but charity hadn't been on his wife's list.

It had been her duty to tend to cottagers with her mother, she had told him. If there was a worse smell than sick, untreated human flesh, she would be surprised to hear of it.

'What do you think it might be with Joshua,' she asked, 'is it aught catching?'

'Hard to say,' he replied, 'fever and scabs. Unpleasant, few want to go near. I reckon myself it might be malnutrition.'

'Fever and scabs and unpleasant odours no doubt, and you want to bring it here in my state? It might be thought you were snooping around. If everyone looked after their own, this galloping around after all and sundry wouldn't be called for.'

'T'is a cold charity that stops at the hearth, Mistress,' he growled.

'T'is a cold charity that doesn't start at the hearth, Husband. I want you to kill me a fowl this morning,' she said.

'God's truth,' said Parson, 'I'm not chasing any chickens. Not this morning. I have my sermon to see to as well.'

'I shall have to prepare the room for the birth,' said the Mistress.'Sidney has to finish the door of the outhouse and Jenny will have to see to the baking, and then the herb garden needs sorting.The sorrel is rampant. I'll feel easier in my mind if all is as it should be.'

She straightened and felt the hollow of her back.

'Don't bother yourself any on my account, Husband,' she said, 'I can always use some of the salted beef I have put down. I had a fancy for a short-legged fowl or two maybe, but who am I to ask for favours?' She sighed. 'I reckon favours are for favourites, don't you, Jenny?'

Jenny nearly choked on her bread, and the Parson declared that nothing would give him greater pleasure than to wring a chicken's neck. In any case, most of the salt beef had gone to Joshua.

When he chased the hens he disturbed the roosters in the alder trees. Their frantic, high-pitched and irregular cackling had not helped to sooth the Mistress's frayed nerve-ends any; Jenny flew down the garden path to suppress her rising mirth.

Her merriment was not yet over. Sidney reported that he had fixed the out-house.

'See,' he said, and proudly demonstrated to his captive audience the opening of the new door which promptly and slowly fell out of its hinges.

'T'is broken, Master.' He scratched his head. 'It needs mending,' he added brightly.

'Isn't it marvellous,' Parson said, 'how Sidney manages to impart a real sense of discovery to the obvious.'

'Aye, Master,' said Sidney proudly, 'I have a way with words, Jenny said.'

When the Parson said the spark of divinity found in all humankind was somewhat dimmed in the lad, his wife said his keep didn't amount to much. It would be even less shortly, she thought; she couldn't inflict his idiotic presence on her coming child.

She had seen Sidney's father and planted the seed that he was a sexual bother to Jenny and it was time they got wed.

'Talking of great brutes,' the Mistress said to Jenny who was deftly plucking the bird, 'did I see that black dog of yours hanging around the yard this morning?'

'I don't know, Mistress,' she said. It was a lie. Parson's wife had nearly tripped over him on the step and the dog had merely turned his head and stared at her.

He was a big beast, half the size of a horse, with a square head and greenish eyes. She had retreated silently on hearing the grumble emitting from his throat like rumbling thunder. No matter, his days were numbered along with Jenny's and Sidney's, and she would get rid of this unholy trinity in one fell swoop.

'Oh, Sidney has made off with my mob-cap again,' Jenny remembered as she washed her hands.

'What a wicked waste, apart from which servants have to have their heads covered. Wind your hair up for the present.'

Jenny bowed her head as Parson was saying his prayers at the dinner table. The Mistress glanced at him covertly as he asked for God's blessing to descend on this house.

Some chance she thought when she saw his glance resting on the child. She observed Jenny intently for a reaction, and of a sudden she saw her as if for the first time.

'My God,' she thought aghast, 'she's not just pretty, she is quite lovely.' Perfect skin, the piled-up, obedient hair crowning the small round face. That high, round cheek, how she envied it, it wouldn't have come amiss on a high-born lady, although highborn ladies wore a bit more than a simple shift underneath their dresses.

Agatha had been tall, stately, her red hair springing

from a low forehead with wide-set, black-fringed eyes deep-blue as a summer sky, her top lip swelling as if from a bee-sting. She had been very aware of her startling beauty.

Jenny was unaware of her looks and naturally neat and tidy. This contrasted with Parson's wife. She, who so loved to be neat, had to fight a daily battle with unmanageable hair, tears in skirts, smudges on her face and twisting fichues with a will of their own.

Jenny made her feel awkward, old and ugly. What irked her most though was the sheer unfairness of life. She had heard that a woman bloomed in pregnancy and these maids blossomed into beauties when they reached puberty, whereas she was not granted a metamorphosis even if she was with child. She remained haggard, the coming child forming a disfiguring lump under her breast. No doubt these maids, sleek, well-fed cats, would give birth to healthy, live children whereas she felt like an animal wintering over in the wild, trusting to nothing but instincts and wits.

'Where is your apron, girl?' she hissed. 'Why don't you look after your cap? Don't you ever dare come to the table again in this state.'

'I won't, Mistress,' said Jenny, 'I'm sorry,' but something else was on her mind. 'The stone wall needs fixing else the cattle might get over it,' she said.

The Parson looked up from his broth, lost in the injustice of a man who couldn't do as he liked in his own house, afraid as he was that the Mistress would find out the way the salted beef had gone.

'The maids will have proper rooms, Mistress,' he announced.

The Mistress picked up the pewter mug and dashed it against the wall with all her might. Then she fled upstairs.

'T'is her condition,' said the Parson, caught between

33

the proverbial rock and the hard place. He had to be both loyal to the Mistress and make some sort of sense of her unfathomable behaviour to the girl.

'The Mistress likes to think things out on her own,' Parson said, and Jenny thought likely sulking was called thinking in houses with an upstairs as she heard Parson's wife roaming above the yellow oak beams.

She was the third daughter of an impoverished land owner and she was plain at that, either a throw-back or a changeling in the family's opinion. The family traits made for dim but handsome, golden-haired, low-browed and square-built people who were easy-going, whereas Mathilda was tall, angular, dark-haired with a high bulging forehead and given to unexpected temper tantrums.

They had tried everything to break her bar walling her up in her room. They had put her on bread and water to cool her blood, deprived her of her sewing and her books, and confined her to the servants' company which she associated with punishment and therefore despised. She had grown into a sullen young woman although very skilled in womanly tasks, but even so, she'll need a good dowry to fetch any kind of a man' was a common enough sentiment. Her sisters had made good marriages, but how many times had she heard her parents complaining about her dowry, as if it was her own fault that she was plain and unlovable.

She had been thirty, unmarried, a spinster of the parish, and as she had said to Jenny, it was not a pleasant state of affairs. Only eight years ago the most likely sexual encounter to come her way had been the sight of her mother's spaniel's enthusiastic but unsuccessful attempts to mount the ginger-cat by the hearth.

And then she had landed Matthew, and she had

loved him at once. When he touched her hand, she thought she would melt away. He loved her, and she walked around covering her eternally smiling mouth. He was learned, although a vicar only, and of a small and spread-about parish of five small villages and hamlets. He wasn't well connected either, no Bishop or Archbishop to help him onto the higher rungs of the ladder, but no matter, he was respected, a big fish in a small pond.

She was proud of him, and she was exalted when God had pronounced their union fruitful. It showed her family that she was a woman who had been wanted by the man of her choice, better than her own father who slept his way around the town, no better than a tom cat.

It had been hot, that summer six years ago, and every morning she had heaved over the pail in the bedroom even though there was nought to bring up.

She had wandered to the window, wiping her smarting eyes, and she had seen Agatha heaving her guts out in the yard below. She was in the exact same condition as herself and through the exact same man, and the pain was as sharp and physical as her desire had been.

She wasn't special after all, and the perfectly formed boy had been born dead, looking like a beautiful waxed white flower lying in her arms after a pain-filled nightmare of a birth.

'It won't hurt very much,' her Mother had said about child-birth, embarrassed; it wasn't a fit subject for conversation. 'In any case, women are made so that they can stand pain,' but she hadn't been able to. She was a failure and she could not look straight at people now. Matthew had no such problems. His eyes were clear and blue and his gaze was steadfast. Nothing could be hidden in the depths of his soul, and he was serene in the day.

It was different at night. In the creaking and secret night, he crept into the parlour. Rest eluded him and she knew his secret, he wrote his guilt clean away at night. It must be so, she thought, although she never found out where the parchments were hidden.

Oftentimes she turned his writing desk inside out, springing the catch on the secret drawer, all to no avail.

The whole village had been brooding for a scapegoat caught in the hedge to lift the curse. In the end it had been easy to plant one; Agatha had been beautiful but stupid.

But now, the very night before last, the stairs had creaked and the man had looked scared, and she had remembered Agatha floating on the pond. She had looked like a flower carelessly picked and thrown away.

Such was the fate of flowers, and she had steeled herself to attend the service the Sunday after, but she had merely recalled the beautiful, uncaring, serene face.

She had been as glad as the villagers that Agatha was no more; it had rained at last.

'T'is certainly her condition,' said Parson again, listening to the pacing from above. 'Did you say something about the stone wall needing fixing?'

'Aye,' said Jenny eagerly, her heart beating wildly, now that her big chance for a private discussion had come, 'but it's nought that can't be fixed, Sidney could do it.'

She ought to ask him why he had crept up to her room the night before last, although the idea became more ridiculous the more she thought of it; there was not enough room to swing a cat in there, let alone a parson.

'Should I go upstairs and see if the Mistress is all

right?'

Parson looked at her.

'Kindly pass the bread.'

He paused.

'Methinks the Mistress would not thank you for meddling. She's a proud woman. It might be thought that you are over-familiar.'

'Me? Over-familiar?'

Two red spots danced on her face, indignation and something else.

Sidney had appeared behind Parson at the window, looking for his dinner scraps no doubt. He pointed at the Master, stuck out his tongue and made out his hands were great flapping ears. She could not suppress her smile.

'What was it now that Pliny the Elder said about pearls,' he said, noticing her pearl-like teeth, interrupted by a great noise from outside.

Jenny would never know what Pliny the Elder had said to the Parson.

Distant cursing.

Parson paused, looking at her over his great stomach on which his entwined arms rested as Jenny danced to the window.

'T'is not Pliny the Elder but Sidney the Simple who has tripped over the pig-swill bucket and fallen into the mud.'

He laughed.

'Pliny the Elder was an ancient Greek Sage,' he said, pursuing his abstract and enjoyable thought taking him away from the present, rudely interrupted.

'Haven't you got any work to do?'

The Mistress.

She went to the dresser and rummaged in a small box.

'Where's my ring?' she said.

'What ring?' said Parson.

'My pearl, left to me by my Godmother,' she said. 'The stone is loose and I placed it in here for safe keeping.'

'If you did,' said the Parson, joining her, 'then it must be here. There it is, safe and sound, hidden by a white cloth.'

He stared at the white cloth as the centre of his world disintegrated and his life fell apart. The box was full of needles. His mind returned to the summer of six years ago, Aggy's summer.

She had stood by the dresser and had turned round awkwardly.

How had it been put at the trial?

The Mistress's bowl had been awash with needles which had manifested themselves in her dish. One had stuck to her bottom lip.

The parlour was kept for eating and as a study for him. The sewing was done upstairs. She had said so herself as part of her evidence and he had borne witness to it. Therefore the needles in the Mistress's bowl had manifested themselves through Agatha's wicked spell.

He couldn't bear to hold the box awash with needles in his hands. He put it back on the dresser before he watched through the window Jenny administrating to the unfortunate Sidney in the yard. His clumsy great body emphasized how small and gentle she was, and just how vulnerable.

Perhaps he was wrong.

After all, this was the woman he had cherished, the woman who shared his bed, the woman with whom he had wept over their dead children. Perhaps the Mistress had altered her routine, he didn't know where she was every minute of the day, he thought as he left the room, and she knew what was in his mind; he would saddle the pony and confess to Squire. But where is your evidence Husband, she thought, haven't you left the needles behind?

She worked quickly and efficiently, five rows of needles to half the white cloth, when he came back, rummaging about on the dresser, the cloth neatly folded in half laid over her arm, the plain side covering the needles.

'You shouldn't have got rid of them,' he said after a while.

'Rid of what?' she asked, hiding the cloth behind her back.

'The needles that were in this box a minute ago. On that cloth on your arm now, I shouldn't wonder.'

'I don't know what you are talking about, Husband,' she said, but she knew she had been stupid; by removing them she had admitted her guilt. Why hadn't she just said the sewing was done in the parlour now?

'Why,' he said, 'for God's sake why?'

She pointed at him.

'You're to blame. Look at you now. You can't take your eyes off her. Like it used to say in the Book of Prayers before Cromwell suppressed it. *Following the desires of our hearts*, remember.'

'*And there is no health in us*,' he said softly.

And then he made a mistake, one that would affect Jenny's future at once and forever.

'Would you like to go back to your mother until the child is born?' he asked.

She looked at Jenny through the window. She put her head on one side, inspecting Sidney before he disappeared from sight, and the Mistress thought that bringing those two together wouldn't work now; there wasn't time.

And leave Matthew here with his evil ways?

'The journey wouldn't be safe for the child at present, Husband, but fear not, everything will turn out satisfactorily. I will see to it myself.'

'And will you see to Agatha, dead through false witness and buried in unconsecrated ground nobody knows where?'

How his wife could make out that it would turn out satisfactorily he did not know, whilst she plotted Jenny's downfall which would have to come soon. Before night fell.

She didn't know how, but something would turn up. In the end it was Joshua's small son. It was as simple as that.

Chapter 5

Jenny came in and said there was a little lad by the back door.

He was no older than her brother Adam as he stood there, twiddling his hat in his hands.

'What it is, Mistress,' he said to Jenny, 'what my Ma said to tell the Parson is that Pa has breathed his last and would he come, the Parson, to see us.'

'Poor lad. Who was your Pa?'

'Joshua, please.'

'I'm sorry to hear it, Peter, isn't it? Your Pa was a right good man,' Parson said. 'You've had a long walk and I'll give you a ride home on the buggy.'

Was there aught to eat at home? he asked him. When the little lad said not much but they had the milk from the goat, Parson went upstairs for a sack of barley.

The Mistress was sitting by the window, sewing and thinking. The boy had called Jenny *Mistress*. Mistress indeed, was that their game?

'I've heard, Husband,' she said, 'best take the rest of the salted beef.'

'Peter says he tried to get the axe out of the felled tree out the back, but it was stuck,' Jenny said when he came down, and this turned out to be a job for Sidney.

Jenny watched 'em ride off in the trap before she busied herself around the house which had become a silent, brooding presence creaking as with night-noises.

Upstairs the bed was ready for the confinement, stiff clean linen drapes on the posters of the bed to keep draughts at bay, the cradle fitted up, the birthing sheet laid out. The Parson's wife clutched the ache in her back and wandered towards her dressing table. When she looked into the glass her face wasn't crumpled like her mother's had been after her father's betrayals, it was watchful and alert. She had known the trick with needles materialising but really coming from her sleeve. She had been told of a similar witch trial.

Retribution had to be quick, before the girl found her wits and her tongue. Funny the things that stick in your mind. She remembered how frantic she became trying to get her lip to bleed. Who would have thought it would be so difficult? In the end she had pricked her finger and smeared it all over her mouth and it had done the trick, blood was blood wherever it came from.

Two children born dead, and now she saw that her downfall was caused by her pride in being a mere shadow, a wife. Fool's corn without seed, she thought, fool's corn, shadows have no will of their own, and then she had listened to the voices below.

She saw her husband sitting on the buggy clutching the reins, looking down at Jenny. She wondered what they were planning now, and then she fell asleep of all things.

When she woke up, she saw it was getting dark.

No sign of her husband yet, she still had time.

Jenny ran her cloth over the leaded windows in the parlour for a final polish. She turned, surprised; Parson's wife had come in that quietly. Shutting the door and leaning against it, she regarded her gravely.

Jenny put what she thought to be a pleasant smile on her face as she looked at her, despite the little maggot of worry wriggling away in her stomach. A door creaked open somewhere in the house. A log on the fire hissed.

'Is there any kind of a mark on your body?' the Mistress asked urgently, and Jenny was deathly afraid now that the mole on her left hip might be called a witch mark, like Aggy's had been.

Why, she thought, she's making out I'm some kind of a witch.

'Why should I tell you that?'

'T'is for me to decide what is relevant for you to know.'

'How very convenient for you, Mistress.'

Nought else to do but to deal with her terrors, Jenny thought. She couldn't figure the woman out. A bird threw itself against the window and she vaguely wondered why a bird would want to fly in and lose its freedom in this dreadful place. Sensible was best, she decided, and sensible meant listening to what her senses told her; she would have to return home.

She had a roof over her head and a family to protect her.

She couldn't be kept here, not against her will.

The Mistress was blocking her way, and Jenny looked around for something to distract her attention. Sudden squalls of wind hurried clouds like inflated sails over the stagnant flat-bottomed ship of East Anglia, interspersed by sudden bright shafts of light from a sun hanging low and threatening.

She saw Parson's wife glancing at her hair hanging heavy on her breast, coloured red by the sun's dying rays, as red as cousin Aggy's had been.

'T'is brown, T'is brown,' she cried, grabbing a handful. Soon the heavy mists would roll along from the fens and envelope the village in darkness and Jenny knew she had to get away before it turned darkness into sticky blackness, but the Mistress was still standing against the door.

'Remember Agatha,' she said, and Jenny minded her Ma who had said that a bully confronted would turn into a crumbling coward. She recalled Aggy popping up startlingly from the slimy greenness of the pond.

Best move now while she was still able to, she

thought.

'It's as well you have reminded me of Aggy,' she said, gaining momentary strength as she stretched out her arms and, like bird in full flight, flew into the Mistress outstretched arms.

She smelt her nearness, lavender and later, much later, whenever she smelled lavender's cloying sweetness she was filled with a nameless dread of unending tomorrows.

'Leave this house, child,' the Mistress said darkly, pressing something round and hard into her hand. 'T'is a golden guinea. Say nought about events in this house. 'T'is yours,' she urged her, 'take it and say nought.

'Say nought,' Jenny shouted, 'why shouldn't I? I tell my Ma everything, absolutely everything,' and the Mistress said she had been a bad girl and was no longer welcome in this house.

Jenny was dismissed.

'Out,' the Mistress screamed.

She opened the door.

'Out, out, out.'

'The once will do quite nicely, Mistress,' Jenny said icily, 'I'm not wanting, nor have I misbehaved either. 'T'is aught to do with me if you and the Master have no time for each other.'

Her arrow had shot home sweet and true. Blood-anger flooded the face before her, but Jenny wasn't done yet. She thought of her belongings.

'And I'll not leave until I have my things either. They might not be much, but they're all I've got in the world.'

'Out,' screamed Parson's wife, 'out, before I lose my control. I'll fetch them myself. Climbing the steps in my condition,' and the door was slammed into the girl's face.

Chapter 6

It was still evening, and a grey one at that. The house looked dark and threatening. The wind blew the fen-fog around her in wispy, torn shrouds. A barn owl hooted, a vole shrieked in its death agonies as another one swooped silently and swiftly and tore it in half.

The killing went on all around her, night and day, Jenny thought and she shivered in the damp evening hour.

I ought to have my shawl, she thought, that would be a comfort.

Accumulated bird droppings by the rooks plaguing the village covered the ground, white and shiny, and Jenny would have been glad if Sidney had been there to point out that it was bird shit and not the long-dead insides of animals, but there was no sign of him and she became increasingly uneasy.

'I won't go without my things,' she muttered, 'I have not misbehaved even if I have been dismissed,' and then she remembered her apron. She had left it on the wall to dry after plucking a chicken in the morning, although it seemed much longer than that.

There was no telling about time, she thought, looking in vain for the Mistress to come out with her belongings. However long did it take to gather her few skirts and bodices?

'I might as well get my apron now while I'm waiting,' she said to herself as she walked a little while on the winding path. Imperceptibly a dark night engulfed her, when she heard footsteps behind her, faint at first. She was afraid, but then she heard the clod-hopping boots coming nearer and she looked at Sidney.

It was dark, but nevertheless she saw that he had a

bright red scarf, small and rolled up, around his neck. As red as St. Agnes's flowers, she thought, pleased that Sidney was with her and that he was holding her hand.

A full moon hung like a ripe fruit in the dark sky, and a chink of light appeared behind her.

'Bundle,' screamed the Mistress, 'off with you,' and the door was slammed with such force that it nearly fell off its hinges.

It would have done if Sidney had fixed it. Everything did.

'T'is fixed, Mistress,' he used to say, 'when shall I mend it?'

'I see things at night,' Sidney said, sporting her mob-cap, 'Ma shuts me out at night oftentimes. She's ashamed of me,' he explained, his large ears sticking out from under her mobcap.

'Sweet Sidney,' she said, as the sight of him had quite cleared her head, 'do you like wearing my cap?'

'Aye,' he said, 't'is yours and I love you. I will give my life for you.'

'T'is ours now,' she said and the lad danced around her in his delight as she walked back to the house. She just had to get inside, as for a start she had to retrieve her shawl. She also had to know exactly what the pair of 'em were plotting against her, and yet it could be dangerous. If they caught her snooping, Parson would chase her home and that wouldn't do.

Ma would think that she had misbehaved, been dismissed, and she needed to explain things clearly and unhindered, in her own good time, and then she stopped.

Just what was it she had to explain? she thought, and her urge to spy on the pair of 'em became compulsive. Then an idea came to her.

If Sidney lurked in the dark distance with her white cap on, Parson might chase after him and the lad could head him off. Perhaps, and the lad was willing, but when she told him that the Parson might be evil, he shook his head.

'Nay, Parson's kind. Parson's good, it's her,' he insisted, and she thought that he was no more wanting than she was as she let herself into the house, except for the little wriggling worm of doubt in her stomach.

She looked around.

Light from the open parlour. The pair of candles on the wall in the hall had been lit as well. She took her black shawl from the hook and wrapped it around her, clinging to the wall as silently as a shadow.

'She's gone, Husband,' she heard the Mistress say.

'But why? I don't know what it is you are plotting, Wife, but I aimed to be ahead of you this time round. I couldn't bear to live if any harm came to her, but Old Joshua has passed away, and I had to comfort his family.'

Silence, and then a pleading note in his voice.

'She's seventeen, yet still such a child.'

A dry laugh from the woman.

'There was nought between Agatha and me then, and there's nought between Jenny and me now. Why, they're maids, not women. *What do you think I am?*'

'I saw what I saw,' the Mistress shouted, 'T'was the morning sickness, the same as it was with me, and if you say Agatha wasn't with child, how do you know it? If you were that familiar with her monthly round you must have had knowledge of her,' and the man sighed.

'Half the village was heaving with the dry sickness, including me.'

'Did you tumble Jenny or did you tumble down the steps the other night? Explain that away, Husband, if you can.'

'I have explained it. The child had the night horrors.'

'An imagination like yours, Husband, is quite

wasted in a small village, methinks. 'T'is a pity Cromwell has shut the London theatres, you might well make a name for yourself otherwise, not to mention a fortune. T'wouldn't come amiss in this house, living off my money as we do and t'is your own fault again, you're too soft altogether with the tithe.'

'Your money has not been touched, and how many more times must I tell you that a tenth of nought is nought, woman. The men give of their time in the fields and with the slaughtering freely enough if they're fit. How do you think a 'state of this size can be managed with nothing but a maid and a lad?'

His fist thumped the table, and she reminded him of the salted beef he had carted off to the dying Joshua's family.

'It will work to our advantage. I can point to her evil eye causing the illness there instead of here. That black dog of hers will add weight to it, a familiar likely.'

'What makes you so evil, woman?' he whispered.

'I am evil only,' she said calmly, 'if evil means looking after my own. 'I'm resolved to rid the village of this pestilence. The family went last time, and so it shall this time, the whole brood of Coopers will go. I gave her a guinea. I packed her bundle in my best shawl, t'is easily recognisable as mine, and I packed a silver ladle in her clothes. She'll be tried at the next quarter session in Kings Lynn, or wherever, for theft and she'll hang.

'An unborn child is a powerful charm and makes the bearer above suspicion. There is nought you can do unless you can swear on the Holy Bible that you truly love me.'

The man groaned, and a pair of bony hands gripped Jenny's shoulders.

'Behind you, Mistress,' she shouted.

The woman turned, Jenny escaped her grip and sped

48

out of the house.

'Harlot,' Parson's wife screamed and took off after Sidney who waved Jenny's cap at her from the dark distance, and Jenny fell into the Parson's arms.

'T'is an old trick of Adam's, look what's behind you,' she sobbed, 'and Sidney will turn round soon enough and grin at her with his great yellow teeth and then she'll know. Is there such a thing as witchery?' she whispered.

'If there is t'is in a woman's psyche. Intuition, whatever it might be called. This isle was pagan afore the Brothers came, don't forget, Jenny. Woman, the giver of life, can maybe impose her will on events. Unthinkingly and from the heart. The Mistress was a good woman once, maybe she was turned by the death of her babes,' he said.

'What must I do now?' she asked, and Parson's wife shot round the corner of the house. Jenny stood close by the old tree as the Parson walked towards the Mistress.

'She led me a right dance, waving her cap at me hither and thither,' she said.

She gasped for air.

'Enough unto the day. Tomorrow will be the same for her as any other day, there's nowhere but the village for her so she will have to leave. This child needs a rest for now,' she said, grasping her stomach with both hands, leaving Jenny in a black fury.

'We'll see about that, Mistress,' she whispered, as a light appeared in the bedroom, outlining Parson's wife's dark form. 'Why should you spit me out as if I was a rotten medlar gone the bad and treat your own child as if it was the first ever to be born?'

The fen fog rolled around her as seamlessly as time, this time and the next, and still the woman stood at the window. Finally she drew the bedroom drapes.

'However long, woman, does it take to take off a dress and to put on a shift,' Jenny whispered, impatiently stamping her feet, and then the light was extinguished. Jenny grabbed her bundle and sped past the house, longing to get home.

She forgot all about the Mistress's silver ladle.

Chapter 7

As Jenny fled into the dark night, Parson's wife's voice echoed and bounced around her little skull like a dropped stone might leave ripples on a pond.

'Leave this village, child. This very night. No peace will be had until you are gone.'

What did it all mean, she thought stupidly, home was home and safe was safe, wasn't it?

She was out of breath when she finally reached her cottage.

Sanctuary.

The girl slammed the door shut and stood against it in case there were intruders, but nobody tried to force an entry and nobody took much interest in her sudden homecoming.

Her Ma was tending to her Pa who was trying to raise himself on the pillow.

Brother Adam was munching on bread and cheese, eyeing the flute which was never far from his side.

'Hey Jenny, listen to my new tune.'

He promptly fell into one of his silent sulks when he saw that his sister was not even listening, and she was not interested at all in this wonderful new tune he had made up.

'Go to your bed, Adam,' her Ma said.

'I want a candle for upstairs,' he said, chancing his luck.

'Candles cost money and your bed isn't upstairs as you well know.'

The room upstairs was a general storing room.

A fire was burning in the fireplace. Smoke was finding its way up the chimney. Her Ma was brewing up some feverfew in the pot over the fire and its bitter aroma bit at her nose as it always did.

Jenny stood transfixed by this normality. It was as if she had never left home. As if Parson's wife hadn't told her to leave the village this very night. And of the sheriff waiting at her door in the morning.

She stood pressed tight against the horror, an outsider, unable to break out and join the charmed circle of her family. She looked at them, unable to find words. Never a word, and she knew how Aggy had felt, why she kept silent.

It was as past understanding as she was to her Pa, who saw a lovely girl standing there.

'Who is this lady? What does she want with the likes of us?'

'Hush now, t'is our Jenny,' said her Ma.

Why didn't her Pa recognise her?

'I was here last Sunday, Pa, remember?' she said.

'I do now, for a minute I thought Jenny was little, knee-high to a grasshopper,' he said.

Blood ran down from her hand and with it came pain and then she realised that it was the guinea that Parson's wife had given to her.

It brought her out of her trance although she found words hard to come by and she just clung and clung onto her Ma.

'She's crazy. She says she'll examine me for witch marks. She says remember Aggy. She can't do to me what she did to Aggy. Parson's wife said to leave tonight and she gave me a guinea. And she said the sheriff will be here come morning. I'll never, ever leave this house and then he can't get me.'

Yes, that was the way out, she would stay shut up in her cottage with the door bolted and then she would be safe, but then her Pa coughed and said they would burn the cottage down with all of them in it and he always knew no good would come of it and he should have taken a gun to the dog long since.

Jenny looked at him blankly.

'A black dog, for God's sake!' Ready-made for a familiar was Stray. Then her Pa coughed again and Jenny saw his face was bright red and she knew he was ill.

Stray, she had called the silent black beast who was beside the field at the edge of the wood where she was gleaning after the barley reapers. He was hurt, and she thought he might be hungry and thirsty. She put some water into a cup and placed her bread in front of him. After he had eaten and drunk his water, he lifted his head and looked straight into her soul.

He oftentimes got up a rabbit for her Pa, if it pleased him of course, for the dog remained his own master.

Roaming during the light hours, when darkness fell he used to silently settle on their doorstep until Jenny left, keeping an uneasy watch till dawn broke.

He needed a name, she couldn't just call him Dog, could she?

'Dog's a dog, ain't it?' her Pa said, and she had said she knew he wasn't a pig or a cow or a hen, and her Pa had said that no good would come of her quick tongue.

'Ain't no need for a name. He's stray. Don't belong nowhere and to nobody. No good will come of it. I'll take a gun to him.'

Jenny didn't worry, wherever would her Pa get a gun from?

Stray, that's what she called the dog, and sometimes he had tracked her when days were safe. Gleaning after the reapers in the barley fields or berrying in the woods, Stray would suddenly pounce on Jenny, licking her face with the greatest concern lest he had frightened her.

Pa was right though. Stray would be her familiar, and the havoc he caused in backyards chasing pigs and chickens would be seen to have been done at her bidding.

Parson's wife had been put out by the dog hanging around on his ground, Margret knew, and she thought likely she would keep the *familiar* threat, although she wouldn't do anything tonight, not in her condition.

Reading between the lines was all too easy, especially the bit about Parson's wife giving Jenny a guinea. She was not lightly parted from her money, was Parson's wife, and that convinced Margret of the great danger her daughter was in.

She would never understand it, folks with a roof over their heads, good health, help in the house, respected in the village and no money worries, and still they were not content.

Word about Jenny would get about. A cow gone dry. A child wasn't born right. The plague of rooks falling onto the fields even now would be laid at her door the minute the seed was planted.

Jenny, a cousin of Aggy's, had a familiar and would be tried. The cooper's cottage would be burned and they would have to go on the road like Aggy's mum and dad. A scapegoat, Margret thought, or more likely a sacrifice, and the name of it was need.

It wasn't hot like it had been in Aggy's summer, but all the same the weather wasn't right. The fog rolled in as relentlessly as if it was winter, and the earth lay in black, sodden clumps. Weather was weather, that was during the light of day, but at night dark superstitions wriggled their unseen heads from every corner.

Parson's wife had it in for Jenny, one way or another, Margret thought, and - good Protestant woman that she was - she crossed herself against all evil. Her girl would have to leave this night. A fifty-fifty chance was better than no chance at all.

'No good will come of it,' her John always said about almost everything and generally he was right, very little good came out of anything and he had acquired a reputation as a sage sprouting words of wisdom, what with his book learning an' all, and some of it stuck to Margret.

'I mind your John saying right off no good will come of it,' villagers said in awe, and Margret remained unimpressed; no good generally came out of anything excepting of course her Jenny.

John said, 'Don't you go and love her too much, no good will come of it,' when she was born no bigger than a pigeon, but Jenny had stayed. A funny little thing, sickly into the bargain. Black tight curls topped a small face covered in freckles, more freckles than face, two front teeth had grown crooked, and the bump on her nose where she fell on the step hadn't helped her looks any either. She was slow to catch up with other children of her age, but once she did, she overtook them.

Take the reading.

Margret knew all the letters, but she never got the hang of fitting them together into a word, whereas Jenny took to reading like a needle to thread. She oftentimes read out loud from the Family Bible of an evening.

It wasn't the whole Bible, just some parts of the Old Testament, and the New Testament and was given to John by the Parson's wife afore this one.

When Margret saw Jenny a few days since at Parson's to tell her to send Stray away for good, the girl came towards her. Carrying an empty basket on her hips, she walked light and straight. Her hair was lovely, softly curling and her skin was flawless. She smiled at her Ma, who noticed that Jenny's second teeth had grown straight. Even the bump on her nose was no longer noticeable.

Margret said that night that the girl was pretty,

lovely really, and when had it happened, and John said that no good would come of it, and now he was proved right once more.

She had soaked some barley corns for tomorrow's breakfast. She cooked them now, fast, throwing more wood on the fire and it was done in no time. She fetched some cream from the buttery and sat her girl right close to the fire with the steaming dish, both lost in their thoughts.

Margret recalled the day when a lecherous humour had come on Squire at the May-dancing where he had danced Aggy into some bushes. Aggy's hair had rippled and glinted silkier than the ribbons on the pole and if Margret wasn't in the same awe of her beauty as most folks, it was because the daughter reminded her of the ill-tempered and foul-mouthed mother.

Brother-in-law James had brought her home from the market and she had been a right vulgar piece with a mouth on her and lazy, if not downright bone idle.

Squire, a tall man surveying everything with pale, lazy eyes from craggy features once handsome in youth had emerged from the bushes with his white hair falling over his eyes, slowly shaking his head, holding his privates, unable to believe his senses. Evidently Aggy had laid one on him on his precious parts.

'Pig!' Aggy screamed, and Kate cackled.

As bad luck would have it, the Morris Men had not started their dance with bells jingling at their ankles, thighs being slapped and a lot of energetic pretend-fighting of Christians against Moors. Moorish Dancing, the Parson had said, brought over here from foreign parts.

They were still sitting together on the dell and some were blackening-up their faces with ashes.

Aggy had made a dangerous enemy in Squire,

however much Kate had tried to play it down. Margret always blamed Squire for Aggy's drowning, Kate blamed the Parson for refusing to help her at the drowning, and yet it had been that fine, upstanding woman, Parson's wife, who had engineered Aggy's downfall, according to Jenny.

Necessity knows no law, Cromwell had said in Parliament that very spring, and Margret had wondered whatever sort of a law that was to live by, but now she thought they all lived by it.

That very spring, Jenny had been at the Parson's by then, Margret had asked the Chapman, who was from London, about the town. He had pamphlets, almanacs and ballad-sheets in a back-pack and sold them around the villages starved for news and predictions.

John couldn't buy an almanac now and had to wait and find out what sort of weather they were having and what impending doom he had to face, but they had fed the Chapman who had selected a two-page pamphlet for John in return.

Margret couldn't read, but the story was clear by the picture, soldiers had cut off the King's head. The King's head wore a crown of thorns. The Martyr King. The King, the Anti-Christ, had been dead for little more than three months, and now this, a blessed martyr.

The King had died well, apparently. He had asked for two coats to wear at his beheading so he wouldn't shiver in the cold and look like a coward.

'Lucky to have two coats,' said John.

She had asked Chapman about London, about Southwark. She had a sister there near St. Thomas' 'spital, a place where sick folk went to get better or to die.

'My sister lives there. What sort of work is there for a maid?'

'Plenty of work for serving wenches and kitchen

maids at inns and coffee-shops.'

Shops sold coffee, a brown brew made from beans from foreign parts, drinking it made you lively, he said.

That would take some doing, she thought, he walked and talked slowly, had a longer face than a horse, and he was totally miserable; most likely he caught it from the Almanacs predicting the end of the world.

Now why had she asked him about London that very spring? It must a sign, she thought.

When it was safe for Jenny to come back, she would tell the girl to head for London.

Finally Jenny's bundle had been packed in the Mistress's shawl, Margret ticking off the items on her fingers.

Something Godly, Jenny's own prayer-book, suppressed or not, and the Bible. Something to keep her warm. Knitted stockings and clogs. Clean set of clothes and shifts. Something to keep her going. Loaves, cheese and apples. Something of her own. The pewter mug and plate. Money, wrapped up in a cloth, for food and maybe an inn.

'Something for luck,' said Adam padding over, offering his flute.

'You'll need your boots for walking in, Jenny,' she said. Parson's wife's guinea might best be hidden there, and finally, she cut Jenny's long hair even if it was unlucky to start anything new on a Friday.

'Keep your face dirty', Margret said, rubbing ashes over the girl's face again and again, no need to let folks know, if you come across any before Pa gets you, that you're young and pretty.'

Grandma's old shawl was large, thick and black. It had never been washed and was good and warm and very near waterproof.

The old shawl enveloped Jenny from head to foot, her own was gripped against her shoulders, leaving her arms free under the shawl to carry the bundle which bumped against her knees with every step she took, and finally Margret opened the door.

Jenny paused in the doorway and Margret just couldn't bear it.

'I'll come with you, Sweetheart. I might be a hindrance like, but we could come back maybe in a day or two when it blows over,' she said, but Jenny shook her head.

'And who is going to look after Pa and Adam?'

'Maybe you're right,' Margret said, and she kissed her.

'Be wise and be brave, and may the Lord take good care of you until your Pa gets better. Hide near here and wait for him to fetch you. Take the best of care, for you are the best.'

She stood well away from the girl for a last look, and then Jenny turned round once more.

'Do we know someone called Bashiba, Ma?' she asked.

'T'is your christened name, a most beautiful name, not spelled right Pa says but it could not be altered, only you were such a small scrap of a girl, so we took to calling you Jenny. Like a little Jenny Wren. Why do you ask?'

'My name isn't in the family Bible against my birth-date, I never thought Jenny was short for Bashiba so she might have been my twin and not lived.'

'Tell Pa and Adam I love them more than anything, and tell Parson I was fond of him and to keep me in his prayers daily.'

'I will.'

'And tell sweet Sidney I thank him for his company.'

They dared not embrace, if they had, morning would come and they would still be clinging to each other.

The smell of damp earth and sweet meadow-flowers

mingled with the darkness which swallowed her child.

Margret sat by the fire and longed for morning. A moth fluttered near, singeing its wings.

'Who let you in,' she sighed, and then she put it outside; likely it liked to flutter for another day.

A lumbering shadow passed her wearing something white on its head, a ring of daisies or a white mob-cap perhaps. Anything was possible this night, she thought.

She put some more logs onto the fire and she thought of dark shapes and demons of the night.

'*May the Lord protect us from Ghosties and Ghoulies and things that go bump in the night,*' she prayed, and after a while it occurred to her that it had been the lad Sidney passing by, but she still wasn't sure what the white thing on his head had been.

'Look after my Jenny,' she wanted to say, but when she looked down the path, he had vanished, and then she noticed a dark shape, a tracking dark shape, a dog, and it came to her that it was Stray.

'Stray,' she called softly, 'here Stray.'

He didn't move terribly well and she thought he might have been in a fight, or else he was hungry. She filled a bowl with oats and milk. When he had finished, she told him to look out for Jenny. He looked up at her on hearing the girl's name and looked straight into her eyes; Jenny would have a strong protector.

She opened the door again. Carried on the wind, but faintly, came the sound of a bell.

She counted its thin tolling, thirteen times. Dear God, what could it mean? she thought. She shut the door, and then John woke up. The fever had broken, and she had to tell him the whole sorry tale. He said that it was bad, as bad as it could get, except he was feeling better and he would fetch Jenny home on the morrow.

'That witch accusation against Jenny,' he said, 'it won't wash twice,' and she remembered the shawl and the silver ladle.

The Parson's wife's white shawl was in Jenny's bundle, but she put the ladle in the hearth and let the fire tarnish it. Then she hung it on the wall with her pots, spoon and forks, all the while thinking that she hadn't told the girl something, but she couldn't recall what it was.

Chapter 8

There was only one way out of the village and the night was boundless, stretching into eternity.

Jenny knew every tree and stone, every house with every porch and every bend in the road.

In the day, that was.

In the dead of night, her bravura and indignation of a few hours ago not even a memory, she felt as lost outside her own cottage as if she was in a foreign place, but there was nothing for it but to put one foot in front of the other.

One foot forward at a time she thought, and soon she ignored all else. Head bowed, her bundle bumping against her knees with each step, she watched where she would put her foot next.

The mist had lifted and every now and then a silver moon threw its light onto her path. She turned her head once and saw smoke from one of the cottage chimneys. It would be her own cottage.

She thought of her Ma and she was glad that Ma, with her bad eyes, would not have to walk the dread path this night. She would soon reach the pond, and she thought it likely that she would be frightened by it, but she only sensed the expanse of water on her left. On her right was the old church, like an upturned Viking boat rammed into the ground by the Normans, the tower - a seeming afterthought - overseeing the darkness of the graveyard.

It wasn't dark though, in the graveyard, not all the time.

She stood still and silent as a shadow, clutching her bundle and she wished her heart wasn't beating so loudly. There were folks in the graveyard and flickering candles, and now folks were looking her way.

Then the moon disappeared behind a cloud and Jenny jumped into the hole of the old elm struck by lightning, although just the roots of it were left now.

It was rumoured there was a nest of adders in there which would turn an arm blue before it fell off. Adders were the lesser of two evils now, for Jenny watched one of the hooded figures detach itself and walk towards her, and then it looked up and down the path.

By its stark features and tall, straight bearing Jenny could tell the hooded figure was a man. Unmoving, he seemed to look straight at her poor white face and she stopped breathing. After an eternity he turned away and went back into the graveyard.

He hadn't seen her face after all.

Then she remembered that her Ma had rubbed ashes all over it. Her face would be as dark as the shawl clinging so close to her, and as dark as the night.

Some sort of an evil ceremony was going on in the cemetery.

The tall man was now at the head of a tomb. In front of him was a skull and two candles, flanked on both sides by two figures.

An evil ceremony, and what it signified she knew not. All she knew was that her life was worth nothing if they discovered her, which they would do once they had finished their business.

She tried to wriggle deeper into the root, but most of her was still sticking out. What was she to do?

If she ran back home they might see her and her whole family would be in danger. Sensible is always best, her Ma had said, so where did ultimate safety lie?

She had two options, she could run past them when their attention was elsewhere, or she could run back home, but she would still be exposed for a stretch and then all of her family would be in danger.

Think on that, Jenny, she kept saying to herself,

think of Ma, of Pa, of little Adam, and then the church bell rang out thin, thirteen times, and sharpened her mind.

Midnight and something else, something unholy.

She slowly raised herself, watching intently both moon and clouds and the hooded figures. They were chanting in awful and harsh sounds at an ever increasing speed.

'*Mae--jes--tor, Mae--jes--tor, Mae-jes-tor, Mae-jes-tor, Majestor, Majestor.*'

One figure was bending down to get something out of a sack, their attention fully on it. It was a small white animal, a little lamb, then a small cloud covered the moon and she sped past the devil worshippers with all the speed she could muster.

A hooded figure appeared in the church door, the bell-ringer. She shrieked a warning and pointed at Jenny.

Run, run, run.

Soon she would reach the corner of the path and be out of sight. There it was.

Only a few more steps and then the terrible moon emerged.

Night was silvery light and they were after her.

Hide, hide, hide.

She recalled blackberry bushes and a ditch just around the corner. Slither round the corner and jump in the ditch. Pray God I make it, she thought.

She jumped, and seconds later she heard the soft murmuring of voices above her. The brambles were but thin twigs at the end of the ditch, even so her bundle stuck.

She tugged at it in great fear and it fell on top of her. When she peeped from under it the brambles were still softly moving. The traitor moon still shone its light on her and she listened to the terrible voices above her.

'We can't let her get away.'

'She can't be far off.'

There was real evil abroad and the village sensed it. Parson's wife had played along with their fear, but Parson's wife wasn't amongst the evil towering above her.

Silk-breeches. He was going to wed Squire's daughter. He was one. The children had made fun of him and had thrown stones through his bandy legs until one little lad had been lost for days.

And Squire de Breville.

It was Squire himself at the head of the tomb with his arms held to high heaven, and his white hair was falling back from his forehead.

'We'll light torches and look in the ditch. No other place for her,' the voices from above, and then silence.

She peeped cautiously from the protection of her black bundle.

The hooded figures had turned their attention towards the road, and from around the bend a figure emerged.

Sidney!

He trotted up to the figures and then he stopped.

'What's amiss?' he asked pleasantly, and they fell on him.

'Run, Sidney, run,' Jenny silently implored him, as Sidney took to his heels, back to the village.

'You can outrun 'em, Sidney,' Jenny willed him on, 'and you can lay about yourself. You know the night well, just don't try and hide in the graveyard, they know it better than most.'

All was silence.

She couldn't sit in the ditch all night, she thought, and then she recalled what the voices had whispered.

Torches!

They would be back shortly brandishing torches and

smoke her out like vermin.

When she peered onto the path it seemed to be clear, and she tried to run on it, except for her knees which had turned to water and her feet, nailed to the ground in terror.

A terrible scream, cut suddenly short.

Dear God, she thought, t'is my sweet Sidney, and she ran then. Faster and faster. She ran past the clunch-pit, on towards the place where the road divided.

On she went, and after a while she could see the woods. Blessed woods, she couldn't wait for their protection, but when the woods swallowed her she felt no safer.

The way ahead was illuminated by the relentless moon and Parson's wife stood at the end of each twist of the path.

'Harlot,' she screamed, and behind her were the whispering voices.

'Pursue, pursue, pursue.'

Jenny knew full well that these terrors were not real but it did not lessen her anguish any, and then she heard a soft rustle from the embankment to the left.

She stopped and listened, and then she fell headlong over a tree-root as thick as a man's arm, barring her way.

As she looked back, she saw the flickering lights of real pursuit, five pools of light held high steadily advancing.

Dear God, they had done for Sidney, and now her turn had come. It was no good, she hadn't the strength or the will left to make a run for it and suddenly there was Stray, licking her face and tugging at her clothes.

She threw herself up the embankment and ran after the dog through the trees.

Run, run, run.

Dear Lord, look after Sidney's soul.

Branches scratched her face.

They had tried to conjure up the devil himself and she had looked on them.

She could put a name to some of them.

She ran headlong into tree-trunks and twigs snapped at her but she knew what the dog headed for when she reached her hiding place by the musky smell of rotted down leaves.

The beech-woods.

She threw herself gratefully face down in this hidden place.

Sanctuary.

Chapter 9

'Stray,' Jenny whispered, 'oh, Stray.'

The dog gently flicked his rough tongue over her face and settled down next to her on his haunches as she unclenched her hand and stroked him. Poor Sidney. He was wearing her cap, a beacon to set them on his path.

'I'll look after it, cross my heart and hope to die,' he had said, and now he had.

To think that she had given it to him because he liked to share something with her!

How many times in the past had Parson's wife, and her Pa, told her to finish with *That Animal*, and how many times had Stray managed to let her know that he was still about?

She should have known that the dog kept an eye on her at all times. Had he been a silent shadow even by the graveyard, she wondered? If only she had known he was there, how much easier in her mind she would have been!

She let her hand rest on his solid body, and after a while she sensed that he was on the alert, ready to spring. His ears pricked up and she felt his hackles rising; he was getting ready to pounce!

Something must be up ahead, she thought, although she dared not think who or what it might be.

'Don't leave me, Stray,' she whispered, and after a while she felt the dog relax. He gave her face another lick and then he gave one of his enormous great yawns.

Jenny put both her cold hands into the great warm cavern of his mouth, held open obligingly until his jaw-bones creaked and life returned to them.

She was not alone. She had faced all the terrors of the night, but she was not alone, and then she remembered that she hadn't said her prayers like she did every night.

'I lie me down in gratitude,' she intoned automatically, and then she stopped.

'Dear God,' she said, 'why do you allow such evil in the world when you could get rid of it?', and then she recalled that something good had happened when she thought the world was all wickedness. 'Thank you God for sending me Stray,' she whispered, 'look after Sidney, Lord. He was a good lad and there was no call to make him suffer. Amen.'

She settled herself against the large and solid trunk of a beech. How dark it was! It was tangible, the darkness of the night under the leafy roof, with no sign of the traitor moon now, when of a sudden Stray sat up on his haunches, and she felt his hackles rising under her hand once more.

Something was up yonder for certain, she thought as he whined softly and tugged at her skirt. 'Not now, Stray,' she whispered, 'I can't cope with anything else tonight,' but even as she said it, she arose.

As Stray melted away, she wound her way a little way through the trees, and then her heart stopped. Five hooded figures were holding flickering torches aloft at the very place she had entered the wood.

Searching.

Broken twigs, bent branches. They had found her trail, and she knew the evil would not let her go when she saw the figures fanning out. Four of them rammed their torches into the ground as they slowly and silently advanced. She could not move, try as she might, for her knees had turned to water, and then she saw the dog silently flitting from tree to tree.

He was on his belly now, creeping up on the one hooded figure holding a flaming torch for the others to see by.

Now the dog was right behind him, and of a sudden the man shrieked. The dog was on his back. The man fell on his face, and then Stray was gone.

The man screamed again and the flames were licking at his cloak.

The dog was by her side, panting, when the four turned Squire over, and when they did, she saw blood coming from his nose and white foam welling from his mouth.

'A seizure,' said Farmer Morrow uneasily. 'It cannot have been anything else. Was there something on his back, something black? Did anybody else see aught?'

'No, we did not,' came the whisper.

'We best take him home. Best make a sling out of your cloak to carry him in, Jonathan. Call off the search for now.'

After a while she crept to the edge of the woods, resting her hand on the dog.

The fifth torch was being held high in front by Silk-breeches, his bandy legs revealed now that Squire was carried home in his cloak like a sack of pig manure.

She watched them until her eyes ached and she saw five twisting paths and untold menacing figures, and then she went back to the beeches.

She searched blindly for her Bible in her bundle, she had to hold something Godly, and after a while she made do with the Book of Prayers. Gradually she started to feel safer and warmer next to the dog's solid nearness.

There was no waiting for Pa, there was no turning back now.

Hooded night figures would turn into respectable village folk, smiling folk, and as upright as saplings, and before she fell asleep she thought about her journey next day through the fens.

70

She had heard tales about the fens, tales of two-headed animals and grunting folk, there would be water and marshes and reed-cutters, but she would have Stray.

She dreamed of Squire's daughter, so near that her face was right close to her and when Squire's daughter opened her mouth, on her breath was the hot stink of fox.

Jenny woke up with a start and looked at the triangle with green eyes. They looked at each other, Jenny and the vixen, as the reality of the day replaced night and its dreams.

The vixen sat and looked at her, her white-tipped brush moving leisurely like a vexed cat, then she melted away, and Jenny knew now what it meant to be a hunted animal. She got up and then she saw that she had been sleeping in a fairy-ring of toadstools. Poisonous fungi, all had hoods covering long stalks nearly reaching the ground, and she recalled the hooded night figures.

Like cures like, her Ma had said when she collected the spotted lungwort to cure a phlegm cough.

Like cures like, so evil had kept evil out. But how had the ring sprung up overnight? So many things she didn't know anything about, the fairy ring and the fox, and suddenly she felt ravenously hungry.

Rummaging in her bundle, she finally unwrapped one of the loaves and gave half to Stray. He was uneasy now and eager to be gone as she knelt over her open bundle. She had heard that wherever the page the Bible opened by itself was a sign, an omen, and she was almost afraid to look where the pages had unfolded.

'*Now we see through a glass darkly,*' she read slowly, '*but then we shall see face to face. Now abide Faith, Hope and Charity, but the greatest of these is Charity.*'

Where would she find this Charity? Faith and Hope might get her through, she thought, and the dog would help, but she didn't put any trust in Charity what-so-ever.

She opened the Bible at random. 'Beware the many-headed beast,' she read slowly. She could do without one of those, she thought, leastways she would recognise it.

The dog had lost patience and had silently melted away before she was ready and fit for the road. Bundled and shawled up, she finally retraced her steps of the night before. It had been dark in the heart of the forest and as she approached its edges, lush greenery underfoot unfolded before her, glistening in the morning dew. Tightly bunched ferns were covered in glittering spiders' webs, ready to trap their unwary prey. A dead tree trunk sprouted some bright yellow fungi next to an elegant plant.

Belladonna. Beautiful lady, they called it, two foot of slender green stalk topped with one single, round, purple and luscious berry held proudly aloft between two curved, shiny leaves. Beautiful Lady, and her taste was mortal.

Jenny scrambled down the embankment as near to the place the night before as she could recall to get her bearings, and she knew she had been stupid again.

A pony and trap stood waiting for her, as if it had waited for her all night, but Jenny could see by the pony's foaming mouth that the beautiful lady driving it had pulled it up very sharply that minute.

It was Squire's daughter.

She was turned towards her, the Lady Eloise, and her hand, with a stone of blood on one finger, laid lightly on the reins.

Her purple cloak was open at the neck and her hood was down. Her hair was parted in the middle and caught over the ears by gold-hoops into long ringlets; around her slender neck she wore a necklace of pearls, like moons.

She looked at Jenny with her shining eyes and pointed to the place next to her.

Jenny threw her bundle up, then she jumped up and sat next to the beautiful lady, and she thought her taste was mortal, although she was loathe to believe it.

Squire's daughter was not only luminously beautiful, but also sweet to look at through her expression of sorrow and concern that touched her deep-blue eyes.

It all depended on the lady's nails now.

'Well, what are you looking at?' said the Lady Eloise.

'The ring, please my Lady, I have never seen the like, is the stone coming loose?' Jenny said, leaning forward, all of a tremble.

Squire's daughter withdrew her right hand from the reins and examined the ring. Her hands were bloodied and Jenny saw the grime embedded under the nails.

Did you bury my sweet Sidney with your own fair hands, Jenny wanted to ask and the Lady gave a short, sharp, laugh.

'Just so,' she said, 'the stone is too big, it needs attention, a new setting. What sharp eyes you have. My jewels bring me luck, I wear them at all times. What brings you luck?'

'My dog does, if you please, my Lady.'

'Well,' the lady said clearly, tugging the reins, and the pony set off.

She was perplexed.

This girl was a traveller. Sharp. Self-possessed. Filthy dirty, dirty old shawl. A bundle. A dog. She was looking for someone from the village in flight and fright.

'Did you see anything or anyone strange in the

night?'

'I didn't see anything in the night,' said Jenny. 'I always find me a safe place in the dark.'

The lady didn't say anything to that and Jenny thought it had sounded lame.

She had to make it more convincing, and she best think fast now.

Far off, she saw the end of the wood, there would be room to turn the trap around. She had to give the impression somehow that she was not alone.

'I was with the others,' Jenny said, 'and then I went mushrooming. When I came out from the wood I fell over a tree root. See.'

She showed her the knee caked with blood.

'I couldn't keep up with the others and then I was lost.'

'We are all lost,' said the beautiful lady, and her voice was the rustle of dry leaves.

'How will you get back to the... others?' asked the rustling voice and Jenny saw the black outline of Stray at the end of the path.

'They generally send the dog to look for me.'

There was triumph and relief in Jenny's voice as the trap stopped and the lady handed her the bundle. Best let her go, she knows nought and she is nought but a dirty traveller, she thought.

Something worried her about the girl's account, but she was too tired to think it through.

Where was Jonathan, she wondered, he was supposed to meet her here. Without him she could do nothing, for the girl had been right, the dog had certainly brought her luck; he could tear her limb from limb if he had a mind to.

As Jenny stroked the dog she saw in the far distance what the lady had seen. The others. A few lonely travellers of the road.

Chapter 10

A pink morning dawned, promising more foul weather later.

Parson's wife had dreamt of a knife being painfully plunged into her back. When she awoke, the pain in her back was real enough.

'You best see to breakfast yourself, Husband,' she said, digging him in his ribs with her thin elbows, 'I don't suppose Jenny soaked the barley last night for the porridge, let alone fetched the water for the morning.'

'How very unreasonable, if not downright ungrateful of her,' he replied, climbing into his breeches. 'Could you not have asked her to see to it afore you promised to drown or hang her?'

He buttoned up his coat, marvelling at his composure; he hadn't missed one buttonhole.

'I shall miss her,' he said, 'I was fond of her right enough, her innocent prattle and I'm fond of Sidney as well, maybe you'll accuse me of unnatural practices with him.'

His voice rose as he got fully into the swing of things.

'I shall have to muck the pony out which is likely flashing its lust for me, and if I mention that the pigs need feeding, I'll do it instead of Sidney, and you'll accuse me of pig-worrying.'

He paused by the door in a black rage. Why had he married her? The parson needs a wife, the wife needs a maid, the wife needs a child, and also, he had loved her in his own fashion.

What now?

'When I wed thee, woman,' he said, 'I put my hand in the manure or shit, as Sidney has it, pig shit and it stinks.'

He slammed out of the room.

Where was Sidney? The lad normally appeared with the dawn, but there was no sign of him in the yard, nor was he in the stable where he sometimes slept. After Parson put the pony out to graze, he emptied the swill bucket into the sty and a pail of corn all over the chickens.

'Sort it out amongst yourselves.'

No sign of Sidney, and when he took the wood into the kitchen, he wasn't there either. A yellow blob of chicken fat floated on the stew pot and the sickly smell of cold broth made him retch.

Parson's wife couldn't wait for him to be gone.

'Yes, yes, yes,' she thought during the Parson's tirade, 'just go, go, go,' for she had found a treasure which would find out his guilt.

Last night, after he finished writing, she had finally found his papers, and they were now all rolled up in the dresser drawer waiting for her.

She had often wondered what he did with them; conceal them on his person maybe, as he never took anything away openly when he finished writing.

Last night she had crept down when he had fallen asleep. She had ransacked his writing desk once again, nothing there as ever, and then her great stomach had touched the little table next to the desk.

Mean and old and ill-made, it housed the Parson's various bits and pieces of old pens and pen knifes in open compartments at the top.

It had long been an eyesore to her amongst her elegant spinet, dresser and chairs. He treasured it though, so she had minded her peace and always averted her eyes from its meanness.

The compartments had moved, ever so slightly.

When she cleared them and tipped the drawer, it

swung half-way, revealing a goodly space which housed his papers.

'Thank you, child,' she said to her stomach, 'and now I shall have him.'

'I'm away to Sidney's to see what's up,' himself shouted up the stairs, 'I might fetch Agnes to help us out.'

She had to be quick. He would return soon and the child would interfere with her plans as well judging by the insistent pain in her back and the full feeling in her stomach, she thought as she scanned the pages scattered on her bed.

Pages on pages, signifying nothing.

Rhetoric.

Recording every day that the Lord had been good to him in his bounty, to him and his dear wife, who was a prop to his needs. A fine record of the weather. Who had passed on and who had been born and what they had left and to whom. Who was ailing and who got better.

The tale of his sore toe, a sorry tale, and she was quite glad when the nail had finally fallen off, a feat which appeared to have taken some time.

'Yes, yes, yes,' she said impatiently, nothing about Agatha as yet, until finally he recorded a black day, and he didn't understand any of it, or so he said, in pages on end. Supping his broth one minute and the next Agatha was drowned, and how he couldn't find her grave to say a prayer over it.

She was buried in hurry. I could not find her, how can the Lord restore her soul now without a prayer being said over her resting place, she read, 'but what did you think of her, Husband,' she whispered

Very aware of her fierce temper Agatha was, and how, despite having no liking for her, he had admired the way she controlled it, despite being intellectually wanting if not to say soft in the head. There, she had him. He had admired her.

Later, her own confession of planting the needle.

'God help us all.'

Finally last night. Jenny, a child he admired for her spirit, hounded out by a demented woman.

Plenty of rhetoric in the beginning though about a handsome and capable woman.

'T*'is the pregnancies turning her head,*' she read. *'After the child is born, please God, Mathilda will come back to me and we will face what has to be faced together.'*

Plenty of admiration in the past, but none for her now.

She rolled the papers up and put them in her dresser drawer.

When he returned, she was crouched on the pot.

'My waters have broke,' she said calmly.

'Your waters broke already?'

'Best fetch Mistress Cooper. Margret,' she said, and he did as he was bid, although he wondered why Margret Cooper of all people should help her out.

Chapter 11

'Seems a body can't eat his breakfast in peace without a Parson sticking his nose into it, don't it, Pa,' said Adam, feeling very adult after Pa had told him he would have to take the cow out to graze by himself.

Father and son sat at the table by the small window eating the rest of last night's barley.

John had felt a lot better once he had been able to control his shaky legs and now nothing would do but he had to go and set off after the girl. Bring her back and get her married off or hide her, he would think of something, but first he had to find her, and Margret had finally recalled what she had wanted to tell Jenny.

'I meant to say to hide in the clunch pit for a few days until it becomes clear what mood the Mistress is prey to.'

John said no good would have come of it, t'was too near and likely water-logged, and then Parson passed by the window like a black shadow.

Jenny had trusted him, but all the same it might be better to keep him in ignorance, his woman had a powerful charm of evil about her.

Parson shouted at the door that the girl should not be frightened this morning.

No reply.

He shouted that his wife was in labour and wanted Mistress Cooper's help, just as the door opened.

There was no need to shout, said the woman calmly, adjusting her shawl in the damp morning air, her sight might not be all it should be, but she was certainly not deaf.

'Jenny has gone to relatives, in Cambridge, before they take her to my sister in Southwark.'

She would go with the Parson, she had decided, she

wanted to find out exactly what Parson's wife would plan on next. Jenny had the shawl. She would also return the silver ladle, not the shawl, and she looked forward to seeing the woman's face when she did, not to mention the unlikely explanation.

They walked silently side by side, Margret carrying a basket, the ladle hidden under her apron.

Splay footed, his calf swelling from tightly gartered black stockings, Parson's expanding stomach nearly popped the buttons off his coat as he walked by her side.

'Look at me, Mistress Cooper, What do I look like to you?'

'A black crow, maybe,' she said thoughtfully.

'Exactly,' he shouted, 'should that generate passion in a woman?'

'There's no telling what a woman sees when she looks at a man.'

'You know, Saint Thomas of Aquinas is reckoned to have calculated how many thousands of angels could balance on the head of a pin,' he said.

'Never,' said Margret in amazement, 'that must have taken some doing.'

'Not as much as fathoming the moods of the Mistress, I can swear to that.'

'Perhaps he wasn't married,' she said.

'Whoever it was who worked out the amount of angels,' she added, 'he can't have been what you might call useful.'

Parson laughed ruefully. He often thought now that the old religion had valuable asset in unmarried priests. A friar of an Open Order, a Franciscan maybe. A life solely devoted to carry out God's work in the community appeared to him now what he was born for.

'I was born too late or in the wrong place,' he said mysteriously, 'or I should never have wed,' as they parted at the back-door of the Parsonage, where deaf old Agnes waited for them.

'I'm Agnes,' she shouted as if she was a stranger suddenly in their midst and not known to all and sundry as Batty Aggy. 'I'm Sidney's Ma. Come to help out, what would you like me to do, Margret?'

'Best go in the kitchen and see if the water is hot and if there is aught bubbling on the stove. The Mistress will need some good nourishment. She has a long travail ahead of her.'

'The kitchen is the room which ain't the parlour,' Aggy shouted. Margret would have to find out what stage the birth was at, although she doubted that she could look at, let alone touch, the Mistress.

'Where's Jenny?' said the Mistress.

'Gone to her kin in Cambridge and onto Southwark.'

Parson's wife said she didn't know that she had kin in Cambridge.

'You don't know everything,' Margret said, 'but you'll be pleased to know that I have returned the silver ladle, Mistress.'

'Such lies these girls tell, such lies,' said Parson's wife, and when Margret forced herself to look at the woman she saw that her eyes were opaque and about her was the smell of fear; and then the birth pains were on her.

She gasped, and then she said she wanted to repent, repent, scrub herself clean and atone. She wanted a healthy child.

She might or might not, said Margret, wasn't there something else, something she might have forgotten?

'Confess,' she reminded the Mistress sternly, 'confess comes first, then repent, and then atone,' but she weakened as she looked at the woman who was in great pain. She would have no child at all if she did not loosen up soon, laying there as stiff as a poker would do nought for her or the child.

'Confess,' Parson's wife gasped.

She beckoned towards a drawer in the dresser table and Margret pulled out a sheaf of papers, tightly rolled up pages on pages covered in Parson's large hand.

'It's all in there. All about Agatha. What he did and what I did. Can you read?' she said, and when Margret said she could read letters but not words she calmed down.

What the Mistress had forgotten was that her John could read, he helped at times to take an inventory when some poor soul had passed on without kin and he always remarked on Parson's fine, large hand.'

He would recognise the writing and then the truth would come out.

T'was Parson's personal confession, apparently he wrote far into the night by candle light, the Mistress said, 'what a wicked, wicked waste of candles.'

Hardly wasted, Margret thought, the papers in her apron pocket. She meant to hang onto them like the grim reaper.

A healthy child in her arms and the woman on the bed looking vulnerable with her braids loose and her eyes warm and pleading would turn into something else.

No hair showing from her starched cap, her eyes as narrow and as green as unripe berries on a foggy morning would be a different story.

'Hang onto the bedrail with the next pain,' Margret said, 'I'll go and see to the hot water.'

The papers rustled reassuringly in her pocket as she wound her way down the narrow stairs.

'My Sidney didn't come home last night,' Agnes said. 'Himself beats him if the temper's on him, and then I lock him out, but last night he didn't come home so I couldn't lock him out. You won't know what it's like with that healthy boy of yours and that lovely maid,' but Margret had an inkling of it.

That feeling of Jenny not being quite right after she was born with a cowl over her face had been a worry to her. Her mother hadn't helped when she had said not to worry, the Good Lord looked after fools and children.

When she looked at Agnes, she saw that her hands were clean enough to deliver a new life.

She brightened up when Margret sent her up with the broth.

'Stay up there,' she shouted after her, it might take her mind off the lad.

When she had busied herself before the birth with the pots she had noticed great fat and rounded larded candles stacked on a shelf.

She picked out the six best ones and placed them on top of the papers in her basket. John had a lot of reading to do, he might as well have some decent light to do it by.

It was a short, excruciating labour but the child had laid the right way for the birth, and a little dear girl popped out like a startled rabbit.

'A lovely, milk-faced little maid,' Margret said,' and wait for what comes after.'

It was over.

The Mistress sat up in a chair while Margret busied herself and bundled it up with sheets for Agnes to burn.

'I had not expected a girl,' the Mistress said irritably, and now she had her healthy child, she became hard and unfriendly. She asked for a clean gown and her looking glass as she braided her hair into thin, hard strands and forced them into her white cap.

'I have no more need of you today after you put clean linen on the bed,' she said. 'What ails you now?'

'You look like the oldest spinster in the parish with

nought but grim death to look forward to, not a woman with a sweet maid.'

'I can tell you are Jenny's mother,' she said, and picked up her child. 'Tell Parson he is the father of a healthy girl, and look sharp about it.'

The woman was up and about a mite early, but Margret minded her peace and also what Agnes had said, that folks had more trouble passing wind than Parson's wife had in giving birth.

She found Parson saddling the pony.

'What news from upstairs?'T'is not a boy? How strange,' he said.

'It has to be either one or t'other, although I have come across a third kind the once,' replied Margret.

Parson was glancing at the candles in the basket, and Margret said it was part of her Jenny's wages and she had taken the liberty of choosing the best ones.

'We got us a lot of reading to do, John and me,' she said.

Parson Wilcox watched her departing back and wondered what on earth they were going to read between them.

His wife was watching him from the window upstairs.

Cradling her girl, she now felt like a person in her own right, the substance, not the shadow. The baby was sucking regularly, looking up into her face unblinkingly. She put her gently into the cradle and was looking absent-mindedly in the drawer for her looking glass when she noticed the papers were missing, which made her smile. Margret had been right deceitful, she thought, and fighting for her own as fittingly as she would in her stead, and it would be a good and even contest.

Even if Margret had been trying to divert her attention away from the papers onto her appearance to give her time to get away, she had been right; she looked as old as a knackered horse. She unbraided her hair and caught it in a roll in the nape of her neck, and then she got dressed.

She turned round.

'Motherhood sits well on you, Mathilda,' Parson said from the door. 'Did you suffer much?'

'Women are used to suffering. Don't pick her up just yet, Matthew, she's resting peacefully. I'm surprised, I didn't think I had a girl that pretty in me.'

'I don't see why not, and I'm sorry that I used foul language on you this morning.'

'I looked at your papers this morning,' she said, 'and now Margret has taken them away.'

'My diary?' He stopped in the doorway. 'She told me her John had a lot of reading to do. I had wondered about it.'

'John Cooper can read, of course, he kept the trial. I had forgotten,' she said, relieved that it could be sorted out betwixt the Coopers and themselves.

The child gave a little cry and she picked it up.

'It won't break us, Husband,' she said, 'I haven't used my dowry money yet, I was in a bad mood when I said that last night,' and then there was great shouting from below, Old Agnes bellowing something about Carew.

'Something amiss, Carew says, and it's urgent, he says,' she shouted up the stairs.

'I must away, Mathilda,' Parson said.

She listened to the voices, crouched at the top of stairs; the cause of the commotion could well be Jenny. She wasn't sorry she had rid herself of the girl, but it would be a shame if the good feeling betwixt herself and Matthew became muddied.

The girl had gone to Cambridge, a lie if ever she had heard one, and it proved the whole family reeked of deceit.

When Carew said that the graveyard had been disturbed in the night she thought it was bound to upset Matthew. Why couldn't anything ever go right for her?

Chapter 12

When Parson heard Agnes bellow for him like a moonstruck calf, he thought that maybe some illness had struck Carew's family.

When he got downstairs, Old Carew was waiting for him in the parlour, although not low with grief like he might be if one of his family had been taken; he was struck down by sheer terror.

'It's like this, Parson,' he said, twisting his hat in his hands, 'I was about my business early this morning when I took a shortcut across the graveyard. Well, one of the graves has been disturbed, last night like,' he said

Something terrifying had taken place last night, he added.

When Margret had told him of the safe delivery of his pretty daughter, Parson's first thought had been that the Mistress would kill the child by the time he reached her. She won't stand for what she thinks of as a rival, he thought as he rushed up the stairs, but the picture of contented motherhood was just as he had prayed for oh, so many times.

Saturn devouring her own children she was not, after all, and for that he had apologised. She devoured other people's children instead, and if normality was no longer a tenable proposition, a semblance of normality had seemed the greater miracle after last night.

'Best not disturb 'em in the Manor, the groom told me in the yard,' said Carew. 'Squire has had a seizure early this morrow and got himself burnt knocking a candle over as well, so he says.'

Carew coughed.

'Is there more?' asked the Parson after a while.

'The grave was disturbed like I said,' Carew said, 'and I noticed it because a white hand was asticking from the black soil. Freshly turned over, the grave was,' he added.

'Oh God,' Parson Wilcox prayed silently, 'please let it not be an exchange. Not one dear maid taken for another.'

'Begging your pardon, Parson, there's quite a crowd gathered awaiting you, and I ought to warn you that you might be upset. 'T'is a large, enormous hand, and well, we think likely t'is your lad, Sidney.'

A howling Agnes is no good to me, how am I going to manage now? the listening woman upstairs thought, and the child in her arms gave a piercing cry.

'You're right, child,' she said, 'what am I skulking on the stairs for in my own house?'

Carew waited while the Parson opened the Bible at random.

'For guidance, Eli, sorely needed this day.'

'What's it say then in the Good Book?'

'*Be still and know, says the Lord*,' whispered the Parson.

And a fat lot of good it was to them too, Carew thought as the Mistress came in on shaky legs, they wouldn't know aught if they be still.

'Best find out what's amiss then, Husband,' she said as well. 'Best fetch your man, Agnes, he can help out in the yard for the present, I shall rest awhile,' she said raising her voice to the door. Likely Agnes was listening and as she was more than a bit deaf, she wouldn't have heard about the dead hand yet, she thought, and finally Parson was persuaded to saddle his pony.

He found Agnes in the stable. She only made out she was deaf so she couldn't hear what her husband had to moan about, and she had made a habit of it as it became useful. If she had been crying her eyes out, she cried because she had had no inkling that Sidney had been in any danger. Her other son Joshua. had gone as a pike man in the King;s army. Nobody knew what had happend to him, likely he was one of the dead on a battle field.

And now Sidney!

When her grief was spent, she washed her face in the pony's water-pail. She turned her apron around to the clean side and rammed her mobcap over her ears. The Mistress liked a clean body about the place, and Agnes had it in mind to become indispensable at the Parsonage.

'You'd like to help the Mistress in the house, Agnes, wouldn't you? Your keep and some money at Michaelmas?'

She looked pleased, then uncertain.

'If she'll have me. She'll likely want a pretty young maid waiting on her, like Jenny maybe,' but Parson assured her she would do just fine as she was.

Parson passed Mistress Cooper on the way to the graveyard. She wondered about the hurry he was in, his fierce look and why he hadn't stopped to impart whatever bad news he harboured.

Margret suddenly felt tired and hungry and she decided to call in on Emily, the village's mainstay, for the fresh bread and start spreading some good news. In case there was something in the papers liable to lead to a parting of the ways betwixt the Mistress and her money.

It was blackmail and it didn't worry her any, what worried her was that she couldn't tell her friend the truth.

'Adam will come with the milk later,' she said.

'Aye,' Emily said, 'put the bread on top of those candles. You haven't made off with them I don't suppose?'

'Parson's wife has been delivered of a fine girl, but

my Jenny has left her employ. The candles are part of her wages. Jenny has gone to Cambridge, my brother-in-law fetched her last night.' She didn't like lying to Emily, but the less Emily knew, the better.

'There's talk today in the village of the graveyard being disturbed in the night and Squire himself having a seizure early in the morning.'

Was there a connection, Margret wondered?

'My sister's man has come into some money which he wants to share with us like,' she added; if money was coming to them from the Parsonage it had to be explained somehow, even if her friend looked unconvinced that good fortune was a sharing experience.

'I'll have it in mind to see Cook at the Manor about Squire's stroke,' she continued. 'If there is aught going on, Cook will know about it.'

Emily grasped her hands. She understood with her gut and not with her head that her friend had to keep something from her.

'Let me know what you find out,' Emily said, 'I'd go with you, but there's another batch in the oven.'

Margret hurried home.

She swept the rushes out and laid clean ones and washed the dishes.

The place looked altogether different and she felt better in the routine of her every-day tasks. She separated the cream in the buttery and she collected the eggs.

'Wonder what's written in there,' she said, looking at the rolled-up papers, placing the eggs on top in case somebody came round snooping.

Washed and dressed in her Sunday-best as always when she visited Cook, she took the short-cut through the fields to the Manor, and after all that effort, the Companion of Squire's Daughter threw her out before

90

she could make sense of it all.

John was drying himself in front of the fire when she burst through the door. She drew a bloodied mobcap from her breast. With shaking hands she pointed to the small tear neatly sewn up.

'T'is Jenny's,' he said.

Margret said last night, was it only last night, she had thought that the lad Sidney was passing by wearing something white, like a ring of daisies, which might have been a mobcap.

'Must have been Jenny's, he was fond of her, and a bit wanting.'

It was a mystery how it had ended up in the Manor, and they agreed that it was connected with Squire's mysterious seizure.'

John had left soon after Margret that morning, after he had seen Adam off a goodly way with the cow.

He got as far as the place where the road divided for Cambridge or the fens to look for Jenny when the fine lady nearly ran over him in that trap of hers, and none too pleased she looked.

"She's abroad early and alone,' I said to myself when she said very nearly the same thing. She turned the trap round towards the village. 'What might your business be so early in the morning, My Man, and what is your name,' she said,' he recalled and Margret hoped he hadn't told her.

'Only my first name, I'm not as daft as I look. I asked what exactly it had to do with her. Was the village missing a girl and a black dog, she asked. When I started to tremble, I explained about my fever, but Squire's daughter smiled then, a secret smile, and said she would have no option to look for the girl herself.

'T'was not right families should be split asunder,'

she said. 'You have a daughter?' she asked me. So I said, yes, but she was at home. Then she asked me if she had a name, so I said of course she did, we weren't heathens. And I let on it was Jenny.'

'Dafter than you look,' said Margret.

'Too right. 'Jenny, her name is, you say,' she said, and then we reached the graveyard, just as Parson was getting off his pony. We followed him.

'Lots of folks around, and when they see him like, they show him a grave with a skull.

'"*Be still and know*,' says the Parson, but the Lady Eloise screams, and Old Carew said he had found Sidney in the grave and now he was gone.'

Well, John said, after the Daughter had gone off with Parson in the trap, he had a sudden thought that Jenny might be hiding in the beeches that she was so fond of.

'It's not so far on Parson's pony, and when I got there, I found something belonging to her in a ring of toadstools,' he said and he got the prayer book out of his breeches.

'It's hers sure enough. She was hiding out in the night there, Jenny was, protected by a fairy ring, and she must have got away early on,' Margret said.

And while he was there, he had looked in his snare and found his dinner waiting for him. 'A rabbit. I took the snare out and threw it away, you never know. When I came out of the wood, Squire's Daughter roared past me, and believe me, her face wasn't any too pretty now.'

He was startled to see the dog, Stray, tracking the Lady Eloise, head down and keeping an exact same distance, so he figured maybe Jenny was hiding not so far off and the dog was keeping guard.

He was glad of the pony, he said, and he rode a goodly way. 'I called her name every now and then as I rode along, but it was bucketing down, couldn't see my hand in front of my face let alone anything else. The barn was blazing, but she wasn't there either, and I rode the pony back to the Parsonage afore anyone could shout horse-thief.'

Margret was more composed now, and she told him that she had been to see Emily first, then Cook.

In the Mansion's huge kitchen one of the maids was coddling eggs. Another other was chopping herbs, the third was preparing eight little woodcocks.

Cook sent them out for more eggs and parsley and told 'em to be a nice long time about it, and then Cook had told her that Squire had been brought back insensible, and covered in dirt. She had seen it with her own eyes.

She was a troubled sleeper, was Cook, and she could not but help noticing what went on at night, and plenty did.

'I am done for,' she said, her face waxen. 'T'is because I can't mind my own business, never could. The girls know aught, that's why I sent 'em out. Every other body in this house keeps their head well down below the covers at night, but not me, I am just itching to know what's amiss.'

Never before though had she heard bells a'tolling in the dark hours, and on Friday, the thirteenth.'

Cook said she had hidden in the great gallery when they took Squire to his room, Farmer Morrow - bleeding heavily - and his son. The Daughter had flung her cloak onto the banisters and Cook had crept down to see what the white thing sticking from the cloak was.

'She showed me the mobcap,' said Margret,' and I pushed it down the front of my dress, because Cook crept to the door, checking for listeners.'

Back to the story.

93

Then the Daughter and her intended came down and went out again, dark night or not, Cook said, and she was that frightened, she daren't venture upstairs, so she crept into the kitchen.

'Farmer Morrow was still about upstairs, and she says it's that dark in the hall, she might have knocked into some of that armour that's standing about,' Margret related.

'So she listened at the kitchen door in her nightshift, and finally dawn was creeping up on her and the pair of 'em returned. She hid in the scullery when they made up a drink, and Cook said, the foul language that came out of the Daughter's mouth is not to be believed. And to think on the sweet girl she was at one time, which was news to me.'

They also agreed to give out that Squire had a seizure in the night and got himself burned by a candle, and that Farmer Morrow had a run in with a bull that broke his nose.

'Then we heard somebody coming down the stairs, Cook and I, and only just in time, so I talked very loudly about Parson's wife giving birth,' Margret said, and added that it was the Companion of the Daughter.

'I know her, a long streak of piss.'

'Aye.'

She had thrown Margret out of the kitchen.

'T'is not the time to gossip,' she said, giving Cook one of her looks. 'Where are the kitchen girls? And might you be the widow woman with the children?' she asked me, not waiting for an answer,' said Margret, and John wondered if he had been dead and buried in their talk.

Turned out he had, Margret had admitted to being a widow readily enough, the Companion had a real menace about her.

'There's one or two widow women with children

about, she won't know the difference,' she said and John agreed. To a fine lady, one who only ever saw a gaggle of village women in church, they would all look alike as petals on a daisy, if not as pretty.

'Off with you,' the Companion had said, and then she had run after Margret and asked what the round thing was that she was hiding under her shawl.

'T'is my belly, if you have no objections,' Margret had said, pretending to depart in high dudgeon, but really she was mighty relieved that she had stopped off first and had hidden the candles and Parson's parchment under the bowl of eggs in the buttery.

If there was kindness as well as wickedness in this world, as Parson had it, John said, why had only wickedness come to haunt them?

'There's wickedness as well as wickedness in this world,' Margret said, 'just you forget all about kindness and read what I have brought home while I see to the rabbit. What was it that Parson said?'

'Be still and know, says the Lord.'

Parson had it right once again, Margret thought. Be still and know. That's what they would do once John had finished reading the papers.

Chapter 13

Squire's Daughter was in a foul mood when she spotted the commotion at the graveyard. She had to stop now and feign interest instead of turning round and pursuing the girl.

How on earth had the body of that lad been discovered that fast, she wondered, and now she was well and truly lumbered with the Parson.

Sat next to Eloise on the trap, his eyes began to focus unwillingly after the horror of a disturbed grave and the mystery of Sidney's disappearance, and the first thing he noticed were her hands, dirty and bloodied.

She was more of a fool than ever he was, pretending he didn't notice her hands.

The idiot gone, as per usual, Jonathan hadn't made a proper job of it, and the girl had tricked her! Cooper's girl, Jenny.

Now it became clear Cooper had been out looking for his daughter, the feeling gnawing at her bones that the girl wasn't telling the truth had been right, and now she knew what it had been; the girl's hands had been clean. Cleaner than her own, and her legs had been clean when she had revealed the cut knee, only her face had been dirty.

She wasn't any ordinary traveller, that was certain.

And the girl had wanted to see her own dirty hands, bloodied, under the pretext of looking at the ring.

When she had gotten the girl onto the trap she had let her go, fool that she was. Her beauty was fading slowly already. Her fine features had gotten coarser, her hair was less abundant, darker. Her appearance no longer caused astonished gasps and she simply could not bear to tolerate it. What else did she have, apart from her beauty?

She recalled her mother's fate, so fair and then so foul, and she shuddered.

'T'is a bad day, Parson,' she said sadly, 'my Father had a stroke come the dawn.'

A tear was rolling down her cheek.

'And he was burnt by a candle, and Farmer Morrow, he was charged by a bull yesterday,' she said as Parson sat up, fully awake now and taking notice.

'A gang of vagabonds was hiding in one of the outhouses,' she lied, 'and you know what Father is like, he does not want to bother his servants if he can help it.' Parson had the smell of a rotten egg under his nose; the Squire was born to command and discarded his servants as the mood took him.

Everyone recalled the German companion told to go back to Saxony when she had outlived her usefulness. Sitting by the side of the road in cold winter, and Emily had taken pity on her, talking foreign or not. She didn't last long, but she left Emily quite a lot of money. Emily deserved it, the villagers said, but those who had averted their gaze from the pitiable bundle by the road cursed their luck.

Why was the Lady Eloise lying? The Parson wondered.

'The ruffians set about him in the middle of the night, the candle burned his gown first and then his hand and left him insensible; we found him at dawn. I have been chasing them all morning to apprehend them, and I have so far not been successful,' she sighed.

A stroke of luck, being reminded of the travellers. It served to explain her father's illness and burns as well as her own journeys, although she began to wish she had thought it out better before airing it.

'Did he have a seizure there and then?' Parson asked.

'Of course,' she said impatiently, 'people do not

choose when to have seizures, do they?'

'In the middle of the night,' he asked.

'Yes, when the ruffians set on him, and left him insensible,' she said.

'So how come, if he wasn't discovered until dawn and was insensible, he was able to describe events?'

She stopped the trap.

'I do not care to be questioned as if I was an offender, Parson,' she said. 'I am struck down with grief and you are supposed to provide me with spiritual comfort.'

He looked at that sweet face and noticed the violet shadows imprinted on the delicate skin under the fine eyes as he took his courage in both hands and followed his intuition.

'Get back onto the righteous road, My Lady, and do not let evil into your soul for it will stay there.'

She glared at him.

'Do not grasp Satan's hand, this life is but a prelude to the next. Keep it in mind at all times,' and she hissed at him like a snake.

'T'is a sign for the pony,' she said, smiling sweetly, and Parson couldn't wait to get out of her reach.

The feeling was mutual. Squire's Daughter dropped him at the Parsonage like a sack of barley and roared off down the road.

He wandered down the garden to the outhouse as in a dream. He tried the door, which fell down when Sidney appeared in the doorway.

Sidney was dirty, but no dirtier than usual. Caked blood smeared the left side of his face.

'Am I glad to see you! I thank God for it. What has happened to you?'

Sidney didn't say a word, and he wouldn't for a long time.

When her husband returned with news about Sidney and sent Agnes to see to him, Parsons' wife thought she would cope easily. She would give Agnes some money and send her home for a period until Sidney became sensible.

Parson could live on bread and cheese for once, and if the floors were dirty, they could always lay rushes. It would suffice for a little while at any rate, but Agnes would have none of it when she came back, leaving Sidney in the outhouse, cleaned up, and with a stomach full of oats.

'Getting up the same day is all right for us like, but it's not fitting for the likes of you, it's just asking for trouble,' she said, carrying the little maid upstairs, following the Mistress whose legs had begun to buckle.

Agnes knew her place. So she coped when Parson fell low to a melancholy humour. He didn't move in his chair because he was uncertain what course of action to take. It was clear to him that Jenny had fled in the night, closely pursued by Sidney, who had come across some evil doing, been attacked, and left for dead. But he had risen like Lazarus from the grave. It had been laid at the doors of the travellers by the evil folks at the Manor; he knew the Lady Eloise's tale was a pack of lies.

Same with the Mistress. She should be made to feel remorse, it was her doing that had led to some of the disasters, but she was so fully content now, he was loathe to disturb her long-fought-for peace. Cowardice or compassion?

Cowardice and compassion, strange bed-fellows?

He gave up. He just sat in his chair, uncaring.

In the end the child, fretful at night, had roused him. 'Some sit and think and some just sit, Babe,' the Mistress said, 'he might as well sit and hold you,' and after a while he walked with the babe round and round the parlour and the momentum, once started, continued into the rhythm of his life.

'How long was I out for?' he asked Agnes.

'Three long days and nights,' she said. 'And my Sidney is still not talking, but he is now welcome at home.'

'Get out!' his father had shouted at him, and Sidney had simply walked up to him and laid one on him.

His father got up and Sidney felled him again. His father never made any more objections, after he had arisen from the floor with a bloody nose, of course.

Strange how things worked out, she thought, and as far as she was concerned she was able to roll up her sleeves with her arms clear of bruises.

Chapter 14

Squire's Daughter had ridden off in a fury from the Parsonage. At first it was directed at herself, at her own weakness. Contrary to popular belief, the devil was hard to get hold of. The day, the date, the hour had been right, and when she finally looked at what was in her mind she wondered; had the devil sat on her father's back?

Her fury was now directed against the escaped village girl; she could not have got very far on foot, Lady Eloise thought, and she was right.

The road was as open to Jenny as it was to the Lady Eloise.

The travellers had disappeared from view long since, and the brooding sky hung low and grey, promising great sheets of rain shortly.

The lady might be roaring back any minute to check that she was one of the group; Squire's Daughter was not that easily fooled.

Keep calm, Jenny thought, don't panic. Girl's got her head screwed on right, her Ma had said, look how quick she had fastened onto the reading. I best act as if I've got a brain in my head she thought as she looked for a hiding place.

To the left was a flat landscape of fields with trees behind and a barn. Her heart stopped. A man with a gun slung on his shoulder was riding towards it.

He got off his horse, and she recognized him by the shape of his legs. Silk-breeches! Without looking round, he entered the barn.

To the right, between two high embankments, was a fast-flowing stream which would carry on into the woods where she had spent the night. She scrambled down to the stream, and then she stopped, looking at the swollen water skipping over polished stones.

Slippery stones. Her bundle! She would topple over, and at that the dog really lost his patience. He grabbed the bundle and, head held high and sure-footed, he scrambled to the top of the embankment with Jenny after him, and then it started to rain in earnest. The ground was flat and marshy and great clumps of green, fat spikes sheltered her nicely.

She had just laid down with Stray pressed close to her, when she saw the pony and trap approaching.

It stopped where she had scrambled down the embankment a minute ago, and she had a feeling that the Lady Eloise knew exactly where she was hiding.

She peered through the spiky leaves, and amidst the rain and thunder she heard a sweet, clear voice.

'Jenny, Jenny. Come home'

The name sighed and swayed amongst the gloom.

'Jenniieee!'

'For God's sake, use the sense you have in this weather, ' the sweet voice implored her, and the dog lying right close gave a short warning growl. Don't you dare move!

'Remember Sidney, he wants you to come home, Jenny.'

'Too right, My Lady,' Jenny whispered, 'and if it's a ploy to show myself it hasn't worked.'

Lightning rent the sky and Jenny remembered the stink of fox on the face in the dream. She saw Squire's Daughter and on her face was the stink of evil.

Young Morrow was riding towards her now and the barn behind him went up in smoke. A hiding place gone.

That gun! Pa didn't have a gun any more than any ordinary villagers, even if he had said many times he would take a gun to the dog.

Young Morrow wouldn't hesitate, and he meant to use it on her in the first place. That's why he looked for her hiding in the barn. Nobody would have heard her cry out or heard a shot either.

The Lady Eloise would not have taken her to the Manor in broad day-light.

'I reckon she's headed for home,' the lady said, 'that stream takes some crossing with a bundle.'

After an eternity, the pony thundered on down the road to the village, the rider took off after the travellers, and Stray jumped down the embankment and over the stream as he tracked the vulpine lady back to her lair.

Jenny waited for him, not daring to move or wonder what would be next, when she heard another voice calling her.

Made out it was her Pa, this other voice, with a break in it as if he was crying, but Jenny wasn't fooled; her Pa never cried, and besides he was in bed with the fever.

'Come home Jenny,' the voice cried, 'please, please come home.'

Her Pa wouldn't have said that either, begging her to come home, he would have said if she didn't come home at once no good would come of it.

Who was it?

She peered through the spiky leaves and she saw a man on a horse. He looked a lot like her Pa, but he was riding towards the village and she knew she had been right in thinking it wasn't her Pa, wherever would he get a horse?

Jonathan returned to the Manor late. He had ridden half-way to Huntingdon without success and he was in a foul mood, whereas Eloise was upset from the trial of strength and cunning won by the girl.

The late Lady de Breville's illness could lay dormant

in her, the physician had warned Eloise, and might come to the fore in sudden shocks.

'Avoid them, my Lady,' he had advised her, although he recognised that by their very nature sudden shocks were just that, sudden and unforeseen.

Sidney hitting Morrow and breaking his nose had been bad enough; he had been singularly unafraid when he had encountered them, more than likely he had come across them before. The knife cutting his cheek and being hit on the head with a shovel would have finished anybody else. Maybe burying him in the disturbed grave had been a mistake, but they had been in a panic.

'Seeing I wasn't able to finish her, the girl is now a witness who could tell a different tale. Most likely she has returned to her home.'

Eloise could help there.

'It seems that a village girl went missing, ran away in the night. Cooper, his name was, he was out looking for her, although he would not admit to it.'

'I know him,' said Jonathan. 'An occasional labourer on our estate. Insolent. Educated. Father says he had been a sickly child and the then Parson's wife took a fancy to him and taught him.'

'It's a mistake to educate that sort, they start to question authority and get uppity, Father says.'

'How is he now after the bleeding?'

There had been no change in Squire, she said, and her Companion said a village woman had been snooping around in the kitchen this morning. She felt certain that Cook had been gossiping with this woman.

'She made out she was a widow woman. Not your run-of-the mill village woman, sharp enough to cut herself, the sort that takes charge in a family, like some do. I noticed that the white blouse against her neck was moving as if she was breathing rapidly, she was agitated Her blouse was dirty on top, with blood on it

Only later did I fathom out that the mobcap that the idiot had worn has gone missing,' she said in her clipped tone. 'Cook must have snooped around in the night.'

'Right,' said Jonathan, 'I'll see to Cook and find out the woman's name.'

'Go with him, Hannah,' Eloise said to her Companion, 'keep the kitchen maids out f the way.'

She went to see her father, who looked dreadful. One side his face and his hair had been burned by the torch to a red mass, dribble ran out of his mouth, and he had messed himself.

'He'll not get any better,' she said when Jonathan returned.

The woman had been Mistress Cooper according to Cook, Jonathan said.

'The girl must be hiding at home. We'll waylay her tomorrow and take her to the barn.'

'You have set fire to it, but it will be the travellers who will get the blame.'

What was it with these village girls?

That red-haired girl who had been drowned as a witch had had her father in a spin ever since she had turned him down very publicly at a May-dance; he had to have her after that, and he had seized his chance before the trial.

He had promised her he would see to it that she would go free, but once an itch was scratched it wasn't an itch any more. But whatever Squire had done, her dying curse had done its work.

Now they had to do theirs.

Chapter 15

It was evening when Eloise and Silk-breeches burst through the Coopers' door, just as the darkness fell, and Margret and John were that relieved when they did they were hard pushed not to welcome them with a grin.

It meant Jenny had got away, because they wouldn't bother to come to tell them that they had found her.

'Look and act simple,' they had told Adam. 'Practice on your worst-sounding flute.'

He looked forward to making a nuisance of himself, although the pair of 'em looked menacing enough.

'I have to ask you to leave. You have no right to burst in on us,' said John.

'None what-so-ever,' squeaked Adam.

But apparently they had. They were investigating a theft, the theft of a piece of beef, taken this morning by Mistress Cooper.

'The only beef in this house has four legs attached to it and is in the stable.'

Squire's Daughter pointed to the pot on the hearth with her whip.

'Rabbit stew,' said Margret.

'Do themselves well, the poor, methinks. Sometimes I quite wish I was poor myself, don't you, Jonathan? Rabbit stew, and the rabbit most likely poached from our estate.'

She looked at John.

He looked back at her and was about to say that rabbit had jumped clean into the stew-pot, but Adam cleared the reed just in time and Margret said it had been caught on the common where their cow was grazing.

'The common land belongs to the common people,' Margret said firmly, 'which is us like.'

'Cottagers poaching rabbits ought to take care to pay on time,' said Eloise, but of course she could not prove that the bones had hopped around on her own ground, so the pair looked around the cottage supposedly for the beef instead, starting with the buttery, ending with the adjoining stable.

Nobody was fooled. They were looking for Jenny.

Margret was sweating in case the egg bowl was over-turned and the parchment discovered and even more pleased that she had washed the blood out of the mob-cap. She sighed with relief when their attention finally turned to the beds, which were overturned and prodded with the Daughter's whip.

'Did I ever tell how I came to wed Margret,' John said, as if he was on a story-telling level with the folks from the Manor. 'Margret's Pa hired the bullock for covering his cows, and her and me and her Pa were sitting on the fence like, a-watching. I told her I felt the same way as that bullock did, and you know what she said?'

He had everybody's full attention now.

'She said to help myself like, plenty of cows there.'

'The fever plays tricks on him,' Margret said serenely. 'It's not helped any by your bursting in on him without any cause,' she added, 'if you don't mind me pointing it out.'

'Are you a friend of Cook?' asked the Lady Eloise, and Margret blinked at her uncertainly.

'Cook, at the Manor? How is she?'

'When did you see her last?'

'I see her regular like at Church, but we don't always converse.'

'Did you see her this morning?'

'I did, I told her I delivered Parson's wife of a fine maid.'

Finally, when no congratulations came forth,

Margret asked, 'Have you brought a message for me?' The man said was it likely; Cook had died this afternoon. The physician was there seeing to the Lady Eloise's father, as it happened. Died of a broken bone, Cook did.

'Folks don't die of broken bones,' said Adam, and Silkbreeches said folks did if it was a broken bone which stuck in their throats.

John followed the pair of 'em to the door as Margret sat down and crossed herself like her mother used to.

He had known Young Morrow as a snotty-nosed lad, and now he was growing into a fast-rising young stench if ever there was one, even if he did wipe his nose on a kerchief and not with his sleeve as he used to, John thought as he followed them secretly into the night to give the Lady her whip back, listening to their talk.

'Ringing the bells at midnight might not have been the best idea,' she said sharply.

'T'is written,' Silk-breeches said, 'thirteen tolls at midnight,' and if there was a better way to warn people to stay in their hovels than by bells seemingly ringing by themselves thirteen times on the thirteenth, a Friday, he would like to know about it.

'Well,' she said, 'they can't say they haven't been warned.'

Follow the shepherd and find the sheep, John thought. A nest of adders and in the Manor, and Parson himself useless, just sitting in his chair.

'And there's Sidney.'

'Who takes notice of what an idiot says? And now, well, what can't talk, can't tell tales.'

John had heard enough. He shuffled forward but then stopped suddenly.

'Come Michaelmas they'll be out. We shall not renew their lease,' she said, and John was angry. Why should they have such power?

'Pitch defiles, My Lady,' he said, stepping forward.

They whirled around, mouths agape.

'Your whip, My Lady, you left it behind.'

She grabbed it.

'Good night to you both,' he said clearly and pleasantly, 'I wish you may both rot in hell.'

They stared at him.

'I said good night to you both,' John said clearly and pleasantly again, 'I wish you both well.'

Jenny had overlooked something unspeakably evil, he said after they left, and Cook had been done away with, but what good would it do to summons the Sheriff for a woman choking on a bone, and in the Manor?

'Poor, poor, woman. I will pay my respects to her and burn a bundle of sage over her coffin. I expect Emily will lay her out,' Margret said.

'I wasn't any too keen on Adam hearing that filthy tale about the cattle,' she added.

'T'is an old one, done the rounds since ancient times, I shouldn't wonder. She says she's not going to renew the lease.'

Margret lit one of Parson's fat candles and John started to read, dropping the parchment in amazement only at the very end when dawn was breaking, and then John told her all about Parson's wife's obsessive love.

Who would think love could cause such mayhem; hate could, but love? she thought. When the time was right, she had wed John. She had known him and was fond of him and she looked after him and helped him, sometimes she made allowances for him and if that wasn't love, she didn't know what was. Love like that of the Mistress belonged to ancient tales.

'Like King Arthur and...'

'Lancelot and Guinevere,' he said, 'and it's to be hoped you're not starting to ramble like Old Martha used to,' he said.

'Who was *your* mother, let's not forget,' said Margret.

He urged her to forget the past and look forward to the future, in particular to a herd of cows.

'I see a freehold in there and a bigger window myself,' said Margret.

'What? With the price of glass?'

"I shouldn't be surprised, and don't forget, we have it from Master Cromwell himself; *Necessity knows no law*.'

Chapter 16

Parson preached a fine sermon when Cook was buried.

He preached about sudden loss, about life and hope.

'God has given each and every one of us different gifts to His greater glory and our greater good. Let us remember and rejoice in the life of Elisa Tanner, although cruelly cut down, who did just that,' he said, and the villagers had known he was right about Cook who was a good cook.

Squire was absent.

Villagers tapped their foreheads and crossed their eyes and reckoned that Squire was there and the candles were burning but nobody was at home. They were not so certain about the other thing, that Squire had disturbed a band of travellers in the outhouse who had attacked him first and also attacked Sidney, now even more of a great useless hulk and who was known to roam at night.

Disturbing travellers? When had Squire last lifted a hand for himself?

The farm had always been in the bailiff's charge. Did Squire even know he had an outhouse or would he recognise one if he did? The villagers kept such thoughts to themselves.

In the end the old saying, that lies travelled all around the country while truth was still lacing up its boots, was as right as ever.

It took some time before the Coopers became freeholders. They had to wait until the Lady Eloise and Silk-breeches departed for Cambridge to determine the price of grain and beef.

'The Mistress is hard to fathom out, I know that,' Parson said to John Cooper,who was negotiating a deal with the help of Parson''s diary while they were waiting until the |Manor was clear of the pair. 'These passions make her into a run-away horse, although it's containable now that it's shared with the babe. She is the one person I know who could find the proverbial pin in a haystack and convince herself it was the farmer's daughter.'

"Jenny told me of it, Parson, and as for the money, well, the whole village knows she brought a good dowry with her. It's her that's guilty and she'll get the papers back with her reputation intact. We wouldn't take aught away from you, you know that,' Margret said, 'but well, it's like this, we want to be here when Jenny returns and not sleeping in a ditch somewhere where she can't find us.'

'Oh?' he said.

'I overheard the Lady Eloise talking to Young Morrow,' said John.'She said our lease would not be returned come Michaelmas.'

'I didn't know that,' said the Parson

'When I said papers, I really meant the papers bar the last three pages, we will keep those until our future is secure and Jenny's back home.'

The Parson never said anything to that, but deep inside he wept. He knew that his nocturnal writings were the proof he was duty-bound to submit to the authorities, as there was truth in the scrawled hand of the last three pages, the pages the Coopers kept; he was allowed to live with his little daughter a while longer.

'Best stay away from the Manor for a good while,' was all he said. 'Young Morrow is in charge now, and he is a mean one.'

He surely was, thought John, and selling the freehold to him was as likely as a man on the moon.

'With his own father ailing,' the Parson continued, 'he has two estates to run, and things are already on the slide. Neither of the bailiffs care now about what goes on, neither do the hands.'

Folks farmed their strips of land first, they started work for Squire late and finished early to make a proper balance of the day, and they helped themselves to what they thought they could get away with, the odd sack of barley, a side of beef and so on, or so the Lady Eloise and Young Morrow had it; only of course they couldn't prove it, they couldn't be everywhere, although they did their best; the Daughter and Silk-breeches were everywhere, and the Coopers grew impatient to secure their freehold.

'At some time or other they will have to leave, setting prices always comes from the Manor in the first place and they get it from the outside in the second,' John said, and if he said it once more, Margret thought she would lose her mind.

At long, long last Squire's Daughter and her future husband departed the village, looking up the price grain might be best sold for at the Corn Exchange in Cambridge and what the beef price should be.

The bailiff ran the estate and he was in charge of the red seal until Squire recovered, which wasn't on the cards, or until the Lady Eloise returned. She wouldn't be best pleased, so they had to make the most of her absence.

Chapter 17

Finally the great day arrived.

Margret and John waited for the Parson outside the Parsonage.

Settling the account with the help of Parson's diary had been men's work. She didn't know how much Parson's wife had coughed up to buy their Freehold, but she didn't mind, as long as Parson had the money on him.

It was a fine morning. They wound their way to the Manor past the pond and past the Church, and they sat facing the Parson and the bailiff, Nathaniel Fletcher, in the Great Hall across the yellow elm table where the deed was rolled out and read out by the bailiff, who signed the deed in Squire's stead - with Parson warming the wax and sealing it with Squire's red seal bearing two crossed swords.

Margret looked about her and up at the Great Gallery.

In one of the rooms leading off it, Squire himself lay senseless. Squire's first wife had lost the de Breville heir up there after riding when with child, and his next wife had spent her last years confined to her room with the dropsy. Cook had hidden there and had crept down in the night, and then Margret's reverie was rudely interrupted as the parchment was rolled up and handed over to John; and Squire's Daughter came roaring back.

Silk-breeches wasn't with her, except - as it would turn out - he was the late Silk-breeches, nothing but a bundle wrapped in a blanket and with his face shot clean off, so they heard later.

The Lady didn't look too pleased about something,' John whispered.

'Out! All of you!' she screamed.

'Not you, Fletcher!' she said the the bailiff.

The Lady Eloise would be even more upset once she found out at Michaelmas that she was a cottager short, John said outside.

'Well, Parson? Can I borrow your pony?' John asked.

'I'll go and see to it myself tomorrow,' said the Parson mysteriously.

'To what?' Margret asked.

Turned out the change of property had to be put onto the Land Registry in Cambridge. While she admired John's knowledge and Parson's wisdom of being someplace other than with the Mistress, they went home without inquiring what had happened to bring Lady Eloise back so soon.

Parson said he would know soon enough, Heaven help him, as they parted company by their cottage where Margret handed his diary over, and then, at the Parsonage, just as he had thought, the Parson found that he had to tell the Mistress that the Coopers had kept the important part of the diary for a rainy day; the part which recorded her ill-doing.

'So more blackmail will come forth from the Coopers, his wife said. 'What say you?'

'I'm off to Cambridge tomorrow,' said Parson.

Silence hung heavily over mealtimes.

Baby Jessica was asleep upstairs, Agnes and her man were chomping away at their food in the kitchen, the roaming Sidney was absent.

It struck Parson how little he communicated with the Mistress. She kept a good house and looked after him well. He had treated her with consideration every bit as he had treated his mother, only, God help him, she wasn't his mother.

She had been a passionate lover and yet he had

imposed celibacy on them without even consulting her. He had left her to roam above with her secret soul and hidden pain while he had talked to others, laughed with Jenny, and written about her in the dark night.

He interpreted the Good Book for his parishioners and they brought their troubles to him freely.

He looked at her, seeing her as if for the first time. Twin creases furrowing her brow, she tugged at her awry fichue, a sudden onrush of milk staining her front.

She looked young, tired and vulnerable and he wished that his heart could go out to her.

Perhaps the wish was all.

He would talk to her like he did to one of his flock.

'Are you quite happy with Agnes and the state of the house, Mathilda?' he asked.

'Yes, I am,' she snapped, 'but I am your wife and not one of your flock, and the running of the house does not fall within the auspices of your good offices as a Parson. I resent your sermonizing and your indifference if you must know.' The Parson comforted himself with the thought that even a stone could eventually be worn away.

'T'is Margret's Jooohn, come to see the Miiistress,' Agnes bellowed just then.

'We will pay the money back if and when we can and we shall not ask for more. All we want is a roof over our head,' John explained to them when he was shown in.

In the meantime, he and Margret, John said, would come and do odd jobs in the house and grounds to pay the debt in kind.

'When I'm fit, of course,' he said, 'I'm given to the fever,' and the Mistress showed him the door of the outhouse which needed fixing and the stone wall which was in need of repair.

He fixed the door and wall the very next day.

'Good as new, Mistress,' he said and so they were, although he didn't tell her that he had buried the papers she longed for under the wall in a strong, black box. Now the stone wall was indeed better than new with the box of papers under it.

Parson was sitting at his desk, planning his sermon.

Ecclesiastes, perhaps, *A Woman is more bitter than Death,* or perhaps not, no need to enlighten his flock on what they possibly already knew, while outside John did his best to be reasonable with the Mistress, to no avail.

'T'is my belief Jenny destroyed the wall on purpose so the cattle can trample all over my kitchen-garden and send the roosters broody,' she said, 'so don't expect any credit for fixing it.'

Never a good word or a wish for Jenny from her, and so he left the Mistress working in the herb garden, not more than a foot away from where the black box was buried. Well, he thought, it was up to God now. If He wanted her to find the papers, she would find them. If not, he would find himself a couple more cows instead. No need to enlighten Margret.

The Mistress watched him depart. It suddenly struck her that everything was beginning to unravel like an old bit of Hessian, that things were becoming just as they had always been, despite the child.

To her surprise, her hands started to shake uncontrollably. She felt no ill-will towards the Coopers; Margret and herself were united, both mixed up in a shady deal.

She had been very hurt by her husband's implied suggestion that she didn't make a proper job of running the house with Old Agnes's help, and she had simply passed her bad feeling onto the Coopers.

If only she didn't feel so tired! Feeding the child and doing all the jobs Old Agnes wasn't up to left her feeling worn out before she even got out of bed.

What was it her husband had said? 'Are you quite happy with Agnes, Mathilda?'

Mathilda, not Mistress. The more she thought about it, the more she thought he could have been concerned for her rather than the state of the house.

The Parson looked up from his desk. She had come in quietly, leaning against the door.

'I'm sorry, Matthew, I thought you were dissatisfied with the way things are just now in the house. It's just that I am so tired these days, but it'll improve with time, Agnes says.'

Careful now, he thought.

'You are the Mistress of the house. All you need do with servants is deal with them gently, or dismiss them if they fail in their work or displease you.'

Not hang or drown them, he thought.

What was it her father had said about her? Cleverness is no bar to silliness? The Mistress thought back to Parson's writings, why should he hide a secret if there wasn't one?

She went to him like a child and when he folded his arms around her, they both wept and their tears made them into one.

'If only I could atone for my sins,' she gasped through her tears, 'I would gladly carry a cross for the rest of my life,' but that was wrong, he told her gently, they would carry the cross together.

Whilst the Mistress had mused on her father's sayings, John improved on Master Cromwell's *Necessity knows no law*. Necessity makes up a law as it went along, he said to Margret, who crossed herself and said it was up to them to act decently in that case now.

She had heard rumours of Silk-breeches' death, but also that the Lady Eloise had been robbed of her jewels and cash when their coach was held up by a high-way robber. She had been in a high old state since her sudden return.

It wasn't to be wondered at, if it was true, which it must be since Emily had told her, and now folks were running towards them as they were standing outside the Parsonage having put a morning's work in there, and her heart sank.

Why do people always run with bad news, she wondered, doesn't it always come soon enough? Then she saw young Adam was running in front, followed by a crowd and a cart, on which laid an old woman.

They had covered her with a blanket.

A thin arm was swinging from it. White hair fell away from her head and she was facing the sky, her mouth was wide open and her eyes were staring at the sky; even so, there was something vaguely familiar about her.

It clearly was a job for the Parson, everybody said so, except Margret recognised the bundle on the cart.

'I found her, Ma, in the woods by the common. I poked a bundle of clothes with a stick. Only it swore at me, so I knew it was a person and I fetched the others. She had an ugly voice,' said Adam, and Margret and John looked at each other. Aggie's mother, Kate! Mad as a March hare, and -as she was their kin- she would be taken to their cottage!

They finally screwed up their courage and took Kate home, but it wasn't for long.

'They want to care for her at the Parsonage!' Margret said the next day when John came home.

Kate had lost her senses and didn't recognise anybody nor did she know who or where James, her husband was, but Parson and his wife had taken it on themselves to care for her, which wouldn't be any kind of pleasure. That much was clear when they took her to the Parsonage.

'Clear off, Parson,' Kate screeched, 'you black-faced bastard,' and the Mistress and the Parson looked at each other; their longed-for cross had arrived good and proper.

If that's what happened to people on the road to a strong woman like Kate, Margret thought, how on earth did Jenny fare?

Chapter 18

Jenny pressed herself into the damp earth for a long time, waiting for the dog's return.

She smelled the earth, she felt its dampness, she was part of it and she was eager to have done with it; every fibre of her body ached to be gone.

The lady's pony and trap and Morrow's horse had vanished into the curtain of rain which could be cut with a knife, as had the other rider.

Making out it was her Pa. They'll send Cook next from the Manor I shouldn't wonder, she thought as she sat up.

Stray was gone and the heavens wept.

It was time she was gone, but she couldn't leave without him.

Had they shot him? she was wondering, when he returned. He licked her face hastily and, with her skirt tied into a knot about her knees so she could run more freely, and her bundle slung over her shoulder, they finally set off over soggy, marshy ground, whilst the skies overhead well and truly drenched her.

Her Ma had said that the shawl was very near waterproof, but how near was very near? It had taken a goodly time for the first drop to find its way through, but after that all the others seemed to follow to keep it company. Her skirt began to cling to her and her feet seemed to weigh very heavy. She had to pull them up with each step from the ground, sodden ground covered with moss, but the dog would allow no respite and she supposed it must be as bad for him; after all, he could be sitting out the bad weather in some barn or other if it wasn't for her.

What made him do it?

She had always assumed him to be a very heavy dog

but now, with his wet fur clinging to him in the rain, she saw that his body was bony and his face square when he looked back anxiously with his green eyes at her slow progress.

On either side pale, slim feathered fronds as tall as she wept into dark-green, ever-expanding flats of water. Bullrushes. Dead Lady's Fingers, they called them in the village. When they popped open, a mass of white spilled out.

At one point, she had to hang on to Stray's tail as he wound his way crookedly amongst the still and stagnant waters, but after a long, long while the ground seemed drier, less soggy.

A few sheep had grazed forlornly on what seemed entirely bald ground near the water, the path becoming visibly more of a path, and in the far distance, low-roofed houses and cottages crowded against a church-tower.

A village, and how safe and cosy it all seemed, until Jenny imagined the big houses with a Mistress inside it spinning a web of deceit; and then she was glad when Stray pressed on ahead.

The dog stopped. A thicket of brambles reaching as far as she could see hindered their progress. Get past this and we'll be safe, she thought, but now of all times she was ready to give up; except Stray was waiting next to the thicket, as it gave birth to a large sheep, followed by another and another. Altogether six more had come out of it, unworried and upright but pursued by a small grey dog nipping at their heels, sitting down and looking pleased with himself.

'If sheep can do it, so can we,' Jenny shouted when she crawled after him through the opening. Emerging on the other side, they walked on again until her legs buckled, but she had finally seen the goal he had been heading for when a small building loomed squarely in the darkening evening hour. Did he come from these parts?

The dog circled the barn several times and finally, when he allowed her to push the door open and to her amazement, it seemed to be full of steaming bodies.

'Are you the others?'

Jenny peered into the gloom of a wooden building, a barn with exposed rafters. Rolled up ropes and old sacks were slung on hooks. Bundles of reeds and straw lined one wall. Farming implements were stacked and hung against the wall opposite to the steaming bodies.

'I'm Jenny Cooper from Ninewells, but I'm a traveller now like yourself,' she said. Stray had inspected them with many a sniff and a shake of his soaked body, accompanied by shouts and shrieks of, 'Get that animal out of it!' by the travellers.

Jenny took no notice, she was in a dry place.

'Hold on. I will presently get him out,' she said,' but he is my friend and he will have to eat and dry out first.'

She rummaged in her bundle and shared a loaf with the dog, getting a sack from the wall to dry him off, and then she let him out. The roof overlapped the ground, so he would have some shelter, although the rain was now but a faint drizzle.

'What a daft thing to say, 'Are you the others,' a lively young female voice exclaimed, 'you and your dog are the others to us, Jenny from Ninewells wherever that is, but we never ask questions do we?'

'Shut up Rose,' said a male voice. They had seen a girl far back on the road with a fine black dog like she had with her, but nobody had caught up with them he said. 'But then, they wouldn't, we make ourselves scarce in time.'

Jenny closed her eyes and sighed with relief, but Rose hadn't given up on her yet. 'Which way did you come then, we never saw you behind us when we turned off.'

'I turned off some way past the woods, past Ninewells, by a barn,' Jenny said.

'Never! They reckon the place's alive with quagmires.'

'What's a quagmire when it's at home?' Jenny asked.

'Poor soul,' Rose cried, 'she doesn't know what a quagmire is, she shouldn't be out on her ownsome. A quagmire sucks you in like the old man sucks in food.'

Laughter.

She had hung onto the dog's tail going past these dangerous places, she said.

'Just as well,' said a male voice 'He's bred, that dog of yours. Lucky to have him.'

Quagmires! The very name induced dread in her, but she was safe here, and after a while silence fell, interrupted by Rose's sudden shrieking. 'Mind what you are doing with that saddle-bag of yours, Nathan.'

After a while she giggled.

'Leastways I hope it's your saddle-bag.'

A child started to whimper in its sleep, Rose was given one more chance to behave herself, and Jenny wondered what this Rose might look like. She sounded lively and good company,

Darkness fell on her fast. An old man was close by and he didn't only look as if he might smell, he reeked to high heaven. His long yellow hair hung down to his long yellow beard. He was cleaning his two remaining teeth with a long piece of straw. Likely he was the one sucking in food. His body was covered in bits of old sheepskin and rotting pieces of sacking, all held together with old roping.

Jenny stopped drying her wet hair which clung to her little skull like a knitted cap and looked again at him through her up-raised arms. The sacks and ropes on the wall. He might get what could be called his clothes from barns, she thought, and when she smiled at him, she smiled a great big smile of relief.

A roof over her head on a night like this! The threat of Squire's Daughter and Silk-breeches removed, other folks breathing, coughing, snoring. They were not friendly, these travellers, but nor were they unfriendly.

Finally she took her boots off. Something clattered to the floor. Something round and shiny. Parson's wife's guinea.

She had never noticed it in all of the long day's walking, and finally she fell into a deep, dreamless sleep.

Faraway, she heard a cock crow, announcing the departing night or the approaching dawn, she was never sure which.

She saw that most of the others had departed with the night; amongst them was the old man, and he had departed with Parson's wife's guinea.

Jenny pushed the barn door open. A warm hand was clamped tightly over her mouth and a strong hand held her fast.

'T'is the reed-cutters,' said a whispering voice. 'Travellers get the blame for everything that goes wrong in the villages. I knew a man once who was hanged for stealing a cockerel.'

'Did he steal it?'

'Not that time, although plenty of times afore that.'

'Why are you a traveller?' she whispered.

'I'm like all travellers, I walk to keep alive.'

'Did I hear a child's voice last night?'

'Aye, two boys here with their father.'

A bit young to be on the road, she whispered, and he whispered age was no barrier to being unwanted. Summer was the good time for being on the road, it was the winter which sorted the weak from the strong unless they found work.

She looked at the men from the village walking slowly, wearing waders, moleskin coats, their long knives nearly touching. With red faces and bent backs, they seemed to head straight for the barn. Jenny's heart stopped beating for a moment but they marched straight past it.

After a while the young man and Jenny slowly emerged into the fine morning drizzle. Against the yellowing morning sky, the men from the village walked in single file, the slow procession of black silhouettes appeared like an animal with many heads.

'Look at that. *Beware the many-headed beast*, like it said in the Bible,' she said, going into the barn, opening her bundle and reading the Bible.

'*Keep to the straight and narrow road*,' she said, 'it's an omen.'

'Land drainage,' he said. Nothing grew on land under water, seeds just perished, so the water was made to run from the land into two ditches, in the middle of which was a straight and narrow road.

Jenny marvelled how they had known about the fens in the Bible.

'Are you Nathan with the saddle-bag?' she asked.

'Aye.'

'Are you Rose's young man?'

'Rose doesn't have a young man, not for long, Rose is what we call a flitter. She is with Oliver at present but it's not me.'

While Jenny was amazed that in this new world girls did not have a young man but flitted instead, Nathan was amazed that he had described Rose as a flitter. He had made it up because Rose was caught between two stools, neither slut nor virgin, but they had this code of protection, the travellers did.

Jenny thought that she wasn't a flitter, although she didn't have a young man either, but then she had never

126

felt the want of one. When the time came she would find one or he would find her, and her Pa always hoped that she would find one who came complete with his own bull.

'Hurry yourself,' he said.

When she was finally bundled and shawled up, Nathan took her outside and showed her three heaps of stones by the barn.

In the village stones were picked up from fields when nothing else remained to be done.

'Say you are heading for Huntingdon, like we all are. Look where these shapes are pointing at crossroads and such and follow the trail. T'is left by other travellers come afore us. T'will lead you to a safe resting place.'

'I understand,' she said. A stone was a stone to anyone else except to this unwanted company which she belonged to now, the travellers. At that, he was gone.

He travelled light and free. He was fleet of foot and free of fancies. He was free of encumbrances, but even as he said it once more to himself, he found himself turning round.

'Mind you beware of quagmires now.'

'I will, if I recognize one when I see one.'

'You will when it sucks you in...'

'...like the old man sucks in food,' she said, sucking in her cheeks as he made a great slurping noise, and they both laughed.

He walked on, and when he turned round again, the slight figure was sitting on her heels, completely absorbed in the stones.

She had already forgotten him.

The black dog was eagerly sniffing at the stone signs and for a brief moment Nathan thought how it would be if they travelled together, the girl and himself.

She was dirty and she resembled a boy with her plastered-down hair, but she had got him to talk more freely than anyone else in an age. Good God, he had even made up a word, flitter, but he dismissed the thought of *walking together* as swiftly as it had come.

Nathan was his own master and ever would be.

The rain had given way to a light drizzle and Jenny had walked a fair way. She judged it to be about noon when she found the smelly old man with the yellow beard sitting by the wayside under a big old oak tree.

He waved to her and she waved back and walked on. Then she stopped. It hadn't been a greeting, she realised, he wanted to catch her attention.

He patted the ground next to him and, like an obedient child, she sat down. He had a useless right arm pegged into the rope holding his clothes together and he pared down a stale loaf with the help of his chin and his left hand.

He offered some to her and then to Stray, and she softened towards him; anyone who was kind to her dog wasn't all bad, besides which he could only use one arm.

He noticed her glance at his right arm.

'Is not bad,' he said. 'In some country, punishment is cutting off arm and also leg.'

Some country, she thought.

It was a kind of ritual, sharing of food, so she gave him one of her apples. He never said a word, but he looked at last year's wrinkled russet as if it was made of solid gold. He sucked on it with his two remaining teeth.

When she got up to go, he held up his hand.

'A moment, if you please.'

Then he fished around in his bundle and gave her back Parson's wife's guinea.

'Bevare,' he said, 'gold brings dangers.'

He spoke haltingly, his hands unfolding like the petals of a flower following each word. English was not native to him, Jenny could tell by his gestures alone.

'Vat brings you on the road, my child?' he asked, his dark gaze resting on her as she stood before him, and Jenny recoiled from the deep concern and sheer kindness that enfolded her.

She could cope with anything, she thought, anything at all, except kindness. Please don't be kind to me, she thought, I want everyone to be an uncaring stranger, and unshed tears stung her eyes.

'Well,' she said through clenched teeth, ignoring the question and unlacing her boots for the guinea, 'you needn't think that I should be grateful, after all, *it was mine*. I can't think why you took it in the first place. I can look after myself, I can,' and she abruptly started on her journey.

The old Priest was sad. So young, so young. He remembered. Pain and terror could be accepted, but never kindness afterwards.

In another life he had been a member of the Inquisition. As an Inquisitor, he had acted for the Spanish monarchy who acted on behalf of the Pope, who was the servant of God. He himself searched out the truth on behalf of the Church.

He had examined a young man as he had done it many times. It was the right thing to do, it was his calling in life through God to rid the world of unbelievers.

It was plain to see that the young man in front of him, a dark-skinned Morisco - half Spaniard and half Moor - from the hills was simple, childlike, and that he trusted him.

The man had come to the city to look for work and

he had become a Catholic. After a while, work had run out and he had returned to his village and fell into practising Islam with his fellow villagers. He had simply fallen into the way and custom of other people.

Like an obedient child, he did what he was told.

When he returned to the city, he had been arrested by the Inquisition. For weeks it was questions and answers. During the day, questions and answers and the young man understood nothing and answered everything with the innocence of a child. He trusted his tormenter and the Inquisitor saw Jesus at night.

How fierce Jesus looked on him!

'Suffer the little children to come unto me!'

The Inquisitor dared not sleep. At night he entered a small cell where he could not lie down and he wore a hairshirt. How cursed he was! He fell asleep every night and Jesus was fierce.

'What must I do, Master?'

'You must do right.'

At the end of each daily session the Inquisitor himself had rung a bell to signal a halt to the proceedings, dragged out as long as he possibly could.

After six weeks, the young man was burned in the market place as a heretic, still not understanding what his crime had been.

He was bursting into flames when he saw the Inquisitor, and the Inquisitor saw hope flaring up even as the flames consumed him. He had trusted him to the end.

The Inquisitor was the mediating Priest during the Eucharist the following day. When the moment arrived and the bread and wine was transformed into the body and blood of Christ, he wanted to ring a bell to announce this to his congregation.

The hand he had used to ring the bell at the trial of the child-like man refused to move towards the bell used in celebration of the Eucharist.

He remembered the pain, the flogging, each stroke of the whip tearing at his body, eyelids flying wide open, but God was merciful. Pain and life were not infinite, but he was cursed, although because of the flight he made he was alive and he didn't know why.

The flight and then kindness, sometimes. He could not cope with kindness. He hated the hands of his friend which had led him onto the boat and freedom.

The girl was too young, her mind must not get so twisted that kindness was spat out.

Last night she had smiled at him.

He watched her disappearing into the distance, a slight figure walking determinedly. By her side was the black dog.

As he made the sign of the cross and blessed her, Jenny was stomping along in a fair fit of temper. His gentle kindness had assaulted her defences and she had never been in a fouler temper.

'I don't need any of you,' she said to the empty landscape around her, scurrying along, muttering further dark thoughts to herself.

'And that includes you, Nathan.'

The sun was getting low in the sky when Jenny found the dog sniffing at a few heaps of stones before he followed a criss-crossing scent with his head down.

Clever, that dog, she thought, as she followed him.

The travellers had marked out a good hiding place for the night, she thought, when she approached the light woods of straight tall trees leading to bunched up willows by the water's edge.

No smoke had been visible from beyond the barrier of trees, and she smelt the food before she saw the other folks. A rabbit was bubbling in a pot on a pole slung between two wooden triangles, fishes were baking between two hot stones, and small loaves were baking on hot bricks around the fire, like Ma's had before she began to go to Emily's for the bread.

'There you are, little lady,' said the young man, Nathan.

'Little lady? Little lady?' said a woman, who had to be Rose. 'Have you gone blind, Nathan?'

'Have you got a mug of your own?' Nathan said, and Jenny rummaged silently in her bundle for the pewter mug.

'T'is a most handsome mug,' Nathan said, and for some reason the girl burst into tears.

'Is good,' the old man said, looking in the girl's direction, 'is wery good, you leave it.'

Nathan had never heard him speak before, and he felt let down that he had extended the traveller's code to nothing more than an old foreigner.

'That's right, what he says,' Rose cried enthusiastically. 'Grief has to come out of a body.'

She stood next to Nathan and looked down at the sobbing girl.

'I can only say that I have grieved in my time.'

She turned around when she heard the low laughter emerging from the circle.

'You can laugh if you like, but my God, I shudder to think how I have grieved and cried and sobbed. I know all about suffering, but there's a time for it like, and in the meantime we all want to eat, don't we.'

'Aye.'

'So pull yourself together, Jenny from Ninewells. We all know you're upset by now.'

T'was not fitting, this sobbing, Nathan thought, just as Jenny wiped her nose, feeling ashamed.

She sat contentedly now, flanked by the old man with the beard and Nathan, whilst opposite Rose and Oliver, a pale man with lively eyes in a nondescript face - but who seemed very likeable - fed each other like babes.

Nathan was lean and long-legged with a sturdy body. When he had removed his hat his hair was dark and falling over his fine forehead. He was right handsome with regular features, dark-eyed with fine brows.

She was eating her fill, and - feeling better - she got up and walked to the mere, a great expanse of clear water. Pollarded willow trees, like bunches of sticks held in a giant hand, were reflected in the water with the evening sky, mingling rosy hues of blue and pink.

She rinsed her mug and after the rippling water settled she saw a reflection. It was the dirty face of a boy with plastered-down hair who might have been keeping pigs that stared back at her.

She had forgotten that Ma had cut her hair short and blackened her face, but she could thank her Ma when she returned to her.

She joined the others around the fire with a clean face topped by her bouncing curls shaken loose and free, treading lightly on bare feet, swinging her shawl, her bodice neatly tucked into her skirt once more.

It was a magic hour.

Rose and the young man, who wasn't her young man but with whom she flitted, temporarily excused themselves and wandered off hand in hand, and two little moon-faced boys in dirty hats fell asleep against their father as dusk fell fast.

She listened to the murmuring voices she was part of now. She heard them say that they would meet up at the Digger colony.

'Where is it?' she asked.

'Outside London,' Nathan said. 'They're digging up the common and they plant and build huts, what it is, they want to do away with property.'

'Property? You mean, what is ours?' she said, clutching her bundle.

'Not *that sort* of property, property is *the land*. If it's common property nobody can throw you off.'

She was about to think about it when music was called for and she thought how her Ma always said that things improved no end on a full and warm stomach.

Music, and Nathan, who became more handsome by the minute, said he wished he had a flute, he had lost his, or maybe it got stolen. At times he earned some money on markets with his music, and you found all sorts there.

'T'is a great shame,' Jenny said, and then she remembered Adam's reed.

'T'is my brother Adam's' she said shyly, 'his best, and he said it would bring me luck.'

Nathan tried the instrument and he was glad of it. The surprise when the child with the dirty face and plastered-down hair turned into one of the prettiest maids he had ever seen was the biggest surprise he had had for many a day.

That little waist! His hands could span it, he felt certain.

When he blew into the reed, it sounded good, with a mellow sound to it.

'Brother Adam and sister Jenny. What is Jenny short for?' he asked, flicking his amazing hair from his amazing forehead.

'Well,' she said, 't'is Jenny for short,' as it seemed too long to go into the Bashiba business of her real name. 'What is Nathan short for?'

'T'is short for Jonathan,' he said softly. 'Can you dance, Jenny for short?'

Could she dance? She most certainly could dance, and dance well at that, she was one of the best dancers in the whole village.

She stood in the circle by the flickering flames of the fire, and when the music began, she wished she had never said it. The melody was sad and the rhythm slow and the music enveloped her body and pulled at her arms and feet in sadness.

Whatever sort of a dance was this?

'T'is called a *Pavane for These Sad Times*,' said Nathan.

Then Oliver came back, without Rose, and he bowed to her.

'It takes two to dance,' he said in an agreeably low voice.

She soon got hold of the dance and the tune which the travellers also hummed. It turned out to be less of a dance and more of a stately, slow sort of prance with a lot of slow walking and turning and twisting.

'Here,' cried Nathan and threw the flute at him, 'you play, give someone else a chance, Oliver.'

Oliver shrugged his shoulders. He winked at Jenny and sat down and played a jig on the flute.

That was more like it, the travellers said to each other, as they marched and turned and skipped in pairs to the music, heavy-footed and with earnest faces as if dancing was a very serious business, and then they clapped to the rhythm of a reel.

Jenny grabbed the hem of her skirt and bowed a deep courtesy to Nathan and together they danced in the circle around the fire. As she moved away from him she looked at him and he followed her, all the while looking at her, their hands now and then clasping and unclasping, and she thought her heart would melt into the flames.

Stray, who had been standing guard, came lolloping in and Rose came back, looking furious. The dog was hungry, and Rose had quarrelled with Oliver who not only got up when he saw her, he also got right up her nose, as she said.

'We are finished. I have told you time and again I have naught to do with your unreasonable demands upon my body, I have told you that, and this time it's final,' she shouted but, to the regret of the travellers, she failed to elaborate on his *unreasonable demands*.

'The boys are asleep,' a man's voice said hopefully, but Rose had spoken her last word on the subject. She glanced at Nathan, and her bodice was half undone.

She flashed her breasts for Nathan's benefit, shoulder-blades with nipples on 'em, Jenny thought spitefully when she had seen the dimple of pleasure appearing on Nathan's face.

Before she went off on her ownsome, Rose looked at Jenny critically in the darkening hour.

'Where did you get that white shawl from?'

It was a most wonderful shawl, intricately fashioned, and oh, so soft and warm.

'I don't know, it might be Parson's wife's, what is it to you?'

'White. It's a daft colour with all the dirt that's about, if you ask me,' said Rose. 'As daft as that curly hair, leastways it would be suitable for a boy. Some of us have got real hair. See?'

She ran her fingers through it.

'Call that hair? I thought it was an old sack keeping the rain out,' somebody said scathingly.

'It might be called hair and not a bit of old hessian if you did something with it, like washing and combing it,' said the same somebody, and Jenny was surprised when she realised it was she who had said it, and she got even more so when she realised she was jealous of the looks Nathan bestowed on Rose.

'Hold hard, girl,' said Rose, 'look,' pointing towards the fire where Oliver and Nathan were fighting. 'Who are they fighting over?' she wondered aloud. 'You or me?'

'Not over me,' said Jenny when Oliver was felled by a blow. 'What is there to fight over?' she said, and Rose looked at her and declared she was a true innocent in the year sixteen-hundred-and whatever it was, and she had better put her healing hands upon Oliver's body.

The spell was broken. The travellers quickly stamped on the remnants of the fire and settled themselves down for the night.

Rose wasn't beautiful but she was lively, good company and Jenny liked her. She wasn't so much thin as flat and she had long, long legs, a long, narrow face, a great mouthful of crooked teeth, big goggle eyes ready to pop out of her face, but her pale skin was flawless, and her long, fair hair was lovely and abundant, reaching her waist.

A yellow moon shone through the trees. They looked at each other, the moon and Jenny. They had talked about the quagmires of the fens. She wasn't even sure that there were any or if it was only an old tale. If they existed, they were dangerous, but feelings were worse than quagmires. They sucked you in who-ever you were. Just look at Parson's wife.

Then she saw the young man called Nathan. In the darkness she saw that he was coming towards her, dressed for the road; he had come for her.

Chapter 19

He took to the road as if all the devils in hell were after him and not just one little maid with a tear-stained face.

What is Jenny short for? 'Well, t'is Jenny for short,' she had said and she had smiled into his eyes. The transformation of her, one minute a dirty child bundled up in an old shawl and the next as neat and comely a young maid as you could wish for, walking towards the fire on neat bare feet, carrying her boots and swinging her shawl.

And then Oliver staked his claim!

The nerve of it!

He had no other option but to land one on him. It was time to be off. He had never fought for a woman before, and he wouldn't again. But with Oliver! Half-sharp Oliver!

As Nathan made his way along the path where the moonlight cast giant shadows out of tall trees he swore he would never think of her again, never ever, but maids were full of tricks.

Nathan did not like travelling by night but he had been on the road for going on four or five years now and had developed a sort of place, a sort of spot in his neck which he could not describe, but which was sensitive and alert to danger and prying eyes. Eyes ahead and this place in the back of the neck and he walked free. He was free of fancies and fleet of foot and his own master.

Nathan liked being on the road.

He came from the North, from the silent people of dark, dense forests and the stone quarries.

That's how his master made his money and his father before him and he learned a lot from Sir Stephen, whose father had been knighted by King James himself, and had been a kind man by all accounts.

The old man had died and Sir Stephen made more money out of the quarries and out of the rescuants, the Catholics who were fined for not attending the Protestant Church services.

They were evil, these Catholics.

Nathan knew it, he had hunted them with his master.

He was looked after by his old Gran, never knowing his mother who had died soon after giving birth to him, and his father had followed, it was rumoured through drink, when he was barely able to speak.

Gran was old, and she was wise and kept her fancies to herself. She knew the healing ways of herbs, and their secret places were no mystery to her neither. She never let on. She looked at folks with blank eyes and repeated their sayings and nobody ever asked her for help and advice; she was only an old woman, with a cat for company in the day until he returned at night.

She was wise, for in the villages of the dark dense forests in the North they still burn their witches and she kept her own council and her fancies to herself, and he admired her for it.

Sir Stephen had been to London in 1642 to fight in the Civil War where he fought with the Parliamentarians, and he had returned with a wound in his arm and also a bride. A pale, tall lady and she had brought a spinet with her.

He had stood bareheaded in the large hall and had listened to the sounds of her music, as lost as the lady. She played under the arched window and he played at night on his flute.

Pavanes and reels, and his Gran had been like the travellers.

'Play something with a bit of life, Nathan,' she had said.

He was good with animals, horses especially, and as

he grew older he helped Sir Stephen's groom with the horses, with the grooming and saddling.

One day he was in the hall, laughing with the lady's maid who was standing next to the lady, and then it all changed.

'Take your filthy hands off Lady Eleanor,' Sir Stephen roared. 'I'll give you a beating you'll never forget. Outside! And wait for me!'

He went outside, slow-like, as if he was daft enough to wait, but he saddled the horse and rode off on it like the wind.

After a good way, he left it tied it to the tree he climbed up. Folk never looked up, and he hid till morning had left with his pursuers and the horse.

A horse is valuable and a groom is not, and he took to the road with the saddle bag slung over his shoulders.

He was a traveller. He travelled on his own, but he met up with other travellers; no-one could exist in isolation.

Sir Stephen had pox marks on his face, he was short and squat.

The tall pale lady with eyes like almonds, her dark hair caught up in a roll at the back of her head and almost too heavy for her neck, she had been lovely and she had eyes only for Stephen, ugly or not, after he had licked her into shape of course.

That was the way of the world and that's how it would be with Jenny who had the look of someone special about her. He hoped he would be in time to get back to her to prevent her meeting and experiencing the power of such men as Sir Stephen had been.

He was Nathan, and right now he was the last, but one day he would be the first, like it says in the Bible.

Chapter 20

As Nathan came towards her, Jenny lay rigid, the dog next to her softly growling.

If he wanted her to travel with him, he would have to ask her.

She pretended to be fast asleep, but after a long while he melted away into the night; he didn't want her after all. She banished his picture into the recesses of her mind although it took some doing and his dark eyes were the last part of him to vanish. She was awake for a long time, but finally she drifted off into an uneasy, dream-filled sleep.

She had woken out of her dream with a start.

The other travellers had gone, all but the Priest.

She knew straight off that he was a Priest who had suffered for his faith when she saw him in the mere.

His clothes lay in a bundle by the embankment and his bare back was criss-crossed with great welts like a piece of cloth cut about deeply and carelessly. Whipped to within an inch of his life he must have been, and she didn't like to pretend that she had not witnessed his agony.

He was a Priest. In some great churches, called cathedrals, she knew, hermits were walled up with just a slit for food being passed through it, and outside their grave was already dug for them.

'And that is no kind of life, that sort of religion makes no sense,' her Pa had said, but the old man had a light about him, and the light was good, she thought, and then the dog pounced.

Running down the embankment he jumped, all four paws splayed out, ears flapping, into the water and he nearly half-drowned the old man.

Later they sat silent wearing clean clothes out of

their bundles, silent and clean with the dog hugging the middle space between them, giving one of his great yawns. The Priest stroked him as Jenny rose to get their boots, drying out after the good scrubbing she had given them.

When she returned, she watched with him as a little bird came out of a nest in the embankment. Its beak was nearly half as long as its little body and it looked ungainly until it rose in a shimmer of blue and gold, poised over the clear water and then dived after a fish as straight as a dropped stone.

Stray had been off after some brown ducks hovering shriekingly in the air, and as he settled down awkwardly again, Jenny felt worried about him. There were perfectly happy and serene moments and then a worry would appear like some fat maggot in an otherwise good apple.

The worry was that the dog didn't move well, and there was no denying it.

The Priest was also worried about the dog, but he said nothing to the girl about the lump he had felt behind the dog's ears. She would need that dog as much as that dog needed her.

'He is fatigued from journey,' he said.

He would keep an eye on her from now on, but from a distance and discreetly; a Catholic Priest was not a good companion to have in Cromwell's Protestant Fens.

Jenny stood at the side of the dyke, looking for all the world as if she was yielding a polite way of passage to someone of importance, although there was only Stray by her side. It was the straight and narrow road as she had seen it in her mind's eye and the very thought of walking on it gave her, who had been hiding, a feeling of exposure, setting her knees knocking and her heart beating.

The Priest had departed earlier and she could see no sign of him nor of Nathan, although she didn't think it likely Nathan would be about now.

The dog pricked his ears up and his tail raised itself into the line of his body as the ground was disturbed by the vibrations of a horse.

They watched as a horse rode by, ridden by a man whose fair hair flew in the wind. They saw him in the distance on the straight road and then he turned round.

Jenny hoped he would come back for her; it would be something to ride and get that dyke behind her.

The Fens.

The fair rider on the chestnut horse cursed the fens.

Miles of unbroken, unattractive nothingness. Sullen people. Bent over. Nothing worth looking at, nothing of interest to raise the head or the spirit.

He rode, and as he rode he thought he remembered seeing something out of the corner of his eyes by the side of the road. A young, slight and pretty girl and a handsome black dog. A right picture they made.

He couldn't have done, but he turned round and she was still there, looking up at him gravely with eyes dark blue and her short hair softly curling, as clean and shining as a new dawn. She was very self-possessed, as if she had known he would come back for her all the time.

'Where to, little lady?'

'Anywhere, if you don't mind,' she said.

'If you want a ride, you better jump up.'

'Would I have to ride in front of you?'

'Where else?'

She thought about it.

'You would have your arms around me in that case, it wouldn't be fitting.'

Jenny knew she should refuse the ride. The Bible

had told her that she had to walk the straight and narrow road and trouble would come if she handed her bundle to the fair rider. He helped her up and she climbed up behind him.

'Here,' he said, handing her a belt. 'Put it around yourself and me, if it is fitting, of course.'

He rode like the wind with her clinging on for dear life. But cling she did, fastened by his belt to him, and as she looked back she saw the dog. He was running after the rider with his paws and ears flying and like Jenny, he had the time of his life.

Chapter 21

They were flying along the dyke, the rider and Jenny with Stray behind them and they didn't notice very much else, although the rider felt the girl's arms about him and Jenny felt safe and warm hugging him, his knees so close to the horse they seemed to be part of it . She smelt the horse's sweat and the leather of the rider's coat.

She was the wind, the wicked child whistling round folks gossiping after Church and Aggy was the water, still and undisturbed.

The dog was glad to be moving forward at last. They didn't notice a lone figure walking towards them, walking fast, and deep in thought.

The horse reared up, the rider threw his weight forward, and Nathan jumped into the ditch as the horse's hooves thundered by.

He looked on in amazement.

There was a fair rider, his hair long and flying in the wind, dressed in leather with a white shirt at his neck, Jenny with her arms about him, and Stray running after them.

Where was he taking her?

It just went to show, Nathan thought, as he turned around once more.

It just went to show, he thought bitterly, climbing onto the road covered in dirt, that you should never break the habit of a lifetime.

Not only had he travelled at night, but he had also returned and retraced his steps, and what for?

For a girl with a pretty face.

He had known a few maids with pretty faces and he would know a few more, he did not doubt. He wasn't an old tomcat but neither was he a monk.

From now on, stick to your plan, my lad, he said to himself, the one he had worked out long ago. He meant to get on in life and not get tied down with kith and kin early on like some had.

The way he saw it, maids and lads were like a cat and a dog, contented enough laying side by side in front of the hearth. Tie their tails together, and the story would be different.

He would go to Huntingdon to a coaching inn and work there for a while. He was good with horses and well liked by all, and a roof over his head would not come amiss for a while whilst he added to the money already in his money belt.

It was for the best; she might have got a hold on him. Pretty enough, that little one, but full of fancies, he couldn't do with that. Let Oliver take her on, he thought, except she had already found someone better. How had she done it?

Jenny rode sedately into the outskirts of Huntingdon.

Pretty white cottages lined the road, some with porches and thatched roofs, like small girls in bonnets clinging onto their mothers. Some had steps, and some had small enclosed gardens with hens clucking about in them.

The rider slowed down, looking from side to side. He was looking for something in particular, Jenny thought, and she was wondering why he had not ridden on alone before now when he slowed down and stopped.

It was the last cottage in the row, it had a larger window than the others, and above it was a piece of wood with the shape of a ship carved on it.

The horse reared up, and he cursed as he secured it to the tying post.

'Your Horse Seems Mighty Afeared Of Something,'

she said, and she talked like Squire's Daughter, as if each and every word was valuable, and she held her head like Squire's Daughter, high and slightly twisted, her eyes quizzical and amused.

'With good cause,' he said in a deep voice.

It was a bolter, he explained, bolted straight home once, getting itself free somehow and Jenny hoped, in her Squire's Daughter imitation, that he had not arrested anyone as a horse thief.

'Not quite,' he said, 'nobody had stolen it.' When he finally returned home, he found it in its stable, unsaddled and rubbed down by the groom, looking at him with his yellow eyes.

And just as he had fully gained its confidence he had beeen so enlivended to have a pretty girl behind him, he had ridden like a maniac along the dykes knowing that horses could sink in the mud, the horse was terrified once more and with good cause.

'Just As Well Then,' she said as they went into the inn.

She had an odd way of speaking, he thought, looking at that amazing face and slight waist, and then Mine Host shuffled towards them, wearing an unwelcoming scowl.

'This is an inn? You are the innkeeper?'

The man admitted unhappily that this was an inn, or more what could be called an alehouse, and he was an innkeeper, or an innkeeper who kept an alehouse, and then he pointed out that the coaching inn was down the road.

'Not far. Not far at all,' he said hopefully.

It seemed that his customer had the look of one of them Parliament Men.

'Who do you serve?'

'We serve them that wants it,' Mine Host admitted after much heart-searching and head-scratching, and finally he was persuaded to depart and hunt out some ale and bread and cheese.

The cottage roof was low, and Mine Host was more than a bit on the tall side; an unfortunate combination, especially when he had been on the rum.

He caught his head a glancing blow on the beam.

'Sodding beam.'

A thought occurred to him and he returned to their table.

'You're not from our Bridget with the girl?'

No, they were not, his customer said, very short-like.

He had an air of authority and confidence about him gleaned from years of being obeyed and having his boots licked. Likely he was a Parliament Man and t'would be best not to upset him. Never knew what came of upsetting a Parliament Man.

He turned round and caught his head again on the beam.

'Sodding beam.'

Jenny looked around her.

The inn was large and square with benches along two walls, a table and chair in the middle, but there was an air of comfort about it, especially about the small bench bed on one wall with curtains drawn around it on either side.

The fireplace with an arrangement of mugs was on the other side and by its side was a chalking board.

A pot of stew, judging by its smell, was bubbling away on a roaring fire, and another one, encrusted with barley broth from the breakfast, was resting in the hearth.

It didn't seem a bad sort of a place to her, although by the looks of the man sitting on the bench next to her it would appear that he had been thrown out of better places before now.

One of the two doors at the side opened slowly and the man shuffled in carrying mugs of ale and a platter of bread and cheese.

He was walking slowly and carefully straight towards the beam.

'Mind that sodding beam,' she cried happily.

Her cover as a fine lady was blown but the fair rider had not even noticed when she looked at him.

'What is that?' she asked, pointing to the small, black bench with the curtains.

'That's a settle,' the innkeeper said. 'Where the maids we ain't got sleep.'

It looked very narrow.

'Won't they fall off?'

'Clean your ears out, it's a settle, it opens up.' He scratched his head. 'The paliarse is in the bench.'

'Mattress,' he added when they stared at him.

The innkeeper was put out. His brain was addled. Always was after he had been on the rum.

They would want to pay and he was worried he didn't know how much, and he was right.

'Mother would know,' he said.

She was in the bake-house and it would be hotter than hell in there and she would be in a fine temper by now.

'One shilling,' he said hopefully. Afterwards he wished he had said two or three shillings or even four shillings, as his customer paid up right as rain.

'She's in the bake-house which is an outhouse, but with a bread oven in the end wall,' he added confidentially, and the rider couldn't wait to get away now. Away from this mean cottage, no place for him or this girl who had dented his consciousness.

'Is there a young man?' he asked her outside.

'Nathan', she said.

Who was Nathan?

She didn't know.

What did Nathan do?

She didn't know.

Where was Nathan?

She didn't know.

What did she know?

Not a lot, but more than he would think.

He looked at her.

'Country girls like you are ten a penny.'

'I never said any different,' she said.

The rider patted the horse which rubbed its head against his chest.

'Oh, look! He has forgiven you!' she cried, looking at him very straight.

'So he has, and so I better go and have him looked after,' he said as he mounted the horse and rode off down the road.

She had looked at him without guile, and her eyes were the blue of the very heart of the flame. Still, it was done. There would be an end to it.

Jenny knew she had not seen the last of him.

She should have walked the straight and narrow road like it had said in the Bible and not become the wicked wind, but now she was lost, well and truly lost.

She might perhaps look at the town; she had wondered what a town might be like, as she walked round the inn and put her bundle against the wall of the bakehouse. She would come for it after she had looked at the town, she thought, although that bench-bed looked more inviting than a night on the road. She could hear voices from inside.

The weak, wheedling one of the balding man, Mine Host, and a strong, clear and decisive one of a woman, but she didn't stop to listen. It wouldn't be fitting to ear-wig.

The rider turned around for one last look at the girl

but she had vanished and he wondered if she had ever existed.

The man was in the bakehouse and they were talking about her and it was hot as hell in there with the large oven which was big enough to roast an ox in and Mother was in a hell of a temper. Always was when she made the bread.

'She was not from our Bridget.'

He scratched his head.

'Tell you something now that'll surprise you.'

The woman, who was short and square and fat as if she had been tall once and then something had fallen from a great height and flattened her to her present shape, cut the last of the dough into four with the sharp black knife.

'He was one of them Parliament Men,' he said and she made two small and then two larger rounds and put the small ones on the top of the larger ones. Then she wrapped them in a floured cloth.

After that she got the wooden pallet and removed half a dozen loaves, hot and fragrant, from the oven and put the last batch onto the pallet and into the oven.

'She was a pretty piece, the one he had with her, but wanting, she'd never seen a settle,' he said as she gratefully slammed the oven door shut. Baking was an exacting sort of thing to do, and she didn't want to waste any more time on it than she had to.

She removed her apron and went into the inn, ready to be surprised although she didn't think anything the man told her could surprise her ever again, but she was interested for a minute.

The girl had looked like their Gideon. Their son, and her own pride and joy.

But the girl had gone and there was no need to make a ritual out of it.

It was a crying shame she had not been the one from their Bridget who kept sending girls who were destined to be Gideon's Bride.

T'would be the third one, he had not liked the other two, neither would he shift for himself and get himself wed, with herself just aching to hold a grandchild in her arms.

'Who does Gideon love?' she asked the man.

'He don't love nobody,' he said, 'that one don't, that's been the trouble. Excepting himself, of course.'

'Well then,' she cried triumphantly, 'If Gideon loves himself he's bound to love one that's just like himself.'

He got up and went into the bakehouse and removed the last of the loaves, she looked so nicely settled.

They were dozing nicely in front of the fire when the woman woke with a start; the fire was nearly out with no wood left to feed it and Father was dispatched to fetch some more.

He was gone some time, and when he returned he scratched his balding head. He said out the back was an old bundle, and sitting by it, well, resting its head on it, was a right handsome black dog looking at him with fierce green eyes.

'Growling away it was something chronic, I thought at first it was thunder rumbling over Huntingdon like, but then I noticed it was the dog.'

They looked at each other, Mother and Father, and then they walked to the back door and looked into the yard, which was as empty of a dog and a bundle as it always had been.

They looked at each other, and in the silence, they heard a faint knocking at the front door.

He thought that it couldn't be a dog knocking on the door, and then thought that perhaps it might be best if he did lay off the rum.

He shuffled towards the door as he thought that he wouldn't do it just yet, no need to overdo things.

Chapter 22

Huntingdon, the town and the market place, was one of the sights Jenny thought she would never see, and of course, Cromwell's country seat was in Huntingdon.

Jenny had known straight off it was Cromwell's place when she saw the house not all that far from the inn. A large, grey house, like a granite fist held up to the sky. A powerful house for a powerful man.

Houses were like folks, Jenny thought. Cottagers fitted neatly into their places with low roofs. Parson's house had so many rooms folks could avoid each other, whilst the

Squire's Manor kept servants in and spat them out when they were no longer useful, like so many rotten teeth, whilst Squire and his family was secure for evermore, a large roof sheltering as many rooms as cottages in a row.

Jenny stopped and looked at the grey house.

On the path around the house maids dressed like herself walked with baskets, and a fine lady on a horse waited for a bare-headed man to hold the gate open for her.

It would always be so, and she thought there was nothing to beat a little cottage, nothing at all.

She came over faint in the market place, which was like a large, square parlour without a roof, lined on four sides by tall houses.

Great round cheeses and cloths dyed in all manner of colours were offered for sale alongside bread and honey cakes and fodder for animals, and animals themselves. Sheep, goats, pigs and chickens.

Quick one minute, and dead the next, and God was played by hard and red-faced men, sweaty and rowdy, who advertised their wares.

Killing live animals, if that was wanted, had left the ground awash with entrails and blood, excrement and urine, and Jenny shuddered to think what Parson's wife would have made of the floor.

She recovered her wits when she saw two men looking at her, leaning against a wall. One looked like a weasel, his hat pushed to the back of his head, holding a dog on a leash. The other man holding the house up with him poked him in the ribs until he winced.

'Steady on, I say,' said Weasel-face, 'steady on or I land one on you.'

'That girl over there,' said his companion, 'over there, see, now she puts me in mind of someone, don't she you?'

Weasel-face scratched his head and spat on the ground, then he agreed, but neither could quite think who it might be.

She was the spit-image of... and they stared at her appraisingly as if she was a horse about to be sold. Any minute now they would be wanting to know how many teeth she had left in her mouth.

'You'll know me next time you see me, won't you?' Jenny said, focussing on Weasel-face, and he told her to clear off before he set the dog on her.

Set the dog on her? The dog she couldn't handle had not been born yet. The dog about to savage her was small, covered in grey fur like a bristle-brush with foam at its mouth. Yapping in regular, high-pitched sounds, it was straining at the leash, and she could see that it had sharp, yellow teeth and that it wanted nothing more out of life than to get free of Weasel-face.

'Go on then,' she said to him, 'set it free, let it go. I dare you,' standing squarely in front of the dog, 'let it go.'

There was pain and terror in the dog's eyes for the man had twisted the collar so that sharp studs bit into the animal's neck. It was begging for some kindness and could barely wait to get to Jenny for it.

'No, best not,' said Weasel-face's companion and she looked at him straight and told him to see to his own business, if it wasn't too much trouble.

That did it.

A dare and an insult by nothing more than a little maid. Weasel-face released his grip and the dog got to Jenny with a bound and a sigh.

'There, there,' she said as she scratched under its neck where it couldn't reach, and the watching crowd laughed and shouted they ought to have placed bets on it.

Weasel-face got himself and his dog away, he and his friend red in the face, and so she had made herself a couple of enemies and nearly got herself another dog, Jenny thought as she wandered away from the market and through the town.

It was still and dark in the road after the open air and bustle of the market-place. Rows of steeply gabled houses faced each other, overhanging the road like big-bosomed women in striped aprons leaning close in heavy gossip.

They were welcome to it, Jenny thought, and then her heart stopped for a moment. In front of her walked a young man. He was sturdy with fur strapped around his legs.

'Nathan,' she said with a sigh, and the young man turned around. Under his hat was a red face with bulging cheeks.

'I'm sorry,' Jenny said, 'I thought you were someone else.'

She fled in the opposite direction, back towards the inn. She might as well retrieve her bundle before she set off on the road again, but she knew she was fooling herself, she couldn't face another night on the road.

She walked around the inn and retrieved her bundle. Stray was nowhere to be seen.

She waited before she raised her hand, her heart beating nearly as audibly as her hand knocking on the door, half-hoping she would not be heard.

The shock of Nathan not being Nathan had unsettled her nerves, and she knew that although she was not the girl from Bridget, perhaps she might do until the girl from Bridget's arrived.

Just one night in that settle-bed, Dear God, she promised, and then she would be on her way. She couldn't face the journey on her own, not tonight.

As she wondered whether to knock on the door again, her mind was made up for her. It was opened just a crack. Then it slammed into her face.

'T'is the pretty piece not from our Bridget's,' she heard the old man say.

The door was flung open wide, as wide as the mouth of the woman who was framed in the doorway, and in the light of day the woman looked ridiculous. Her mobcap was rammed down to her ears. When she stepped aside to let Jenny in she walked with the uncertain gait of someone who had not seen where their feet were placing themselves for a long time, which was nothing but the truth. The woman was fat, to say the least.

Even so, Jenny took a liking to her, as if she might have met and liked her in some other time, some other place, and the memory of friendship had merely been forgotten and was being rekindled.

It seemed that this feeling of friendship was returned; she was invited inside with an expansive gesture.

'Step inside, step inside. Come in and out of the cold, my girl.'

It wasn't cold outside, said Jenny, it was a warm

summer's day, but the woman said she hadn't been outside for nearly fifteen years, had she, she asked Mine Host who agreed; any rate he nodded his head, and the woman laughed.

'He almost always agrees with me, don't you, Father?' and he nodded his head once more.

Come in and out of the cold, my girl, said the spider to the fly.

Chapter 23

Jenny lingered by the window. She had drawn the curtains like Mother had told her to, and through the filthy glass she had seen him walk by. He had told her to call him Father Bernard, that was the name he had adopted, and she had pictured him in some other country. He looked like a vision from some other place with his long yellow hair and his long yellow beard. He walked slowly, his left arm leaning heavily on his stick which made no sound on the dirt-track. Where would he rest his head tonight?

The woman who had been so pleased to see Jenny was Mother, so the old man called her, and she called him Father and in the evening he was well into the rum.

Mother did not say a word, she was eating. She always did one thing at a time she had informed Jenny, and Jenny saw that now she was eating.

She had fetched a plate for Jenny and filled it to the brim from the pot Jenny had seen bubbling away that morning. Barley corns and great chunks of pink and white bacon and bread freshly made with a large slab of glistening butter. Eating like this was one of life's pleasures, she thought, although chance was a mighty fine thing.

The woman's teeth were grinding away; the man didn't eat much, but sipped slowly at his mug of rum and looked at Jenny like a pig clean out of acorns.

When the woman stopped eating, she asked Jenny to wash the dishes by the hearth. The girl fetched some more water from the stream running behind the cottage and she had lingered awhile, but there was no sign of the dog.

When she came back indoors, the woman was slowly sipping ale out of a large mug. She took a sip and then she placed the mug back on her chest, which made a nice little table, never spilling a drop.

Sitting in front of the fire, she was transformed. She had taken her mobcap off and although she might have looked ridiculous in the clear light of day now, in the soft light of evening with the fire playing on her regular features and her amazing white hair streaming down her back, Jenny thought that she looked right handsome.

'Did you think you were the only one what's good-looking?' said Father, looking mean and menacing.

Jenny had no answer, but she asked where she could wash.

'Too much washing is not good for you,' said Father, 'there's no protection in it,' although he did not say what dirt would protect her from, and Mother asked how often Jenny washed herself.

'Well,' the girl said slowly, 'in the Parsonage we washed...'

And that did it.

No matter what, from now on she was firmly labelled as a Parson's daughter, and Mother said Parson's daughter or not, Jenny had come in out of the cold night of her own accord, same as Bridget had, and the Parson's daughter accepted her status and that the balmy summer day had been a cold winter's night.

'The girls from Bridget are sent as brides. Intended as brides for Gideon, only he didn't like any of them, said Mother.

Gideon was their only son who would not shift himself and fetch a bride for himself.

When Jenny asked if he had not taken a fancy to Bridget, Father looked at her as if she was daft; she was knocking fifty.

Strong and hardworking these girls that Bridget had sent, and snapped up they had been, and now they were raising families for other folks.

'See these arms?' Mother said, lifting the sleeves and revealing muscles like curled up hedgehogs. 'I intend to hold Gideon's child with these arms and so I see to the bride myself, like I do to everything else.

'Now, we like you, Father and me, and we forgive you for being a Parson's daughter, and we ain't kidnapping you. Stay and see if Gideon would like to wed you. If you don't like the idea of it, well, then there's the door. Is it a bargain?'

'Well,' Jenny said thoughtfully, 'what if I don't like Gideon?'

Mother always did one thing at a time, and now she was laughing.

Jenny was the one for her Gideon right enough. The others said, fearful like, 'What if Gideon don't like me?'

It was on. Fair was fair and a bargain was a bargain and it was agreed.

Gideon and Jenny were both on trial, that was the difference, and she would agree to almost anything to lay down in her bed and draw the curtains around it.

There was no sign of Gideon that night. She was overcome with the delicious drowsy feeling of sleep and warmth and safety and a full stomach, and then, just before Mother and Father wound their way upstairs, they issued a stern warning.

Jenny had to promise never, ever to go upstairs. She not only had to promise, but she had to get out of bed and get her Bible from the space under the bed. She had to kneel down in front of them and swear it on the Bible.

What on earth did they keep upstairs, she thought. She hoped it wasn't Gideon.

Chapter 24

Before she had finally fallen asleep, Jenny had said to herself quietly and firmly that she would be packing her bundle and be off with the departing night.

Quite menacing, the pair had looked before they had rumbled off upstairs but now, in the light of morning, she changed her mind, no harm done if stayed awhile. After all, the old couple had taken her in and fed her and let her stay the night, a perfect stranger.

When she had risen, she saw that the sun had beaten her to it and was already high in the sky. Whatever time was it? Whatever time did they get up?

Of course, they had all sat in front of the fire with a candle burning away and they had talked far into the night, whereas at home, folks rose with the sun and went to bed with the night.

There was still no sound to be heard from upstairs and she looked through the window. Maids passed the cottage dressed like herself, walking lightly and carrying baskets. Men on ponies rode by, balancing large baskets on either side. Sullen these men looked, like the men on the market and quite menacing, with their dark hats pulled low over their red faces.

There was no life outside the back door when she stepped out, no pigs or chickens or cows.

The morning air was soft and mellow with the sun playing on the wilderness of weeds and bushes. Elderberries were still tight green bunches and not ready yet for picking.

She walked further on to the dark stream of the night before. Further on was the barrier of light trees, the start of woods. T'would be a safe place for Stray, she thought, and wondered where he was now, although she knew he could look after himself.

As she washed her face in the stream, she wondered

if folks would have been as kind if her face had been different, if maybe she had a wart on one eyelid pulling it down or if she had walked with a limp through a faulty hip, or even if she had been as beautiful as Cousin Aggy.

Beautiful Aggy might have been, but as nasty as an unfed pig, especially to her mother. The times she had put her foot out so her Ma would stumble and fall over, the times she had nearly pushed her into the fire, the times she had told lies to get other folks into trouble. Her Ma had sent her to the Parsonage; that would sort her out, she said, and look how that turned out.

Jenny straightened up, out of her fancies, and went back into the house. When she went into the larder, there was a large yellow cheese, as round and golden as Parson's wife's guinea, and half a side of bacon hanging from a hook. Beef was salted down, a lot of barrels were stacked, and the sourdough, flour and water for the bread was in a large dish.

'What you snouting about in here for?' the old man demanded from behind her, and then he jabbed a grimy finger in her face. 'I hope you haven't been up them stairs.'

'You must be dafter than you look if that's possible, which I doubt,' she said, 'you've only just come down. Besides, I promised not to.'

Mother came down with her mobcap rammed down to her ears.

'Give him as good as he gives, mean as hell when he's sober and maudlin as a new lover when he is at the rum, and there's no in-between. He's all I got, apart from Gideon, and he gets what makes him content.'

She looked at the girl.

'It's not real rum from the molasses like, but from the malt, but we calls it rum just the same. Next door's empty, and next door to that belongs to a gentleman in

London. Him and his wife come down once a year in their finery and bring a housekeeper with them. Fine folks can't sneeze without them about who wipe their noses for them.'

'Their shitty arses, you mean,' said Father.

'What are you still here for?' Mother cried. 'Get your hat on and see to them loaves, make sure they pay proper for it and keep your ears open while you're at it.'

Father rammed his hat over his head and picked up a basket full of loaves.

'Next door to that died without kin, further down the road he's ailing, and nephews and nieces crawling about him with hampers like worms about a corpse while he can still sign his will.'

The one flaw, as far as Jenny could see and work out, was the question of money. The money for the stocking up. Where did the money come from for buying and stocking up with food like that?

Not from selling the ale to the men who came in for the drink that night, that was for certain.

Who were they?

Them that wants it, men from the village, sitting on the benches, the candle in its holder flickering over them; they had their own stone mugs hanging from hooks over the hearth and they knew their own mugs from the chips that were missing and the cracks in them.

'Keep your hands off this girl,' said Mother. 'If you want to feel a woman's backside, go home to your wives and fondle it, if you can find it.'

'You might have noticed I said *backside*, because Jenny is,' she paused and waited for silence, 'a Parson's daughter.'

'Right, of course she is.'

They nearly fell off their benches with laughter.

Suddenly a knife was flashing and then clattering to

the floor when Mother twisted the man's arm behind his back and marched him to the door.

'Settle your old score somewhere else. Father, door, if you please.'

'They certainly mind Mother,' said Jenny to the old man.

He said she had arm-wrestled a strong man once.

'And she won,' said Jenny.

'As it happens, she didn't,' he said, 'she broke his arm. And a horrible sight it was, all bloody, with the white bone sticking out.'

'As it happens,' Mother said later, 'it's nothing but a tale. He's heard it so many times, he's like the others, he believes it.'

She paused.

'I don't think it would be possible to do,' she added, 'but it means they do mind their manners.'

One thing wasn't clear to Jenny; nobody had come in the previous night and when she asked about it, Father had looked at her as if she was half-sharp.

'You drew them curtains yourself, didn't you? They don't come when them curtains are drawn, do they?'

It was a signal. The curtains had not been drawn that night and a candle had been placed by Jenny herself in the window instead, but the money question remained. Pennies and not shillings changed hands, and nothing was chalked up on the chalking board by the door.

It was all very strange, Jenny thought laying in her bed after *them that wants it* had departed and the candle had been put out. Just another day, she thought, and then she heard the neighing of a horse out the back and the stairs creaking; someone was coming down once more. She took a careful peep through her bed curtains and saw the woman was at the window and the curtains were drawn tight.

There was a cold draught from the back door being opened. Father's voice and Mother's voice and another, younger voice, very melodic.

'What you brung us this time?' Mother's voice.'

'That's right good.' Father's voice.

Gideon was a good son, Jenny thought, he brought presents when he visited.

She cautiously peered through the curtains around her bed once more and by the light of the candle on the table she saw the famous Gideon.

There was a bloom on his cheek which wouldn't have shamed an apple blossom, his hair sprang soft and curly from a fine forehead, and his eyelashes laid black and long when he lowered his eyes.

He yawned a great yawn, and his teeth were as white and straight and even as petals in a daisy.

Folks were right, Jenny thought. Gideon was like herself, just like herself. Only much prettier.

Chapter 25

Jenny never got to meet the famous Gideon after all, for he had fled with the shadows of the night when he had heard what was lying in wait for him with the curtains drawn around. He had fled with never a look at her.

Apparently he would sooner look at a new corpse in a coffin than at a new bride.

'Another one, Mother', he said, 'not another one, Mother,' and he said sadly that he had thought she would knock that particular game on the head.

When Mother told him that not only was she certain he would like this one but that the girl was also a Parson's daughter into the bargain, he said Mother was as daft as a brush without any bristles, and that he needed a drink to help him digest the grim news.

Father joined in then and sprung to the old woman's defence.

'This one,' he said with pride and emotion and rum nearly choking him, 'this one was just like Mother had been when she was young. The very spit image of Mother herself this one is.'

Jenny went more than a bit pale when she thought that in her old age she might turn out like Mother and rest a mug on her chest, but not half as pale as Gideon.

The spitting-image-look of Mother sent him as pale around the chops as a chalk pit on a winter's day.

Mother said that this one was a bit like Gideon, and Gideon said he wished they would make up their minds. One minute the girl was like Mother and the next she was like himself.

'What makes you think I need one with hair all over her face I shall never know.'

The pair of them didn't go to bed after their pride and joy had left them, and Jenny understood just where she had got herself to in her search for comfort when she listened to the soft murmuring of voices afterwards.

T'was not much he had brought this time, said Father, a couple of silver spoons, but Mother thought it would have to do. One more good haul, Gideon had said. He was tiring of the life and he had made a plan already. Still, all in all, it would work out for the best, Mother said, and she would tell them of the plan next time they came round for the arrangements.

Father was told to take it upstairs, and the old man took a good look at her then and poked her in the ribs to make sure she hadn't heard anything. She pretended to be fast asleep, just giving out the little moaning noise of an interrupted sleeper.

She was in a den of thieves sure enough, and she thought she ought to leave, although she had to be honest with the woman at least as she felt she owed her something.

What was she to say to her though? Gideon is a thief and you sell the stolen stuff for him and you live off it yourself?

Would they let her go her own way if she knew and could tell all? And if not, what could they do?

The little bed still brought her a lot of comfort that night, however much the voices lingered on in her mind. She curled up and stretched herself in it in turn. That was the trouble, they could make her very comfortable. They had given her so much comfort that she felt she never wanted to move out.

She needed some sharp and almighty kick to get her going and onto the road again.

The Diggers were outside London, Nathan had said. The Diggers would be ordinary folk earning an honest living and she might see Nathan again, but London would be a big place with many outsides. She would head for there, but not just yet, just one more day, she thought with each passing day.

She needed some sharp and almighty kick to get her going and onto the road again, but for now, she was just too comfortable.

Father had taken himself off to church on quite a few times times,on so many Sundays, on so many weeks, Jenny thought, but as she had lost count, she was none the wiser. And Parson's daughter or not, she always refused to go with him.

When he said she would be just like Mother, bound to the house, the woman told him sharply to go.

'Life comes to me inside, so it's not a bad thing.'

Jenny started to clear a patch out the back for vegetables, carrots and onions, which was a good thing; however, getting to grips with the filthy laundry beggared belief.

'Those whites are not whites,' Father whined, 'those are yellows and browns.'

'Not for much longer,' Jenny said, and Mother became interested.

'How do you make them white?'

'At the Parsonage,' Jenny said, 'we had the blue from the low lands, at home...'

'Which is the same thing...' put in Father.

'...we used soap and urine,' she finished.

'Plenty of urine here, just ask Father, and I will get some soap.' said Mother, and Father reluctantly filled a big tub out the back, first with water.

She spread the clothes and linen over the bushes and the sun did the rest, while Father wondered where the yellow went when they were dry, although he was triumphant that the brown was still there.

'Them's your breeches, you daft sod,' said Mother, but she said it fondly.

Father took himself off to the market one day and

Mother was plucking one of the cockerels he had fetched back; not outside, she hadn't been outside for fifteen years.

'Life comes to me indoors just the same as it would outside. I might have told you that.'

'How about going to Church then?'

As she already knew, Father went on his own and very smart he looked in his black hat; Parson, not one of the men that wants it, thought he was a fine, upstanding widower.

'Life comes to me like you have done yourself and of your own accord.'

The plucking and the cooking were done and they feasted with the curtains drawn.

The cockerel had been roasted. Great drops of fat hissed into the fire and Mother had made a dish of eggs and bacon fit for a king, only there wasn't one now, and then they plied her with rum.

Father didn't need persuading.

'My God,' he said, 'if it ain't the best drop of rum I have ever tasted,' and Jenny knew then that it hadn't been watered down.

But why not? What was so special about tonight?

She said she wouldn't touch a drop. She never had drunk rum - and she never would - but the pair of them were insisting that she drank up, looking at her over their mugs with mean little eyes. They had never done that before, Jenny thought, why was it so important now? Then it came to her that company was expected from which she was excluded.

She yawned, and when the pair looked at her expectantly, she said that she thought she had heard a noise.

'By the back door,' she said, and they both left the table in a great hurry.

She had barely enough time to pour her rum into

Father's when they returned, by which time she was sucking her fingers dipped in rum and nursing an empty mug.

'They all come to it in the end,' whispered Father, 'Parson's daughter or not.'

Not, thought Jenny as she went to her bed as meekly as a groom on his wedding night, not changing into her shift.

She said her eyelids felt very heavy, and they were not surprised.

'Drink does that to you, my girl,' Father ventured, helping her to the bed, and finally there came that knock on the back door they had expected and recognized.

Folk came in shrouded in great whisperings and muted footsteps.

'Keep the noise down,' said the old woman. T'is Gideon's new bride. In the bed like.'

'Not another one,' said a sneering voice. 'If you ask me, you're flogging a dead horse with Gideon, he is not like other folks in the breeches stakes. T'is best not to stand with your backside to him.'

'What goes on in his breeches is nought to do with the likes of you, and I'll have you know that the girl is a Parson's daughter.'

Jenny laid on her side listening to the voices, and she was remembering how hard it had been to keep her fluttering eyelids still as Nathan had looked at her that night, when footsteps came near.

A flickering light. Curtains round the bed being lifted, and then a long, soft whistle of surprise.

T'is the girl you set the dog on in the market.'

The girl had tamed the dog with one look.

'I've put the dog down since.'

Another voice.

'No good for the baiting once they goes soft.'

171

Departing footsteps.

Jenny parted the curtains. In the flickering light of the candle, she saw Weasel-face and his companion sitting by the table.

They both grumbled that it didn't amount to much, two small spoons.

'Silver,' said Father.

With a crest, it was not worth turning out for, it couldn't be flogged safely.

'You've cleared us out, I'll have you know,' said Father, 'I'm buggered if you haven't, that's all there is,' and the woman said Gideon was tiring of the life. She would like it known and kept within their confidence that Gideon had a plan in his mind.

Disparaging noises and Weasel-face spat on the floor.

All worked out, that plan, said Mother One more good haul, that's what it amounted to, he had said, and then he would settle down. T'wouldn't be long now and could they make the arrangements like, and then she talked about Gideon again and how he would settle down with the girl.

'Settle down with me,' Jenny thought, 'not if I can help it,' but this time she wanted to slap Father around his chops when he started poking her in the ribs to make sure she was still asleep.

'Get off,' she said sleepily and crossly, 'go and poke some other body,' and she planned a few games of her own. She would keep 'em sitting in the dark hours waiting for her to go to sleep, making a great pretence of yawning and stretching and tossing and turning in the narrow bed; but she suddenly felt uneasy, recalling the sneer in Weasel-face's voice.

'She's sharp, that one,' whined Weasel-face, 'sharp enough to cut herself one of these days.'

'Do you reckon?' Mother asked silkily.

'Sooner rather than later,' said Weasel-face, and Mother and Father laughed uproariously as they saw their night visitors off the premises; they got positively hysterical when Weasel-face's companion ventured that they could all depend on a come-uppance.

'Oh, my God,' gasped Mother after the door was locked, 'we've been set up.'

'Good and proper,' said Father, 'it took a while to sink in, then it dawned on me that they acted all along as if they had the upper hand like.'

They sat at the table, looking up at Jenny uncomprehendingly when she got up. Mother gave a sharp laugh and said it saved a lot of explanations all in all.

'Have you been listening all along?'

Jenny nodded dumbly.

'They must have made a deal with the Sheriff, but why just now?'

They tried to figure it out. There was nought incriminating left on the premises, it was as they said, they had been cleared out.

Gideon must have made a straight deal with them some time ago and cut Mother and Father out, Jenny ventured.

'Little as I know of it,' she added, but Gideon hadn't carried out this plan he had talked about yet to their knowledge.

'Not to our knowledge he hasn't, but somebody else might know that he has, and that somebody else might know that the plan has gone awry.'

The Sheriff's men.

'Must be serious if they are prepared to do a deal with that vermin.'

The last time Gideon had been here nothing unusual had occurred. He had come in, grumbled a bit, upset Mother, and then he had gone out again, said Father.

'No,' said Jenny, 'that's not right. Before he left, he went upstairs.'

They looked at each other, Mother and Father. Mother clasped her hands until her knuckles went white as the old man shuffled up the stairs.

'Is it gone?' she asked when he returned.

He nodded.

'It's the pistol, Jenny. He has taken the pistol.' She paused. 'But he wouldn't be daft enough, would he?'

'He would,' said Father.

'For what?' asked Jenny. But no answer came forth.

'He knows how to handle it, he liked to practice when he was quite young,' said Mother. 'And he's got a horse. Where did he get that from?'

'Why should Gideon bring his trouble home to you, especially if he has done the dirty on you?' Jenny said uncomprehendingly.

Mother said Gideon was likely frightened if he realised he had been caught in a trap.

And where else would a frightened man go but home?

'I wouldn't,' Jenny thought, 'not if it meant trouble for the family.'

When the woman came down in the morning she found the girl bending over her bundle, reading the Bible.

'What's it say in the Good Book?'

'Something about an informer and a fire,' Jenny said thoughtfully. It was impossible to find the same place again even if she knew it was in the Proverbs, but the woman had made her jump and she had lost the place.

'We know about the informer, but try and find out about the fire.'

Jenny took the Bible into the light of a fresh new day. God's voice sighed through all the rustling pages. The special place remained lost as it opened

174

somewhere new: *Chapters*.

The woman asked Jenny not to leave her for a while and she promised; whatever might happen, the woman said, she would make sure that Jenny would be safe.

'I'll see you safe, my girl,' she said.

She was as fond of Jenny as could be, she said.

'Trust me,' she said, 'I need something young and shining around me a while longer.'

'What about the Bible and the fire?'

The Bible was always right, Jenny said, and she had a gut-feeling that she should be long gone from this place, but the woman said to trust her. She would see her safely on the road when the time was right.

Trust me and stay a while longer, said the spider to the fly.

Chapter 26

Jenny looked at the panicking pair, puzzled.

'Just what are you so worried about?' she asked.

They looked at her as if she was half-sharp.

'We've been set up, haven't we?' said Mother.

'Good and proper,' said Father.

'But Weasel-face took the loot last night, didn't he? Or have you got more upstairs?'

'Weasel-face?' said Mother.

'Old Tanner,' said Father, and she didn't know what was good for her, earwigging like she did and knowing about Gideon, but Mother said the girl was right. They had clothes and boots upstairs, but nobody would know any different.

'Gideon might have the good sense to stay away,' he said, and Mother said you never knew with Gideon.

Then she fetched a cloak down and said Jenny might as well leave.

'I can't recall where I first got it,' she said, fingering the soft blue garment.

Nothing she could give Jenny was come by honest, the woman said.

The cloak was a beautiful blue, like the colours of the night and the morning air mixed together.

'If you ask me,' said Mother, 'there's not a body in the whole wide world that's honest. A body aims to breathe in after breathing out.'

It all came down to choices, and Jenny thought that her Ma and Pa might be honest as she twirled around in the cloak.

Father was quite overcome; she was just like Mother had been in that cloak when she was young, Jenny was.

Mother had to fetch some more clothes for her. As she tried them on, the old woman threw Jenny's old clothes on the fire.

Blouses with sleeves falling like water from the shoulders, and tight, white bodices. She matched one with a brown skirt the likes of which she had never seen, just yards and yards of soft material gathered into a tiny waist.

'There's pockets in there that would hold a couple of dead cockerels,' said the women. When Jenny put her hand into one of the pockets, it didn't come out with either a dead or a live cockerel, but with a little comb inlaid with blue.

They sat all day uneasily within their thoughts.

The old man remembered a young woman with a little boy by her side.

The woman sighed for her lost beauty, recalled by the blue comb from which black hair had tumbled for evermore; whilst Jenny just itched to be gone from this place, and yet she lacked the courage to hurt these two old people.

As the day advanced, her old clothes would shortly be nothing but ashes, and in the dusk they heard a horse neighing and then a loud noise.

Someone was banging on the front door.

Father shuffled to answer it at long last as the two women listened.

A low, authoritative voice.

It was the fair rider, and Father told him they saw to the rough trade, and that there was a coaching inn down the road.

'I need to speak to the girl. It's urgent.'

'It's that Parliament man for you,' said Father, slamming the door in the man's face, 'don't bring him in here.'

Jenny talked to him outside by the old black poplar tree.

It was getting dark with the moon like a pale face

sinking into a shroud in its halo of soft grey clouds, and she saw the white blaze on the horse's head.

'It is you then,' he said, tearing his hat off.

'It is,' she said. 'What is the name of your horse?'

'Blaze,' he replied.

'And right lovely you are, Blaze,' said Jenny, patting him.

And Blaze let her, that was the wonder of it, he thought.

She looked quite lovely, he thought, they must have treated her well. He had heard some talk though which had disturbed him, and furthermore he'd been told that a young girl, foreign to these parts, was mixed up in it.

'Get thee gone from here,' he said suddenly and abruptly, his concern reflected in his deep voice. 'This is no place for a young girl, you must see that. T'is a den of thieves and there is an informer. It is common talk.'

'Maybe so,' she said, 'but they have been good to me. But I thank you most kindly for your concern.'

She laid her hand on his for a second and looked up at him.

'I'm just a country girl,' she said.

'The word '*just*' will never apply to you,' he said.

He looked vulnerable for a minute.

'Take good care of yourself,' he said.

He rode away from her, thinking that he had done his duty and so he was done with her, as he always did.

It was what Jenny needed; this man had touched her spirit, but Mother said she had looked out of the window and he was not one of them Parliament men.

'He's one of them Royalists.'

'Likely he has lost his seat, and the House of Lords has been done away with,' said Father, 'and he is on the run. Let him find out what it's like to be without.'

They had heard about the informer, it might well concern Gideon, and the woman thought she should explain herself to Jenny.

'I have known the true love of a man and I found a sanctuary. Not many can say that. There we were, Father and I, living on waste ground, afore it was enclosed. We managed and laboured as farmhands, but then when the child was due, it was that cold I thought it best to go to the village for the birth. A parish has to take care of a child born there.'

The ground underfoot crackled with frozen snow and the landscape looked blue.

'Blue, everything looked blue,' the woman said, 'and that included Father and me.'

They reached the village and they knocked on a house.

'A goodly house it was too,' said Father, 'with a light on inside,' but the door was slammed on them faster than it had opened. When it opened once more, they were chased away with sticks and she gave birth in a broken-down shed without a door, to a little boy with a face like a flower.

'In the morning they came looking for us and arrested us for vagrancy,' Father said, 'the thing is you leave footprints in the snow.'

She was eighteen and she had the child about her, and he was flogged for being a vagrant. Couldn't pay the fine, see?

'There's a law against vagrancy, but Father lost his place at the farm after a drought and we had nowhere to go. They flogs you for having no roof over your head and then they set you on the road again so they can flog you once more, I reckon.

T'would never happen again to us, we said, so we thieved. Robbed anyone.'

After a while they stole for the thrill of it, anything,

anywhere, keeping a proper balance between rich and poor, but careful like.

Gideon was good at it, right enough, and they had shown Gideon the gibbeted man who had been caught thieving.

'He has a language of his own, a gibbeted man, creaking at night and swinging in his sack. There's always a gibbeted man as a lesson.'

'The lesson is, don't get caught,' said Father, 'and Gideon was smart enough to know that.'

'We kept on thieving. We found this house, empty, and walked straight in, over the door laying on the ground as it happened. We stayed and when nobody objected to us, we opened an inn. You get all sorts which explains money coming in and you hear about things.'

Jenny had run into the night and she had barely fended for herself. If she had had a child to look after too, there was no telling what she might or might not do.

'We kept on thieving,' said the woman. 'If we had kept a proper inn, we would have made a living, but it gets into your blood, taking from them that have it and make laws against them that don't.'

After a while the woman said for Jenny to look into the Good Book again to see exactly what was meant by the fire. When she looked into her bundle for her Bible, she saw that the woman had put some rolled-up clothes as well as some food in it.

Jenny would be able to go at a moment's notice, but Mother begged her not to go just yet.

Stay awhile longer, said the spider to the fly, and then in they trooped, them that wants it, and by then it was too late.

Chapter 27

Jenny took the wet cloth from the casks in the pantry and the old man filled the mugs himself, mixing it with rum. That explained their custom.

'Which one of you is the rotten apple in the barrel?' she asked, swinging the cloth in the air. 'Come on now, own up.'

Weasel-face said she didn't make any sense, they had come to drink up and not to own up, and he complained that it wasn't his mug in front of him.

Jenny cried loudly that the Ale Was The Same, Wasn't It? Had he frightened any good dogs lately? That shut him up.

The woman staring into the fire turned around, surprised to see Weasel-face there, but she said nothing.

One round would do, Jenny thought, and then she announced to them that wants it that the ale was on the house.

She walked to the chalking board like the woman did to signal that time was up and they all trooped out with no trouble.

She swept the rushes out and she left the door open to air the room while she walked to the stream to fetch some water.

It was dark and still.

There was no sign of the dog, but neither was there any sign of men posted around the cottage. After she had laid fresh rushes the air in the inn was sweet and clean. She rinsed the mugs and she washed the table like the woman normally did.

Everything was neat and ready for the next day, and then she fetched the rum and she sat the old man by the table in front of it.

She looked out the back once more for any signs of trouble.

She felt different since she had spoken with the rider. She walked light and free to the stream and washed her face. The water was cold but not as cold as the water from the well in the village. It must have been a very deep well, she thought as she waited for a black shadow to pounce, but there was no sign of Stray.

It looked like she might have to leave without him after all.s

And now there was only living and breathing and waiting. When she looked out the back once more, she saw a black figure bending over something only a few yards away. The shadowy figure straightened up and turned into Gideon.

'Is it safe?' he whispered.

Without waiting for an answer, he crept past her.

He was pale and shaking and not looking so pretty now as they went into the house.

'Is this the girl?' he asked, looking at Jenny as if this was some great social occasion, taking his hat off and shaking her hand in a most charming manner.

'I like this one, Ma,' he said, and Jenny wondered at the dirty state of his hands. 'It's not too late, is it, Ma?' he asked.

He rummaged in his pocket and he looked at his Ma like a small boy would wanting praise. Then he put two gold hoops, a pearl necklace and a ring with a stone like a drop of blood on the table.

'Haven't I done well, Ma?' he said, and Jenny's heart stopped beating for a moment.

She remembered a pale hand with nails embedded with grime, pointing to a place on a trap. A ring with a stone like blood and gold hoops holding curls in place and round the slender neck was a pearl necklace.

She hoped with all her heart that she was wrong and

182

that it had not been Squire's daughter who had been robbed. She would be an evil one to cross, that one, one who would never give up.

He had been holding up a trap, Gideon said. 'Cambridge way. By the Ford. Well, before you get to it. Then it all went wrong.'

Gideon's mother turned around slowly and watched him with amazement, although more in sorrow than in anger.

'The lady was beautiful and the man was some sort of a lawyer in silk breeches.'

Squire's daughter, Jenny knew it now, and she thought God help us all.

Gideon patiently explained why it had gone wrong.

He made them get out of the trap, and, as he said, he merely intended to fire through the man's bandy legs to frighten him.

'Only there was summat wrong with the pistol, and I shot his face off instead. She was screaming, and I rolled the dead man in a blanket and put him on the trap, and she made off.'

Then it went wrong again.

As he rode away, his horse caught his leg in a deep mole hill and broke it, and he had to shoot the horse.

He could always get another one.

They had a lot of cash on them, the pair of them, and he had it all.

'I've got their loot,' he said,well pleased, but he was tired now, worn out. He had been on the road for three nights solid.

'I need to rest up.'

He had buried the coins in the plot that had been worked out the back, Gideon said, and his Ma gave short shouts of laughter, punctuating each sentence in turn.

How dreadful that his pistol didn't work.

It didn't bear thinking about.

'It's a comfort to know where you were when it happened.'

'It's a comfort to know you buried the loot right here.'

'I told you never, ever to take a life, so now you are on your own.'

Her voice had risen to a crescendo as she grabbed Squire's daughter's jewellery with one sweep of her hand and threw it on the dying embers.

Dawn was breaking, and Gideon had spent the night trying all the hiding places with the intelligence a headless chicken might employ.

Behind the curtains on the bed.

In one of the empty barrels.

In the oven in the bakehouse and back again, like a neverending circle, and he left sooty footprints just about everywhere.

It was past Jenny's comprehension how the son could endanger his Ma and Pa like he had, his sins coming home with him to roost. She thought if he had anything about him at all he would have gone in an entirely opposite direction.

Gideon was crammed on the settle bed once more they saw, watching him as if he had been conjured up in some sort of a bad dream, when they finally and abruptly fell asleep over the table.

When the woman woke up with a start, it was morning.

She rammed her mobcap over her ears and then she gave a gasp and hurried over to the fireplace.

'Get a cloth girl, look sharp.'

Her hands scrabbled through the dead ashes with lightning speed.

There was the stone of the ring come loose from it, and the pearls were all sooty.

She knelt there wrapping up the evidence, wondering what to do with it and what to do with her son, when a loud knocking on the door put the fear of God into her and set her trembling.

Gideon took his fate into his own hands when he saw there was no help to be had from that direction.

As he fled out the back, Jenny grabbed the jewels and put them into her skirt pocket.

'Kindling and wood, Father, look sharp. Put an apron on and then see to the door, girl, and look sharp.'

The front door shook on its hinges once more.

'All right, all right, I'm coming,' Jenny shouted, dancing to the door in neatly slippered feet, tying a clean white apron over the brown skirt, with a neat bow at the back. She couldn't exactly say why, but neatness seemed of the utmost importance to her just now.

When she opened the door it was one of the Sheriff's men who surveyed a scene of serene domestic bliss.

He contemplated the happy scene.

A pretty young girl was opening the door for him, standing aside politely.

An old and tidy woman was up and about early, clearing out a fireplace.

A Bible on the table.

An old man shuffling in carrying kindling and wood.

He scratched his head, pushing his hat well back over his head and then he went outside, Jenny after him like a shadow, but all he did was look at the sign of the ship carved on the wood by the window, and then at Jenny, and back again to the sign.

He carried a pistol, Jenny saw, when he motioned to her with it to proceed him into the inn. She had a mad desire to take to her heels and run, run, run, but she could hardly move her legs enough to go inside again.

The Sheriff's man didn't look at anyone inside.

The old couple had got a hold of their senses after a fashion, and Father said the inn wasn't open yet, but there was a coaching inn down the road like.

The man wasn't impressed.

He looked for Gideon Hutch at the Ship Inn, Huntingdon, and was he right in saying this was the place?

He continued when Mother assured him it was.

Men had been posted at the said Gideon Hutch's boat on the river Ouse, at the Port of London, and also at the home of a certain Bridget Miller residing in Ramsey.

'Are you Robert and Marjory Hutch? Are you the parents of the said Gideon Hutch?'

'Yes,' said Mother, 'you and your fool questions, Aaron Fletcher. You know full well this is the Ship Inn and that we are Gideon's parents. Father has supped the ale drawn by Gideon with you yourself many a time in the past, afore you went up in the world of course.'

'What's Gideon supposed to have done?' asked Father, and the pair of them went pale around the chops when the man read out charges of murder and robbery on the highway, to be punishable with death by hanging. The official declaration of Gideon's crimes in the clear light of day made his get-away a seeming impossibility.

The man didn't say anything, but he looked at the rushes in front of the bed. Finally he picked up a bundle of sooty rushes and held them up high.

'What might you call this then?' he asked no-one in particular, pointing to the soot Gideon had left on the rushes when he had come out of the oven, practicing where he might hide.

'We call them rushes around these parts,' quaked Jenny in a high voice, and the man wondered how long Jenny had been around these parts; vagrancy was still a punishable offence.

'You might well be wrong there,' said Father. 'I've heard tale that vagrancies are not strictly enforced like these days, too many of them on the road.'

'Hmm.'

And Mother came up trumps.

Gideon had brought the girl from Bridget some time ago.

Bridget always sent girls to help her like at the inn.

'Just one more good haul, and then Gideon will settle down with the girl,' the man said, 'isn't that how the story goes?'

Jenny went pale remembering the night voices, but Mother didn't like to be interrupted when she was in full flow and she said the girl was a Parson's daughter.

'Does she look like a vagrant? I ask you,' she said.

The man walked over to the table and opened the Bible, Jenny still after him like a shadow.

'It's not the full Bible,' she said, 'it's some of the Old Testament and the New.'

'Hmm.'

'John Cooper, Anno Domini 1605' he read out, and after a while, 'Bashiba Cooper, Anno Domini 1632.'

He turned to Jenny.

'Is that you, this Bashiba Cooper?' and Jenny agreed, trying to hide her amazement. She had forgotten that this was her real name and she wished that her Ma and Pa had chosen some other name for her.

'T'is after some fine lady in the Bible,' she said.

'She is a Parson's daughter,' said Mother.

'I'm called Jenny. For short,' Jenny added, but the man only commented on her Pa's fine hand.

Then he drew his pistol and shot through the curtains of the bed.

He loaded again and walked into the larder and shot through a barrel, and the ale gushed in spurts. He loaded the weapon, and then he went into the bakehouse.

'Some oven,' he said to no-one in particular. 'Some oven.'

Mother did on occasions bake for the big house up the road if they do like, a wedding or some such event, Father said, 'help out like,' but the man cut him short and told him to fetch kindling and wood.

The oven door remained shut as the Militia man set the flames under it alight with the taper.

He waited for quite a while, although a good fire was roaring away fairly quickly, but there were no screams, or smells, of a man burning alive, and Jenny thought that they might be in the clear yet.

Proof was needed of the robbery but they were safe, always supposing he didn't ask her to empty her pockets, but he must have read her thoughts.

'Empty your pockets,' he pointed with his pistol to the three of them. 'All of you.'

They stared at him.

'Turn 'em inside out.'

He looked at the group, a picture of desperation and guilt unable to masquerade as innocence. The old couple's pockets hung as loose and empty as their mouths and Jenny thought he would ask next what was still in her skirt pocket, but he didn't.

The Militia man aimed for surprise.

'What's out the back?'

Out the back was a black dog starting to dig the black earth.

'Call the dog.'

'Stray!' Jenny called, and he was at her side.

The sheriff's man began to dig. He found something and he held it aloft.

Gideon's loot!

Chapter 28

The Sheriff's man had left them huddled together like lost sheep.

'Don't any of you move.'

The words hanging over them mingled with the smell and smoke of the powder and added to their confusion.

'He could have shot someone in that bed, he could have, no wonder she's white and shaking,' said Father, nodding at Jenny.

White and shaking did the trick, Mother said, and of a sudden she felt that she was in control. Now was the time to act. Shaking wouldn't do, but time was of the essence, it wouldn't be long before men were posted out the back, cutting off any escape route.

If the girl was to get away they had to act fast and think long, the old woman said. 'You'll have to get away. There's no need to involve you in our trouble.'

Then she put the blue cloak around the girl.

Fletcher had seen a pale, slim girl with fluffy dark curls and when Jenny emerged he would have to see an entirely different girl.

She scraped every bit of hair away from Jenny's face and secured it on top of her head with the blue comb.

'Put the hood up. Fasten it.'

She tied it in a bow in the front, and then she pinched Jenny's cheeks sharply several times, adding colour to her cheeks.

Fletcher would see a rosy-faced girl without any curls.

She placed the bundle high on Jenny's chest and secured it tightly under her cloak with the belt. It was more of a cape, and her hands stuck out idly through two slits on either side.

'Basket, Father.'

She stepped back and looked at Jenny.

'She could be thought to be with child and going to market. God speed you on your journey, child, and remember, don't worry about me and Father, we have got out of bigger holes before now.'

'Not many,' said Father, but Jenny realised she had to leave by herself, except for Stray who was by her side.

She would have to go out the back, hiding behind the trees to sneak into the cottage next door. Its back door was not locked, although the front door had a bolt which would have to be drawn from the inside. The dog would certainly be a problem, but Jenny said the dog had a good sense of what was wanted of him.

'Don't look like it to me,' Mother muttered, 'but if Gideon hadn't dirtied his own nest things would be different.'

'She'll never be strong enough to draw that bolt by herself,' Father said, 'I best do it for her.'

They walked out the back, Jenny, the old man and Stray, and Jenny felt very different with her hood up, almost invisible.

They ran along the back behind the trees and to the back door of the empty cottage next door. Although the wood had warped and needed an almighty kick of Father's foot to open it, it was not locked, like the woman had said.

She walked through the empty room smelling of damp and decay and Father drew back the bolt on the front door.

Stray shot out of the back door when she pointed to it, following the shuffles of the old man while she opened the front door.

She saw that the Sheriff's man in front of the inn was not paying any attention to her at all; he was busy issuing instructions to his men, pointing down the road, the bundle with the loot at his feet.

Walking slowly backwards, she walked briskly forward when she saw him turning in her direction. As she walked past the Sheriff's man, it looked as if she had come from further down the road.

The man touched his hat and the girl stopped.

'Trouble?' Jenny wanted to ask, but her voice stuck in her gullet; but had he only pushed his hat back for a good scratch, he had not noticed her at all and was talking to one of his men instead. She might as well stop and listen to what he had planned, she thought, making a great pretence of being highly pregnant and rubbing her aching back.

He wished that he had not withdrawn his men late last night and set them to look-out by the river, he said, but his informer had told him that the couple had no idea they had been set up. He pointed to his informer who was sitting by the old poplar.

Weasel-face.

'He'll get his come-uppance. Might as well have another villain for the gallows.'

They had nothing to charge them with at the inn. Nothing at all on the premises.

'Isn't that the loot?' asked his man pointing to the bundle, and the man said no, Gideon had made off with it, but they would get him.

'I didn't let on they were in the clear in there. I'll make' em sweat for a while longer. This,' he pointed to the bundle,' is Gideon's dirty linen, a shirt and waistcoat with blood on it as a matter of fact. The dead man's blood, likely, but a bundle of dirty linen isn't any kind of evidence. We'll have to catch him with the loot on him.'

The woman at the inn always did one thing at the time.

She had got on with the living and now she got on with the dying. They had aided and abetted a robber and a murderer, there was only the noose beckoning in the distance.

She would wait until she saw the girl passing by the window safe and sound, though. Now was the time to pay the bill for living on this earth. There would be another day and on that day the dead would be raised and there was no telling what would happen then.

She wasn't afraid of death itself, what she dreaded was the unknown, the passing over.

'Well, Father, is it to be a hanging or a burning?' she asked.

'Burn the place, and it's best if we are insensible when it happens,' Father said, 'and make sure the place burns well. We have to go up with it, dying is best done in private.'

He was right, she said, and she recounted all the steps she would have to take for their dying, like she did with the baking.

First she made the fire up. Make sure he was well into the rum so he would never know much about dying.

All the same, when Father said to fetch the taper and set the curtains ablaze, she said there was no reason not to put up a bit of a fight, life was sweet.

She walked to the window.

Old Fletcher, gone up in the world and now a sheriff's man, was talking to one his men outside by the tying-post, and Jenny had stopped close by. She was rubbing her back and listening intently to their talk.

'Dear God. Father, come here and tell me that this ain't our Jenny a-busying herself ear-wigging out there, and dear God, whatever does she think she is a-doing of now?'

Jenny had never felt so happy in her life, as, near giddy with relief, she listened to the men talking. She very nearly fell into the inn door, which opened at the exact moment she was about to knock on it.

She was shaking like a leaf as she fell into Mother's arms.

'I need a strong drink, strongest you got.'

The rum nearly burnt her throat, but it steadied her almost immediately.

'The bundle. It's not the loot. It's Gideon's dirty linen, it's all they got on him,' she gasped. 'He must have made off with the loot after all. The sheriff's man knew it all the time. He was going to make you sweat in here a bit longer, he said so to this other man with him.'

They stared at her.

'Well, I'll be buggered with a red-hot poker,' said Father.

'First time that Gideon ever did anything right in his life, even if he meant to land us in the shit leaving it with us, which I will never forgive him for,' said Mother. 'Wouldn't have put it past him to run away and off to the Americas with a bundle of dirty washing.'

They looked at each other, then they hugged each other, and then laughed and laughed until tears ran down their cheeks and their sides ached as they conjured up images of Gideon fleeing and holding onto his rags for dear life.

It was a wonderful, wonderful feeling to be alive and to be given a second chance, Mother said.

'Except Weasel-face is for the gallows,' said Jenny. 'And Gideon will be hunted down.'

'I was about to get my angel wings, I intended to set fire to the cottage, I can't abide the outside,' said Mother.

'I would have got wings myself,' Father said looking

193

forlorn, and Jenny suddenly felt a great wave of affection for him and Mother.

'I expect you will join that scruffy old man in sacking with the beard that walked past the first night you were with us,' he said, and Jenny thought Mother had been right, Father did have an uncanny knack of finding out what was important.

She and Father were old and tired, Mother said. If Jenny saw a likely girl on her travels, she should send her this way.

'And a likely man for the heavy lifting,' said Father.

'And why not?' said Mother. 'Didn't the Bible say *Chapters*? New chapters, a new beginning.'

Mother opened the door as if hustling Jenny to go to market with her basket, their very last pretence.

'I want a word with you, Aaron Fletcher. It's about making repairs to our cottage and persecuting innocent folks,' Mother shouted to the sheriff's man as Jenny set off down the road, 'and you best tell him,' pointing to the tree where Weasel-face was sitting amongst a crowd of men, 'that he is no longer welcome in our house.'

'He best do his drinking some other place, or else,' said Father, keeping up the pretence.

'You mean old Tanner? He's for the gallows,' said Fletcher, or so he thought. Turned out that Weasel-face was now the late Weasel-face. His mouth was frothing, and when one of the men touched his shoulders he toppled over and a knife was sticking out between his shoulder-blades.

'Whose knife is it? It's a good knife with a pewter handle,' he asked, drawing the blade out.

'In that case, it's his own, he thieved it and boasted about it many times,' said one of the men.

'You will have some explaining to do to your betters, won't you, Fletcher my lad?' said the old man.

'Terrorising innocent folks, destroying their goods which is the means of their making a living.'

'And letting a man get murdered under the very eyes of yourself and *with his own knife*,' said Mother, before Fletcher could point out only one barrel of ale had been shot through.

Jenny walked on as if in a dream.

It was raining and she felt cosy in her hood.

Before she was very far along the road, folks coming towards her asked her if she knew aught about a murder, but she shook her head, and she wondered how on earth rumours got around as fast as they did.

After a while she took the belt off around her middle and let her burden fall to the ground, leaving the belt in the basket by the roadside for Father to find.

She soon got used to walking like this again, and then the dog pounced on her.

'It's all right, Stray,' she said, stroking his warm, solid body, 'everything has turned out fine and now we will find Nathan.'

They reached an inn of sorts by the sign that was swinging from a gabled house with a double-flight of steps outside reaching the first floor, and by the looks of the coaches and horses in front of it.

She only noticed it because the dog stopped dead in his tracks.

He sniffed around a good deal, and finally he shot off around the house through a big entrance which led into a yard with stables and outhouses in the back.

When she followed him, there was Nathan.

Chapter 29

Nathan was grooming the fair rider's horse, Blaze.

Dirty water lay in puddles floating with dirt, and a comely maid with some white geese cackling around her skirt was laughing fit to burst at something he said. Her head was thrown back and she showed off her gleaming white teeth. It was something rude, something to do with a goose nearly up her backside, Jenny thought.

Nathan scratched his head when he saw Jenny.

'Jenny,' he said, 'is it you? Why are trussed up like a chicken?'

'A blue chicken,' said the maid. 'Never seen a blue chicken afore now,' and Nathan laughed.

'What do you want with me, Jenny?'

'I don't want anything from you, you great big twerp,' she said, 'I just came to see what was amiss with the dog.'

The maid walked away, her hips swinging, looking over her shoulder, a deliberately daring look, leaving Nathan in a fair quandary.

'Make your choice,' she said.

He made a good living here, and lanky Rose who had come with him hadn't lasted more than a week, like he had thought.

He thought about it all, and then he fetched his saddlebag.

The road and Jenny had won the day, but it had been helped by the horse. He had groomed and coveted it. He had polished the brass in its stall to ward off evil spirits, he had exercised it when Sir Richard and borrowed a horse from the stable, and he had thought that shortly the day would dawn when he would he ride off on it.

Before Jenny left, she had said good-by to Blaze. If she knew the horse's name, she had to be well acquainted with its rider, he reckoned.

After a while he was by her side.

They walked out of Huntingdon as the fine drizzle lifted. The sky was covered in torn clouds which let out a halo of golden light. It would be a fine day after all. A while passed, and then they caught up with someone else, an old man with long yellow hair and a long yellow beard, a white lambskin slung over his shoulder.

Nathan wasn't too pleased to say the least.

The old foreigner had sheltered in one of the many out-houses attached to the inn. Nathan had warned him early that morning to sling his hook or else, but now he was sorry; he should have left him there undisturbed.

When Jenny said something about an old woman and an old man at an inn, he didn't enquire any further. He could picture it. A long line of folks. Jenny at the head, then the dog, then the old foreigner, then himself, then a member of the aristocracy, and then an old man and old woman shuffling at the back, not forgetting Oliver, all swaying through the country-side.

Just what was it about her that made folks stick to her tighter than a bad smell?

Chapter 30

'Bad news, bad, bad news,' said the innkeeper, wringing his hands.

If the innkeeper was apologetic to this customer it was only good sense, so his wife had said, and she was right for once.

After all, his customer was a very fine gentleman, one who brought great credit to the inn. Well thought of in these parts too was Sir Richard Bennet, and his father had sat in the House of Lords. Not now of course, it had been done away with when they had done away with the King.

Sir Richard had taken supper with Mistress Cromwell herself, even though he had supported the King's cause in the war.

What was good enough for Mistress Cromwell was good enough for the innkeeper, although the difference was that he saw to it that Sir Richard was well served with his suppers, dinners and breakfasts and hired his horses out so that the Chestnut horse could rest. He would recall it all when he presented the bill to him.

Sir Richard's son, well, now he hadn't supported the King. Unlike his father, he was a Parliamentarian and not a Royalist.

T'was rumoured he was going to stand for Parliament when he returned.

Riding home now with Cromwell, Sir Richard's son, and they had tamed the Irish in record time. Heathens all of them, or else Catholics, although Sir Richard had said the Irish were a race with their own culture.

He was welcome to his opinion, but all the same the innkeeper could not help admiring Sir Richard's wisdom of keeping one foot in each camp. Better than keeping one foot in the grave and the other in prison any time.

His customer carried on eating, seemingly quite unconcerned.

'What was this bad, bad news?' he asked after a long while, wiping his hands with the napkin.

'The new groom has cleared off, leaving the brushes all in a muddle,' said the innkeeper.

'I'm sorry to hear it, he was as good a groom as I've come across.'

'T'is the new groom what arrived with his sister the same day as you yourself did, only she was not up to the mark. T'is the handsome one who snouts around inside where he's got no business to.'

'Half-groomed, the horse is,'added the innkeeper.

Sir Richard kept on eating his breakfast, but then he wasn't an innkeeper but a mere customer.

That wasn't all, the innkeeper said. There had been a real casa... casar...casatrophy like.

'Catastrophe,' said Sir Richard, reaching for the bread.

A catastrophe gave the innkeeper pleasure, as long as it didn't befall himself, of course.

'A murder. There's been a murder at the inn down the road, the one we talked about only last evening.'

The man put his fork down, losing all interest in the smoking dish of eggs and bacon, the innkeeper's best, and anyone with half an eye could see that, fine gentleman that Sir Richard was, he was as interested as the next low fellow in a real disaster even if he did know all about long words.

'Anyway, the woman they call Madge or Marjory, she makes the best bread hereabouts on account of her strong arms, it's the kneading what does it, and the man, Robert, or is it John? A thin fellow on the moody side, he was and, oh yes, the new girl as well and there was talk of a black dog, but that might well be rumour.'

'Who was murdered?'

The innkeeper didn't know, could be any one of the three, but he had lost his audience. His customer shot off like an arrow fired by a strong arm and the innkeeper shouted after him that his horse was unsaddled, but Sir Richard shouted back that he had saddled a horse himself before now, and that he would return to settle up shortly.

'The informer was found murdered,' said the Sheriff's man outside the inn, 'knifed with his own knife by that very poplar. Sir.'

'How about the people in the inn?'

'Nothing was found. Sir.'

'How about the girl?'

'The girl? Seemingly she was a Parson's daughter, it takes all sorts.'

When further questioned, one of the men said he had seen a young woman heavy with child coming down the road towards them. She had worn a blue cloak, but the Sheriff's man saw that this information was of no use to the gentleman.

He went into the inn and Mine Host shuffled forward.

'There's a coaching inn down the road,' Mine Host said. 'We had an incident like last night.'

'Where is the girl?'

'Girl? Mother would tell you where she got to, but Mother's in the bakehouse. The girl, she took off,' said the old man, so Sir Richard did the same.

He settled his bill at the coaching inn and then rode on.

As he rode he thought he remembered seeing something out of the corner of his eye by the side of the road.

A group of people sitting together, amongst them a

young, slight and pretty girl in a blue cloak and a handsome black dog.

By her side was a young man, the groom from the inn, and an old man with a beard.

He turned round and she looked up at him gravely, her short hair softly curling over the rim of the hood, as clean and shining as a new dawn.

Heavy with child? But of course - she would have concealed the bundle under her cloak when she made her get-away.

They had all arisen, and the groom from the coaching inn removed his fur hat.

'This is Nathan,' she said. 'And this is Bernard.'

The old man inclined his head and there was a rare dignity about him despite his crippled arm.

They were heading for the Digger Colony which was outside London, Jenny said.

'Folk who keep themselves,' Nathan said.

He knew well enough where it was. Walton-on-Thames, and General Fairfax himself was looking into it that particular problem right now.

The local people had complained bitterly about vagrants settling there, digging up their Commons, felling their trees for houses and clearing their land for crops.

That was the problem. How common was the common land?

The girl could be placed upside down into a dung heap and she would emerge smiling and smelling of violets, he thought. All the same, he would keep an eye out for her, as it seemed to him she wore the look of a sleeping child woken up rudely.

He would look out for her just in case, he thought he as he rode on, although there seemed no doubt that the young man, Nathan she had called him, and Jenny were made for each other.

Something delightful had crossed his path and brightened his life. He couldn't involve her in his troubles though. He had a letter at the inn from his bailiff; he was safe enough for the present and no warrant had yet been posted for his arrest at the Port of London as a Royalist.

He knew all about that nonsense that was spouted about him. *As if he would dine with Mistress Cromwell! As if his son was riding with Cromwell*! His son was at home, digging his father's grave. He was waiting for a letter at the Swan Inn, and in the meantime he had visited friends for a place of refuge, one in Gloucestershire, and one in Cambridge, and the news wasn't good.

He had a mind to go abroad after he had spoken with his son and got some money together. It was right and fitting that these two young people, Jenny and Nathan, should cleave together, so his senses told him, but the memory of an upturned face haunted his heart.

Oliver had cleared off when he saw Nathan, and Father Bernard had gone his own way because he could sense the division he caused between the two young people. Stray whined and Jenny sighed. She always felt better when she was in Bernard's company but Nathan felt differently about him.

'Good riddance to foreign rubbish,' he said.

'He was a foreigner, so what? You would be a foreigner if you were in foreign parts.'

Him, a foreigner? Was she mad? He was an Englishman and ever would be. He came from a place where men and women knew their places and women hid their fancies like they should. He came from up North, he did, the best place in the world.

'My Gran lives up North,' he said proudly.

'Surprise me,' she said. 'If it's so wonderful up

North, what are you doing in these parts?'

She followed Stray who was playing about in front, his black nose well down, criss-crossing the path and taking off after strange scents, leaving Nathan in a fine quandary. He was not a follower but a leader, always had been, but then the cloaked figure had transformed herself into a pretty girl once more and he thought to himself that she was full of tricks, that little one, and he had better watch out for himself.

Chapter 31

Stray was playing about in front, delegating responsibilities of leadership and guardian angel to Nathan, who followed, loathe as he was to follow and not lead.

The dog seemed well enough to Jenny. Resting up while she had been at the inn must have done him good, she thought.

At times it had seemed to the girl that the heavy light of the fens was being sucked into the watery earth but now flowing light played and danced along young beeches puffed up with tender green leaves. It danced about their heads as they walked side by side, and they sat close together when they rested after a while, but they were but strangers to each other.

Nathan recalled arriving at the inn and seeing the red horse being rubbed down. It was evening then and Jenny had been on his mind. He had recognised the rider, fine gentleman or not, as the one Jenny had wound her arms around riding on the dyke. What had Sir Richard done with her?

Nathan had got short shrift from all, in fact he was thrown out of the house when he searched Sir Richard's room, although for what he was searching he did not know.

All but the serving maid. A bit of an animal when it came to the coupling and he had enjoyed her, but she wouldn't do for the settling down. All the same, he had strung her along and kept her sweet and it turned out well. When the black dog shot into the yard he knew Jenny would follow shortly, and she would be left in no doubt that she was not the only maid in the world.

Jenny felt as dead inside as the outside of the dead tree they rested on. Layers on layers of hopes fell about her heart.

'Any wild pigs in these woods then?' she said listlessly to fill up the emptiness around her.

'No,' he said, 'leastways I don't think so.'

Then he grabbed her arm.

'Don't move,' he whispered in the deadly voice of a whispering wind. 'Don't move.'

She sat bolt upright, straining for sights and sounds of the Sheriff's men in hot pursuit. He looked at her and thought how pretty she was, and he looked forward to the sport.

She shook his arm off. 'You and your games.'

He would take her in his arms after he had frightened her and then there would be giggling and falling onto the ground together. It was a love game in which maids played along with men when the time came and no more was thought of it, he said.

'I would sooner die an old maid,' she said, grabbing her bundle ready for the off.

They walked all the day and then the shadows of the night came when the yellow light faded into the distance like a slowly tilting candle. It was snuffed out by a cold gust of wind.

Nathan found a deep clearing. The exposed root of an ancient tree hung over them like a threat as he made a fire. The flints sparked and caught the rustling leaves the first time and he was relieved.

What was up with her?

It was only the way of the world and he had not invented it, while she thought of the woman at the inn. Mother had given birth and Father had been flogged but they had been together, and Jenny thought, what if she had a child?

'I left you in the night,' he said, 'but it didn't take you long to find another. Nearly ran over me, Sir Richard did when I walked back for you that morning.'

Nathan had come back for her!

She buried her face in her bundle.

'Come here, Jenny for short. Let's never fight again,' he said and they made a vow not to fight or argue ever again.

'Come lay with me,' he said, 'if it's a child you're worried about, I know the way to prevent it. No maid of mine was ever left with child.'

'And neither will this one be,' she said. 'Good night, Nathan.'

She listened for Nathan's reply, but none came. The moon was sieved through the delicate twigs of a dead tree and she clutched her shawl to her face in her loneliness.

She opened her mouth to call out his name and the night was drowned with the shrieking and wailing of all the dead lost souls in the world. The dog jumped to his feet and both of them looked up at the white saucer of wisdom in the tree above them.

'Hush, Stray,' she said, 't'is but an old Billy Owl.'

Nathan caught a rabbit the next day and they fed well, or they would have done; the meadows fairly twitched with them, but after a day or two Jenny had watched so many rabbits of so many sizes that she would not touch them now. After a while she found that it was beyond her. Nathan insisted one day that she should eat a rabbit stew and her stomach had promptly thrown it up.

Even Stray, laying with his muzzle between his paws next to her, took no notice when the rabbits had come out of their burrows in the soft evening air. She knew them so well, the little ones learning not touch thistles or nettles once they had stung their delicate noses. It accounted for the way these plants flourished and grew so tall, while everything else was chewed down to its roots.

Eating rabbits seemed like a betrayal of life to her although she knew better than to say so to Nathan. Instead she emphasised that if they acted prudently there would be enough food to last them for a long while, what with the cheese and bacon and loaves now hard as rock, all neatly wrapped in cloth. A cockerel as well, would you believe, plucked, drawn and roasted! When had Mother put it in her bundle?

'Wasn't she good?' Jenny said.

He would never understand her, not in all of his life. Thieves and murderers and she called them good! She had an awful lot of fancies in her head, he did not doubt it.

Good night Nathan, he thought bitterly.

Trust him to pick on a maid who came complete with a four-legged, black-furred and sharp-fanged beast of a dog-faced chaperon. She was always surrounded by someone who he couldn't abide.

The Priest for a start. Spouting forth his Catholic spells now which he had never done before. And Sir Richard, power and money, and him a Royalist, more than likely a Catholic as well, and both of them always turning up when they were not wanted, leastways not by Nathan.

He avoided other travellers, even Rose and Oliver, and he had never done that before. He had always enjoyed their company at the end of a day in all the time he had travelled on the road.

But now it was different, what with the Priest and Sir Richard, and Jenny and her fancies, while she thought she ought to explain herself.

'Trouble just came to me all of a sudden,' she said, 'and of its own accord,' and Nathan begged her to tell him, if she didn't mind too much, something he hadn't heard of before.

'And you left your village in the dead of night because the Parson's wife wanted to see if you had a witch mark on you. Quite reasonable seeing she had harboured a witch under her roof before.'

He looked at her sideways.

'What did Sir Richard think about that mark of yours that the Parson's wife wanted to see?'

Why should he know about that mark *when she didn't even know him* and why was Nathan never on her side? But when Nathan came back with the water from the stream he said he would swear by all that was holy never to leave her again.

Then they fell into a heated argument about what was holy and the Priest figured very largely in it.

It was the last time that Jenny argued with him, and she only mentioned Father Bernard once more, but that was later, much later.

There were other ways to reach Nathan, but she was glad she hadn't lain with him. She wasn't hankering after being wed. That would involve banns being read and witnesses and above all, it would involve a Parson who likely had a wife.

She knew that life wasn't all dancing around flames and looking into each other eyes, as Nathan pointed out many a time. Jenny had to live on this earth, even Adam and Eve had had to; they had started it, according to the Bible.

Jenny was going to say that Adam and Eve's first-born had turned out to be a murderer when she saw that Nathan's fire, just like Cain's, had smoke which curled like a snake along the ground, but she minded her peace.

Then she remembered that the lovely clothes she wore were from Mother. The pocket in the skirt was, just as Mother had said, big enough to hold a dead cockerel; her arm sank right into its depth well up to her elbow.

There was a comb in there and something else besides.

'Nathan,' she said before she could stop herself, 'you know Mother at the inn said this pocket would hold...' and he went wild. Never, ever, was she to mention Mother or Father at the inn or Father Bernard or Sir Richard either.

As Nathan stomped off, Jenny thought that she now had a good idea what Nathan looked like from the back.

She investigated what else might be lurking in that pocket aside from the comb. Her hand came out with a fistful of jewels.

She had forgotten about them, and she thought it would be best not to mention them to Nathan.

Get rid of them, she thought.

She pressed the pearls, all sooty, and the gold hoops into the ground like so many seeds. Try as she might, she could not bear to part with the great red stone.

A red deer advanced daintily, its ears like large butterflies on its small head. It sniffed at the red stone and then it melted away into the undergrowth. Stray, resting by her side, barely had time to put his lolloping red tongue back where it belonged and Jenny smiled when she rejoined Nathan.

'What are you smiling at? Seen somebody you like? Like Sir Richard?'

She didn't say anything, there was no point.

At one time they had walked along a path by the wood banking onto fields. Passing from light into darkness, darkness into light, Nathan was handsome, but passing into the shadow it looked as if the saddlebag was part of him. He became an old, deformed man, and he looked dark and threatening, like he was someone else.

The memory of it lingered as sunshine gave way to

rain and she was glad of the rest when the dog tired. She didn't feel well. At times she lost her balance, and most of the food was not worth eating as it did not stay down long enough.

Some days it was just as it had been when she had first left her cottage in the night. She had to concentrate on putting one foot in front of the other and she wondered if Nathan was right, and that she had imagined more than she saw in the graveyard.

'It was dark, wasn't it?'

'How about Squire's Daughter?'

'She looked for you, didn't she? Might have been sent by your Pa, she might have.'

Jenny wondered what was real, but she went along with Nathan; she was lost in a strange country.

Perhaps it was just Nathan's way of talking that separated them, the harsh sounds of it and the way he went straight for the throat of an argument as if it might be a threatening animal just begging to be throttled, but sometimes the rider's image arose unbidden in her mind. She was laying under a large elm at noon. Thick black shadows lay heavy on the ground when she saw him riding in the long meadow grass towards her on Blaze.

'What makes you so fair?' he asked her.

'Not fair enough for you,' she said, 'but I owe Nathan, he takes care of me.'

Ramblings, and she looked around guiltily in case Nathan was around.

Sometimes, when she squatted by the fire getting their meal, she thought that the rider was leaning on a tree behind her, watching her, smiling at her, approving of her.

Who is playing games now, she thought, walking the countryside with one man and dreaming of another?

Although their progress was slow and leisurely, Nathan did a fair bit of dancing around. It was gnats, they were about him like a fine curtain of rain, there were that many of 'em, and they wrought havoc on his handsome face.

'Why don't you rub one of those large green leaves, dock or whatever, on your bites,' Jenny rashly advised him one day, 'and leave off scratching, you'll soon find yourself healed,' but Nathan informed her that the world was full to the brim of what you might call green leaves.

Just because gnats never touched her it didn't mean that she was an expert, although gnats and green leaves were not added to the growing list of Nathan's unmentionables because they worked.

The dog lay close to the ground warmed by the sun, stretched out with his head resting on the earth, his eyes looking at her and his ears pricking up at unwarranted sounds. She thought Nathan would tell her next that the dog was part of her fancies as she picked poppies from the meadow, a black imprint on each red leaf, like the black smudge under the Lady Eloise's eyes.

So delicate and so beautiful, these poppies, and yet there was such a bitter smell hidden in the white stickiness inside the thin, hairy stalks.

A tight bud, folded up. As Jenny peeled the leaves and unfolded the silken, wrinkled petals and smoothed them into whole flowers, an image arose in her mind of poppies blooming between Father Bernard's hands.

Nathan was right, she was full of fancies; Father Bernard had only one hand that he could use.

'Playing with flowers?' said Nathan when he came upon her, and -just like that- Jenny had enough. She had run away and made it on her own, and she could again as soon as she had a chance.

It was difficult to find safe places for them to rest; these woods were full of masterless, homeless men, men who took the law into their own hands, said Nathan.

Somebody had told her that the vagrancy laws were not strictly enforced now, somebody at the inn, but she didn't think she ought to mention it.

'Dangerous men,' he said. 'I heard tales of them that would make your heart stop. Nobody is safe from them.'

He glanced at her as she picked up her skirts as daintily as if she was some fine lady or other. She was different from the other maids, and, he supposed, she was what he had been looking for, except for her fancies.

She read the Bible in the morning looking for omens; now that was odd, he told her.

She looked up.

'Odd? How odd? Where did you learn your reading?'

'Here and there,' he said.

'Where? From the almanacs? Did you have a Chapman from London visiting you?'

Almanacs and a Chapman? he wondered.

'Of course,' he said, because no way would he admit he couldn't read, 'where else? But Sir Stephen didn't hold much with book learning.'

He talked a lot about Sir Stephen who had hunted Catholics who wouldn't attend Church. Sir Stephen, who knocked some sense into his beautiful wife.

'It's always Sir Stephen,' she said. 'Didn't you meet some other man who you could learn from?' and he stormed off again, but he came back at once and said that she just had to mark his ways and she would be a fine woman sometime in the future.

'Do I want to be a fine woman?' she asked Stray as she hoisted her bundle and set off. Anywhere away from Nathan would do her just fine, whereas Nathan would just be pleased if he knew where he was.

He had looked at the north star and aimed to walk away from it to the South, but how was it that they never got any further, and then his nagging anxiety turned into a rising panic. He had started to cut notches into trees, and he recognised one after a couple of days' walking cut on the large elm she was laying under at noon.

Jenny had dented his confidence both as a man and as a traveller, and he was desperately seeking his way towards the Digger colony to show her he was man who was always right in what he did and what he knew.

These masterless men made no effort to cover their traces; gnawed bones and rubbish were strewn around and camp-fires barely stamped out, but probably some time ago, he thought. As he had told her, they were dangerous. Even if the vagrancy laws were not enforced now, masterless men were rounded up. Branded and flogged or else hanged, and it didn't make them any more docile.

When he returned to the place where he had left her, she was gone. *She had run away from him. After all he had done for her!*

'Vagabonds,' he said, looking around him fearfully, 'I must find her before they do.'

He ran ahead, as she would have done he thought, and when evening fell, he found her in a clearing.

'Get out of here, quick. Vagabonds head for clearings. Quick!"

She followed him when they heard distant voices.

'Find a tree with lots of foliage,' he urged her.

He threw her bundle and his saddlebag into some bushes and told her to climb high up into the nearest oak and sit in the nook of thinning top branches. He had been here before, Nathan knew by the notch on the tree.

'Take that blue thing off and wrap yourself into your shawl,' he said, looking across to where she was sitting a yard away from him.

'That's better,' he whispered, 'lash yourself to the branches, and for God's sake don't drop anything.'

'I feel sick,' she said, but all thoughts of it vanished when she saw a collection of rough men passing beneath them. One of them stopped and relieved himself on their oak, and had he looked up he would have looked straight into her white face; but he didn't, he merely looked uneasily from side to side.

As she listened to the vagabond's noises in the night was there a scream.

Jenny thought that she really did owe Nathan now and she would stick with him come what may, whilst he thought that he had shown her he was worth something.

When morning came at long last, the men's voices faded in the distance and finally disappeared.

Stray appeared suddenly beneath the oak, looking up at her, so it must be safe now, Nathan said in a shaking voice, thank God for the dog. She climbed down after him and then the dog pounced on a thick shadow which had detached itself from a tree. He was standing on the man's chest, his fangs not an inch from the man's frightened face.

Nathan walked over to him.

'Mason, it's me,' the man gasped, 'for God's sake call the dog off.'

'Leave, Stray,' Jenny called.

The morning air was cool and she put her blue cloak on with the hood up over her cold neck and picked up her bundle from the bushes. Nathan and the stranger, known to him from his travels as Marston, set off beside her and Stray towards the Diggers.

He himself was aiming to get lost in London, but seeing that the colony was that way, he, Marston, would guide them there by the quickest route.

'Anarchy let loose. They're for the drop, the vagabonds,' he said looking around uneasily, 'and I'm for the knife, I know too much.'

'How did you fall in with a bad lot like it?' Nathan asked, but Marston, a tall, bearded and dirty man, said how were you to know which lot were bad? Especially if they had women amongst them? By the time he had known it, it had been too late.

'Where is the little lady from?' he asked Nathan, as if Jenny was deaf and dumb, and when the girl said she was Jenny Cooper from Ninewells in the shires of Cambridge, the man scratched his head and said he was darned if it didn't ring a bell.

'From Ninewells, Ninewells, in the shires of Cambridge, and a Cooper,' he repeated, and then it came to him. Some time ago they had picked up a couple, he thought it might have been Coopers from Ninewells, a poor old couple they had been too, hardly survived yet another winter, so the man had said.

James and Kate, but it was the same with men here as it was in the village, folk ever used surnames amongst themselves.

'Did the woman have red hair?' she asked, but Marston said she could have had green hair as far as he was concerned, it was covered with a black shawl.

'She had an ugly voice, and her language was foul.'

'What became of them?' she asked in a small voice; it had been James and Kate, driven onto the road after Aggy's drowning.

The man had been knifed for an old pewter mug and had been slowly bleeding to death, the woman had screamed and torn at her hair and cursed them. They had laughed and left him to bleed to death.

Marston was a kind man, as kind as a man can be without home, kin, money and pursued by vagabonds. He had turned Kate in the direction of Cambridge before he took to his heels.

After a while, Marston carried Jenny's bundle, and after a while, Jenny was between him and Nathan, her arms through theirs, her legs dangling like a rag-doll, and the dog limped beside them, never taking his eyes off Jenny.

'I leave you now,' said Marston, 'you're near the colony now.'

As he disappeared into the gloom towards London, Jenny collapsed. She lay like a dead thing and Nathan wrapped her up in the cloak and told the dog to guard their belongings while he walked on to the Digger colony.

The dog looked at him with his green eyes. He understood full well what was wanted of him, but one word from Nathan and he did as he liked.

Nathan carried her in his arms and walked for about an hour and a half, and he thought that was how it should be. The man strong and looking after the woman, and the woman pretty. He couldn't quarrel with her on that account, she was a pretty girl; as for him being strong though, who would have thought that a little thing like Jenny could weigh that much?

Chapter 32

A young man who said he was a Ranter - whatever that was - greeted them in the colony's clearing, where huts of sorts surrounded a large cooking pot.

'There are some oats left in the pot,' he said, 'but only goat's milk.'

'Goat's milk, mother's milk, it's all the same to me,' said Nathan.

The young man laughed. They would get on.

He had watched Nathan strolling in tall and long-legged and handsome, a white-faced maid in blue laying across his arms, a black dog half the size of a horse trotting by their side, like a picture of love from some far-flung romance, like Lancelot and Guinevere perhaps.

'She was as heavy as a barn door,' Nathan said, and the Ranter couldn't picture Lancelot saying Guinevere was like a barn door, but then he wouldn't have to carry a girl like Nathan had for a day and a night like Nathan had told him he had.

With that his mind turned towards a rider who had ridden in on a fine chestnut horse. He hadn't been from General Fairfax who was dealing with the villagers' complaints about the Diggers right now, but this rider had had something private on his mind as he enquired after a young couple with a black dog.

He hadn't lingered, and the Ranter wondered if there was a connection between them.

'A fair man on a handsome horse? Not *that* rider,' Nathan said, aghast. He had thought some breakfast and sleep would sort him out before he took to the road by himself, but now he thought, Why should I? Why leave the field free for Sir Richard after all the hard work he had put in looking after Jenny?

Winstanley, the leader of the commune, had left that very day to plead the Diggers' case before General Fairfax. Nathan had to have some breakfast with him and he had to listen. He had no choice in the matter for never, in all his born days, had he come across anyone who talked so much and so fast.

The Parson had headed the opposition of the villagers to the settlement; last time round, they had a lawyer to speak for them, he said.

He spoke in Latin, that lawyer did, and Winstanley himself had said that the law should be in English.

'Makes sense,' the young man said, 'don't it, because the law is common to the people of England which includes us,' and they should understand the law.

The Diggers had been let off the last time with a warning and the soldiers had ridden through the settlement with their sticks. There had been a deal of noise and women running round screaming and the cooking pot had been turned over and inside the huts everything had been demolished.

But nothing had been set fire to, and starting again was not that hard.

'The common land is common to folks who live in a commonwealth.'

Only, the common land was more common to those who lived near the common land than to strangers and Nathan's head was reeling under the onslaught.

'You see what I'm getting at, common, a common heritage, only the villagers, they don't see it like that,' and neither did Nathan.

Some folks were destined for other things than merely keeping alive, and it was property which made the difference, thought Nathan.

Then he listened once more to the solitary male voice now issuing a warning; there was no telling what would happen to them this time.

But Nathan decided to stay awhile until Jenny got better. A bit of company wouldn't go amiss either.

'As for myself, I am a Ranter, and I tell you now what I think.'

Travellers came and went and some stayed and some were from other Digger colonies. Some were stragglers from the many sectaries to whom the Lord had revealed himself when the King was on the losing side, like the Ranters, the Levellers, the Fifth Monarchists or the Quakers. Cromwell's New Model Army had provided an ideal place for these ideas.

'*Wherever two or three are gathered in my name,*' the Lord had said, '*there I will be also.*'

No church and no preacher and all the fuss that went along with it, and the Ranters were so filled with the wonder of it all that they shouted the good news from the rooftops.

It was an awesome event, England no longer a Kingdom, and it set them free of the old ways.

If Jenny had a dog about her, Nathan had a Ranter about him, panting after him and spouting hot air. His breathing was real bad, Nathan thought, but the Ranter was full of the good news.

'When they cut the King's head off, it meant more than just the King's head in a basket,' he said. 'Before that, they dragged Archbishop Laud out of his Chapel and his God didn't save him, his head came off just the same, the King and his Bishop. We were all equal now, equal to God himself.'

The Ranter was full of energy and he strode the world in long strides which never bestirred his long greasy hair hanging around a face which was what the Ranter called his trouble, face full of lumps and bumps.

'Wild bees. Put my foot in a nest of them climbing up a hill. Sore as hellfire, and can't leave off scratching.'

Nathan liked him well enough now. He had thought at first that this trouble might have been hiding in the man's breeches, the pox, but he knew well enough what a face full of bites felt like.

A roof over their heads would be most welcome, especially one roof for him and Jenny, but for now he would have to share a hut with the Ranter and the Poor Law, he thought as he departed to fetch their belongings.

Nobody took much notice of Jenny apart from Rose, who had put Jenny into the cabin with the other unattached women where she was laid on a mattress and covered with a blanket. As from a vast distance, Jenny heard disembodied voices discussing if she should be bled, purged or poulticed.

'Not purged, Maria,' cried an enthusiastic voice, 'not that, she is far too weak. My God, I should know about purging and suffering and poulticing and that. She needs a herb-tea to break the fever,' and Jenny hoped that Rose would win the argument before she drifted off.

Jenny felt better and was almost fit again. She had been ill for about ten days, but time was pretty meaningless for her at the best of times. And then the Priest was there, real quiet, and she told him about the pain in her ear. She would scream soon and they would all be kept awake. He held her hand and then he told her to separate the pain from her body and follow its path. It worked well enough while she was strong, but finally she screamed and then she fell asleep. When she woke in the morning all the pain was gone and in its place a mess of yellow and red flowed from her ear, but her fever was still on her.

There was a merry dancing in her head. Parson's

wife was shouting and Ma opened the door to let her out and in came Silkbreeches with no face on him and Squire's Daughter was carrying a cockerel and Mother was sitting in the bakehouse plucking the bird.

'No good will come of it,' her Pa said and she rode away with the rider.

She felt better and opened her eyes. Stray looked up at her, and she saw that a fine film was covering one of his eyes and nearly covered the other one. He was going blind and she would lose him shortly.

She hastily dried her eyes when Nathan came in but it was too late. Crying after a dog who was still alive!

'Has he been about then?'

'Who?' she asked. 'Aren't you pleased I'm feeling better?'

'Likely', he said, and later he said Winstanley had come and gone. It had not gone well with General Fairfax and Winstanley had gone to talk once more to the villagers themselves, although Jenny didn't pay much heed. After she was free of pain she felt shriven by it, absolved of all decision-making.

She had taken a fancy to a couple of small boys, a round-faced boy and his adored, god-like blond brother.

She was sitting outside trying to catch a rare bit of sunshine when the two boys planted themselves in front of her.

One was about four, with traces of babyhood still hovering on his plump little face; his brother was about eight, a pretty child with delicate features and a halo of soft, golden curls.

'Are you better now, lady?' asked the smaller one, not pausing for an answer, and with much fiddling of his trouser-belt. 'I said to Joshua is that pretty lady dead then when they brought you in, didn't I Joshua?'

He looked up to his brother for assurance.

'We came to see you one night to see if you were

dead, didn't we Joshua, but you were in the bed ill and not on a table. When our Ma died they put her on a table, didn't they Joshua, and the old man with the dead arm came in and made you better.'

Father Bernard hadn't been a dream after all, but who were these children with?

'We're with our Pa, and we saw you dancing round a fire with Nathan once. I can't remember where it was, can you remember, Joshua?'

'T'was near Huntingdon, Sorrel,' his brother assured him gravely, 'but you were going to ask the lady about the dog, remember. Why she calls him what she does. Stray.'

'I forgot. Why do you call your dog Stray?'

'I call him Stray, I suppose, because he's a stray and often he strays.'

'What do you call him if he stays? Joshua and me would like you to call him something else, wouldn't we, to see if it would make a difference.'

'Could you call him Stay just the once?' Joshua said and when Jenny did, the dog wagged his tail just the same and the boys were delighted, it was just as they had thought; but their delight was short-lived when their father collared them.

He was a nondescript man, hat crammed over his head, and sparse-bearded.

'He thinks laughing and larking about is a crime, I suppose he's a Puritan, whatever that is and he's always got his beady eye on me, and as for that beard, I have seen better body-hair on a man many a time,' Rose said.

Jenny wanted to hear more but Nathan came up.

The allegations of village harassment and moral laxity were untrue, neither did they lay a claim to the land they cleared and cultivated, but the outlook for them was bleak; their supposed misdeeds were written on tablets of stone.

Jenny didn't pay much heed. Nathan was building a hut for the two of 'em. What was all that planning for? She often watched Sorrel and Joshua and their father. He hadn't planned for the boys to have only one parent, life wasn't like that, it couldn't be mapped out, but all the same she wanted some assurance that they would stay with the Diggers and make a settled life for themselves.

Being wed was an answer, but the problem was that the village Parson hated the Diggers and if a pair from the settlement was seen to properly uphold moral standards, their high-handed approach would be in danger of collapsing. He couldn't refuse to wed them though, but they were advised not to ask any kind of a favour of him.

Nathan thought privately that before long Jenny would suggest that the Priest should wed them, although he looked a lot better now with his hair cut and his beard trimmed in a decent manner, wearing a hat and regular clothes.

He couldn't stomach being wed by him though; better that they should be entered in the parish and wed by a proper parson someplace else. But she wouldn't hear of taking to the road again; they had reached an impasse.

He was with the Ranter one evening watching Jenny and Rose who were sitting close together, whispering, talking and giggling, before, during and after supper, as was their wont.

'Those two make me ill, don't they know aught about life and how hard it?' Nathan said.

'She's but a girl in girl-talk, don't be so hard on her,' the Ranter cried.

'Probably, but there's no understanding women,' said Nathan, 'there are better women hereabouts for her to talk to,' and the Ranter said the chance to understand a pretty woman like Jenny would be a mighty fine thing.

She had a mind of her own, had Jenny, Nathan argued, and the Ranter said why not?

'Being equal includes women, don't it?'

Staggering though this assertion was to Nathan, he didn't mind it much; he simply relished the Ranter's male company after their solitary walking. It was plain to him though, a woman had to mark her man's ways and follow his example in all things, including what company she kept.

'You'll have your work cut out with Nathan,' Rose whispered, 'he's the sort who'll tell you when to breathe in and when to breathe out and when you do he's apt to tell you that you done it all wrong.'

'Well,' Jenny said, 'likely that's so, but I owe him, he looked after me for weeks when we were walking in the woods and I didn't know where we were.'

'Of course,' said Abigail, a moon-faced and totally joyless young woman who was sitting next to Rose.

'What?'

'The others arrived weeks before you did,' she said. 'He took you into the woods on purpose so you would be grateful to him.'

'If he had taken thee into the woods, Abigail,' said Rose, 'he would have taken to his heels.'

She started to giggle.

That did it. When Rose got the giggles there was no hope for Jenny, it was as infectious as the sneezes.

Abigail flounced off, and Jenny's mind turned to matters in hand.

'If we get wed, will you be my attendant, Rose?'

'No, I would not,' she cried, 'not in thy dreams. We would look ridiculous together. I would have to wind my hair upon my head and I would look even taller. We'd be like a maypole and a daisy growing next to it.'

'Well, you could stand well away from me.'

'An attendant is supposed to attend upon a bride and not wave to her from the edge of a crowd,' Rose said and they both gave way to laughter again.

'You have lovely hair, Rose, lovely and long and fair.'

'Oh, I thought it wasn't hair but a bit of old hessian to keep the rain off.'

'I'm sorry I said that, but I thought you had set your cap at Nathan.'

'I had set my sights upon him but when I worked with him at the inn, I soon changed my mind.'

They laughed again, and Nathan, watching from a distance, got madder and madder, and the madder he got, the more Jenny laughed. If she laughed with a will, it was because she knew that the laughter would have to stop shortly, for now their hut was finished.

It was big and rough and made out of logs, fashioned in the shape of an A.

Although Jenny knew what she was in for, she was nervous about it, she confided in Rose. Rose said they might chase Nathan and Jenny to their bridal bed, but Jenny would be that glad to get shot of the crowd and be alone with Nathan.

'You just have to sort of lie there and leave the rest to Nathan. I have done it so many times, I could do it in my sleep. Come to think of it, I have done it in my sleep,' said Rose.

When they stopped laughing, Jenny wondered how Rose knew she had done it if she had been asleep.

'It's not to be believed, there are tell-tale signs. A true innocent in the year of Our Lord sixteen hundred and whatever year it might be. How did you manage to keep him away all those weeks walking by yourself anyway, and didn't you want to?'

'I had the dog to keep him away, and I didn't know where I was in the pathless woods and meadows and I didn't know the places, and when I ran away from him, I ran into danger. It wouldn't be fair on a child.'

'There isn't necessarily a child afterwards,' said Rose. 'I am barren, that's why I am free and easy with men. I'm used to their company as well. I had lots of brothers. At home it always was, 'Get thee up Rose and let thy brother sit down. Waiting on 'em and cooking for 'em and letting 'em sit down.'

Her father had been nice to her at times, but when the mood was on him he beat her something chronic. One day a few coins went missing. Pa took his belt off and said for her to tell him the truth.

'I didn't take them, I said, what would I do with money?'

Rose hadn't been able to sit down after the beating.

She ran away, and sometimes she wondered if she was barren because of all the beatings; maybe her Pa had broken something, although she wasn't any too sure what exactly happened down below.

Their shared experience seemed to cement their friendship.

Nathan got more and more insistent that they moved in together. He liked the Ranter well enough but not enough to spend all of his remaining nights on this earth in his company. If he didn't talk he snored.

At least he could count on his talking; it was different with the snoring, because it was like sharing a room with a slowly cooking pot, you never knew when it would bubble up again.

All the same, the Ranter had an answer of sorts to the problem of who would marry them.

'Ain't we all equal and in the sight of God who is one of us now?'

He would undertake it, and Rose did the bidding to Jenny and Nathan's wedding personally.

'Listen everyone,' she cried after supper, 'Jenny and

Nathan will get wed tomorrow early in the morning. You better be there, washed and spruced up, mind you.' She was followed by the Ranter at great length. He always had plenty to say for himself and the gist of it was that he that he would take charge himself.

Next day, when the sun rose.

'Let the fire on the cooking pot go out tonight,' he pronounced like some biblical prophet, although nobody knew why, and nobody asked him, he would only tell them when he was ready.

They lingered awhile, until a scream rent the air.

'A white devil!' Sorrell cried. 'Look, there' pointing at a white, triangular face.

'T'is only a goat,' said Joshua.

'That's what comes from ignoring the discipline,' his father told Sorrel sternly, 'you should have been abed long since,' but he carried him about in his arms for a while, rocking him gently to sleep.

'He loves him after all. I do wish he would let him play sometimes,' Rose whispered.

Eli unfolded his face and favoured her with a rare smile.

'I like for them to play well enough, but they'll have to fend for themselves one day soon, and they miss their mother. I miss her right enough, a right saint she was too during her lifetime.'

'A right cow she was more likely when she was alive,' Rose said when Sorrel and Joshua finally disappeared into their hut, 'she had sainthood conferred upon her when she died, that one did,' and Jenny wondered before she fell asleep, did Rose have feelings for Eli? Not possible, she decided, nobody could be jealous of a dead woman, could they? And then she fell into a deep, deep sleep.

In her sleep she was chasing a great, white bird, over

and over again. A noise like the wind, and the great, white bird flapped overhead. When she turned round, Father Bernard was there holding poppies which were blooming out of his chest between his hands, and somebody was screaming.

Somebody was shaking her, shaking her, and it was Rose.

'Wake up, Jenny, your wedding day is upon you.'

The girls hastily threw their shawls over their shifts and ran past the silent huts in the grey light of approaching morning onto the dell.

Below, two men had already lit a fire and were slowly turning a pig on a spit, closely watched by the dog.

As the girls milked the goats on the dewed grass, a rosy dawn gradually began to replace the early morning grey.

'Drat,' said Jenny, 'T'is going to rain after all, and on my special day.'

'Never mind, you are special, and you're getting wed if you want Nathan around. Do you?'

The question hung in the still morning air and Jenny saw a picture in her mind of a man on a horse by an old black poplar. A halo of clouds was around the summer moon in the night sky. He held out his hand to her and he looked vulnerable and yearning.

'I think Sorrel's father has taken a liking to you, Rose,' she said brightly but Rose wasn't fooled.

'You get settled first, that hog yonder hasn't breathed its last for me, but for thee. Do you love him, and I don't mean do you owe him.'

'I don't know,' Jenny said at long last, 'I feel that I am just passing through.'

'Long enough for your wedding feast I hope,' Rose said, but Jenny had a strong feeling that events would

228

shortly overtake her.

Chapter 33

The Ranter performed the ceremony. At least he was going to but now somebody was actually listening to him he didn't know what to say exactly. He didn't know what to say at all.

Words were like an endlessly flowing stream to him, but of all the times to choose, the stream had dried up on him and words failed him altogether.

He opened and shut his mouth like a stranded fish and he scratched at one of his riper spots with a dirty fingernail, and he thought and he thought.

They could tell he was thinking by the frown on his forehead and the strange silence about him.

The fire had gone out and on a piece of wood over the cooking pot sat the Ranter, next to Jenny's Bible.

It was not yet raining, but there was a promise of it; there always was.

'We are all equal in the sight of God and God is one of us now, ain't he.'

The Ranter had thought of his opening remarks when the dog made his appearance. He settled down next to Jenny, giving one of his enormous yawns and looking around in a not altogether disinterested fashion.

The Ranter started again.

They were all equal in the sight of God, and God was...

'Where's Sorrel and Joshua?' Rose cried. 'Come forward, you two.'

He stopped.

He could only see half of his congregation, gathered as they were in a round, some at the side, some at his back.

'Move forward, will you, all of you at the back of me, so that I can see all of you. That's more like it.'

They were still equal in the sight of God who was indeed one of them now and then he saw Nathan. He carried his hat in his hands. The rest of the men were all bareheaded too.

'What have I been saying just now?' he cried. 'If we are all equal with God we do not take our hats off, do we?'

Jenny and Nathan were in front of him, standing out against the drabness of the motley crowd like a rainbow against a dark sky.

Jenny wore one of Mother's blue dresses with a white lace collar she had found rolled up in her bundle. Her auburn hair had grown and was now held with the blue comb she had found in her pocket.

Nathan, tall next to anyone at the best of times, seemed even more so beside her. He wore a clean white shirt open at the neck and tucked into his breeches. He had scraped every bit of hair back from his face into a pony tail.

She looked up at Nathan and she thought she would remember him as she saw him that moment for the rest of her life. His blue eyes, his square jaw, his confident stance next to her, but the basic problem remained for her. What was she supposed to be to him? What sort of wife?

The sprigs of rosemary for remembrance she kept twisting in her hands were probably placed there by Rose for her to recall that she had better turn up.

She looked nervous, fragile, like a startled fawn, and Nathan's eyes never left her for a moment.

What motivated Nathan, the Ranter wondered. Was it passion, anger or sheer contrariness that made his blood course through his veins?

Whatever it was, he would have to take care or he would destroy Jenny. He had never once taken his eyes off her in all the time the Ranter had known him, and his every action had been designed to force and focus her attention on him.

'She has to be fitting for me, that's all there is to it,' he had said, and that could mean any number of things.

'Get a move on, will you,' came a voice from the crowd.

`'Are we having a ceremony or what?' Sorrel's Pa demanded.

'Or what,' echoed Sorrel.

'Do you listen with your backsides? We do not need ceremonies conducted by one who is higher up in authority if we are equal, do we?'

The day began to disintegrate.

It was pointed out to the Ranter that he, sitting next to the Bible, was higher up on the cooking pot, his non-congregation was fed up to their back-teeth and backsides, and then Old Maria fought her way to the front with a ribbon. She laid it over Nathan's and Jenny's joined right hands.

'Nathan Mason, will'st thou look after this woman and love and cherish her?'

'Aye.'

'Bashiba Cooper, will'st thou look after this man, and love and cherish him?'

'Aye,' shouted Sorrel, and 'Aye' shouted the congregation.

'Amen,' said the woman.

'Amen,' said the Ranter.

'Amen,' said the congregation.

'Bashiba?' said Nathan.

'Her christened name, I looked it up in her Bible,' said Rose.

'This has been promised in the sight of all of us,' said Maria.

'Amen to that,' said the Ranter.

Amen, such a good word, it signified an end to it;

and now for a song, it needn't be a hymn, said the Ranter, and Nathan was passed Adam's flute.

'My Pa knows a song, and Sorrel and I could sing the *hey-ho* after it,' suggested Joshua. 'Please, Pa.'

'Hush now, and I will presently think of something suited,' said Eli.

At four times seven
I must take a wife

And a hey-hoo, and the wi-ind and the rain
and the rain
And the rain
it raineth e-e-very day, sang Joshua and Sorrel.

Thinking thereby to thrive
And leave off
My wanton ways.
To save myself from disgrace.

And a hey-hoo, and the wi-ind and the rain
and the rain
And the rain
it raineth e-e-very day, sang Joshua and Sorrel.

So fare thee well,
Companions all,
For other business
Does me call.

And a hey-hoo, and the wi-ind and the rain
and the rain
And the rain
it raineth e-e-very day, sang Joshua and Sorrel.

He sang with a strong voice and then he looked around

him.

> *And a hey-hoo, and the wi-ind and the rain*
> *and the rain*
> *And the rain*
> *it raineth e-e-very day,* the congregation joined in.'

All the men wore their hats now and Jenny wore her cloak with the hood up. The rain was bucketing down like the song had it, and Jenny and Nathan were married. Well, sort of. Did nobody else notice that she hadn't said 'Aye'? She sat amongst her thoughts. It was as well they had that ceremony else she might never have known what his second name was, except, didn't someone once before call him Mason?

It was her name now, Mason, well it might be, but, married or not, she could settle down here and not roam the roads. She thought she would help the women soon who got on with the food and the baking for the night's feast.

There had been a certain amount of grumbling when she had been ill and her legs wouldn't carry her and she collapsed by her bed; some wished they had legs like that. But now it seemed that her hut would have to be to be decked out with flowers.

Old Maria said Jenny should make the most of her day, as she had the rest of her life to work her fingers to the bone. As for fetching her own flowers to decorate her marriage bed, that meant bad luck for certain.

Jenny said she didn't need any more bad luck, although some of the women said she couldn't have everything, she had wed Nathan after all, but her marriage bed should be bedecked with flowers.

The Ranter mentioned unwisely he had seen some purple flowers hereabouts, and Maria said likely they were wild orchids.

'Go get 'em, what are you hanging about and getting under my feet for?'

The two men discussed the wedding ceremony or lack of it as they walked along. There had been something missing, Nathan said, but Jenny had sounded really excited.

The Ranter didn't like to mention that the 'Aye' had been Sorrel's.

What worried Nathan was their task.

'Pick a bunch of flowers, I ask you, and to be sent out by a bunch of old women!'

'God-forsaken bitches out of sodden hellfire, all of 'em,' cried the Ranter enthusiastically, and he promised that he would kill them all, one at a time, and stamp 'em into the sodden earth for good measure.

'Steady on, I say, let me have my wedding night first,' said the bridegroom, and then he started to laugh. His companion was setting about himself with his hat, aiming at a solitary bee humming innocently about its business.

'Bees I meant, not women,' said the Ranter, and both of them were laughing as they scrambled up the embankment; the Ranter had been right, the flowers were lovely, carpeting the slope just as he had said.

Ain't that a pretty sight, the soldier thought.

He watched them in amazement. What was England coming to? Grown men going in fear of an insect and daintily collecting flowers!

He looked at his empty cart, and his solitary state worried him.

Along with some of his fellow soldiers he had parted from the rest of their company when rumour had reached them that General Fairfax had resigned in protest at the planned invasion of Scotland, and that Cromwell was now Commander in Chief of the army.

Then illness had struck, and a few had died of a severe belly-ache or according to a physician - of something severely unpronounceable.

T'was not the plague at any rate, but most had thought it an ill omen brought on by what some now thought of as desertion.

They had dispersed quicker than seeds in the wind after that. The soldier had always taken his orders from Fairfax. If there was trouble between the two generals he would take arms against Cromwell, and now he aimed to find out what had happened.

He had it in mind to find some more men and these two would do nicely for a start.

Two strong fellows and they would do more than pick flowers and chase bees and laugh daintily when they were fighting in the army. London first and then on to Scotland.

He clubbed the Ranter and Nathan with his pistol just when they were reaching out for another flower. He tied their hands behind their backs when it came to him that these two could furnish an excuse in case it was thought that he had deserted.

These two were the very two deserters he had chased a long way. That's why he had left the army behind, and it would be the noose for these two instead of himself.

He shoved a gag in their mouths in case they came to, then he threw them onto the cart.

As he turned around he turned his pistol round as well when he saw that a great black dog was about to take a running jump at him. He shot the black beast through the head.

He kicked the dog down the embankment, where its descent was stopped by the trunk of a pine tree. There it rested, slung away and discarded and of no further use.

The cart rumbled off down the road.

Chapter 34

Most men had stayed on and lingered awhile until the rain ceased. When it finally did, they thought it best to wait for Winstanley's return from his talk with the Parson; they might as well, no sense in working if they had to get out, besides, that roasting pig smelt better and better.

Jenny had packed her belongings into Ma's shawl and placed it out of the hut, ready to move into her own hut that night. Adam's reed, Pa's pewter mug and plate and the family Bible had been much admired by the women, as well as the fine clothes Mother from the inn had rolled up for her.

She put the great red stone into the pocket of her blue wedding dress and listened with the rest of the morning's congregation for other noises to come nearer after the shot had been heard.

It was muffled and in the distance, and they thought it might have been Fairfax's men.

Jenny slung her blue cloak around her shoulders as she shot outside to get her bundle. She put it down uncertainly when all was quiet, and after a while the women carried on with their chores.

A shot, Jenny thought, a shot. The Sheriff's man had fired through the curtains around the bed and into the barrels and he had said what's out the back. Out the back was a dog, frantically digging and bringing her a present. A black dog, and no good will come of it, her Pa had said, and I will take a gun to him even if he didn't have a gun.

Stray!

She found him easily. He hung with his poor head broken and Jenny hunted for something to place over him so nothing could hurt his broken head any more.

Twigs, and some large, bent-over ferns, and she placed the green fronds very carefully over his head like a cage before she heaped dead leaves onto the dead body.

He deserved better.

A death with kindness now he was nearly blind, that would have been a good death; but there were no tears in her eyes, her grief was beyond them.

A shadow above blocked the light and when she looked up she thought for a minute it was Parson Wilcox standing there, coming to her rescue.

It wasn't Parson Wilcox but it might well have been him. From his pointed black hat to his white Puritan collar, down to small black shoes and black gartered stockings, it might have been him, except this man's mean features huddled close on a small red face, not kindly as on a white butter-ball.

This parson was different, and she hated him for not being Parson Wilcox.

'Get out of my light,' she wanted to shout as he touched his hat.

The Parson mistook her for some lady or other with her hands being so white as if work was a stranger to them. He looked at the blue cloak and the comb inlaid with blue holding her hair now it had grown, and he wondered what a fine young lady might be doing alone and abroad so early.

'Two of the ruffians gone, I see,' he said in a high, nasal whine, 'the rest will follow shortly, that you may be depend on.'

He thought she looked unimpressed.

'What ruffians?' she asked, puzzled.

'The two ruffians from below,' he said, pointing down to the clearing; perhaps she didn't know about the Diggers, being strange to these parts.

'Where would they have gone, these two ruffians?' the lady asked.

'Press-ganged for the Navy, to fight in the Dutch war, I should not wonder.'

'Is there a war with the Dutch then?' she said, and he said if there wasn't a war now there would be one, indeed, there should be.

A war just to please him, she supposed. Nathan and the Ranter had been press-ganged then, she thought by the way he had indicated the direction of the ruffians.

'Who shot the dog?' she asked.

'Why, the soldier who took the ruffians,' he said.

Her first thought was that Nathan, with the way he felt about foreigners, would fight well and they had better look out for themselves, if it was him.

The Parson wasn't finished.

'T'is said their land is but what the tide fetches with it from our shores. Nothing but our leavings, their land.'

'Whose land?'

'The Dutch, that's who,' he said irritably; she hadn't paid due attention but she did when he said more than likely the two ruffians had been taken to the Port of London.

She had to go to the Port of London, Jenny thought, wherever that was. She turned to go down the embankment to fetch her bundle, only the Parson wouldn't let her go, insisting that she listened alongside of him.

What was he expecting to happen and what was she listening for? Was there no end to this awful day?

She listened and then she heard.

Horses' hooves thundering and shouts and screams mingling with the dry, great crackling of fire. Flames licked the trees below and she recalled the Bible warning her of a fire.

The smell of burning from the clearing told her that Fairfax's soldiers had arrived.

The orange tongues of fire had taken over, and men

and women wept and wrung their hands amongst the leaping and dancing flames in the morning air when she ran down and into the way of the two little boys, who walked flanked by their father and Rose.

Sorrel hid his face in his father's coat and Joshua said gravely that his brother was upset, all his belongings had been burned. There was nothing left for them here, his father said, except now they had Rose.

Rose said they would stick together, Eli and the boys, they would get back on the road and find some other place willing to accept them.

'I couldn't do it without Rose,' Eli said, 'I couldn't do it at all,' and he picked the younger boy up and held him fast. There had to be another place for them, he said, but it was not for Jenny, this other place; she had to find Nathan.

'I know of someone who would be more than pleased with you,' she said. 'It's an inn, and the old people there will welcome you with open arms.'

'Me as well?' asked Rose.

'She'll love you, Rose, like everybody does.'

'T'is so,' said Eli.

'Even when the mood is upon me?'

She didn't know aught about moods, said Jenny.

'Where is this place?' asked Eli.

'Marjory Hutch's place, the Ship Inn, Huntingdon. Near Cromwell's place.'

She couldn't linger, she had to find Nathan and she had to find her bundle, but she had it in her mind to give Adam's flute to Sorrel.

She had left the bundle in the open, but now she couldn't find it. She thought the horses might have trampled it underfoot because it could not have vanished into thin air, could it, and then she saw Abigail with what looked like Adam's reed in her hands.

'T'is my brother Adam's reed, I believe,' Jenny shouted above the noise of the panicking crowd. 'T'is my brother's, and I want it back.'

'Take it back then,' shouted the young woman, looking at her with glittering eyes, and they both tugged at it as if their lives depended on it.

'Dirty thief,' shouted Jenny, and with that the flute left her grasp and her opponent fell backwards into the mud, revealing a pale linen skirt as well as a brown one under her black one.

Maria, who had performed the wedding ceremony and who had looked after Jenny when she was ill, shouted at Jenny to leave poor Abigail alone, and that she was disappointed with Jenny's shameful behaviour.

'Disappointed with my behaviour?' screamed Jenny, one foot on the girl's stomach, wrestling for the flute. 'She's stolen the reed which belongs to Adam. She's stolen two skirts and she's wearing the shawl which belongs to Ma, and the bodice which is mine.'

Tears of anger ran down her face.

'Nathan has been press-ganged and Stray has been shot. Sorrel's belongings have been burned, and you are disappointed by my behaviour?'

She turned towards the old woman as the younger one got to her feet. Running past Jenny, Abigail grabbed the flute and sped by with her bundle.

Jenny watched her stop and turn round at end of the clearing, waving the flute at her before she stuffed it down the front of her dress.

'What shameful behaviour,' said Maria, grabbing her arm, 'what would that decent young man think of you now? He paid for seeds when you arrived, and for the pig for the feast. You haven't been here five minutes, and you take it all for granted.'

'Let go of me,' shouted Jenny, 'I want my things back. What do you know?'

'Don't you give me any of your lip,' cried Maria, but Jenny didn't care, she had to go.

By the time Jenny was back on the road, Rose, Eli and the boys had gone.

There was no bundle to carry and no black dog at her side, but she had Father Bernard and she gave a great shuddering sob.

She didn't cry though, the Priest saw, and Jenny was glad that he hadn't said it was a mercy the dog was out of his misery, merely that they had been true friends to each other.

Aye, t'was the truth. The other thing was the truth as well but Stray hadn't deserved his poor broken head.

Together they walked on, the Priest and the girl. They walked along hilly ground, and she looked above and below her at various stragglers from time to time.

'I got me some business to finish,' she said.

With that she took a flying leap at someone walking below her.

'You pig,' she shouted at a young woman, Father Bernard saw, and Jenny's flying leap had knocked her to the ground. He had assumed that he had seen everything in this world that there was to see, but now he had to revise his opinion as Jenny set about this young woman like a wildcat.

First a black skirt came off and then a pale one and a brown one, and then a black shawl and then a white bodice. There should have been a naked body before now, but this girl had more skins on her than an onion.

Jenny opened the girl's bundle and she set about it like a bird clearing out a dirty nest. All sorts of things were flung over her shoulder, but some she kept. Ma's shawl, Adam's reed, Pa's pewter mug and plate and the family Bible, as well as her fine clothes.

'If you wanted some of my things, Abigail, why

didn't you just ask? Is there anything you would really like?' Jenny asked the woman, sweetly and reasonably. Even old Maria would have approved.

When she ha*nded the white bodice of A*bigail's dreams to her, Abigail tore it in half and told Jenny, sweetly and reasonably, to wipe her arse on it if it wasn't too much trouble.

'I just might,' Jenny screamed, and Abigail screamed back that she had intended to give everything back to her.

'Think I was born yesterday?'

'No, but I'll make you so sorry for not believing it that you'll wish I had never been born.'

'Ha, can't even get that right, can you Abigail? I should be made so sorry that I wished I had never been born,' Jenny shouted after the departing woman, who turned around and screamed that it amounted to the same thing.

Father Bernard laughed a great, rumbling laugh; Jenny joined in and they both laughed until their sides ached. Abigail ran off and shouted that she was glad she didn't have anything belonging to her, they were both crazy and it might be catching.

Laughter stopped when they reached a village where the church looked to them grim and grey, the graveyard an untidy mess of weeds and toppled-over wooden crosses, a menace to the dead and to the living.

The Parson was now talking to a man sitting on a cart piled high with sacks and baskets; he was going to the market at Covent Garden.

'Either that, or I might find stall holders outside London,' he said.

That would do.

They waited patiently until the Parson ran out of awful things to say about the Diggers, and then Jenny asked the driver if she and Father might get a lift, she had a guinea to pay for it.

The driver said he wouldn't dream of taking money, it was all the same to the horse as well.

'Best not touch the peaches and grapes,' he said, 'but you and your father are welcome to an apple or two.'

They sat with their legs dangling, like small children on a bench, on the back of the cart. The Priest fished around in one of the sacks.

Apples! Jenny had never seen the like, yellow and round and not sour like the cider apples, and when he shook an apple she could hear the pips dance around inside.

'There's goodness in the world after all,' said Jenny looking at a ripe apple with black seeds, and when the cart started off on its rumbling journey, the Parson found the lady in the blue cloak sitting amongst the sacks at the back.

'As you said, there's goodness in the world,' whined the Parson at her. Jenny beckoned to him nicely and neatly, and when he walked up to her she spat the black pips right into his face.

'You've got a home to go to, haven't you? So count yourself lucky.'

A token gesture, but it made Jenny feel a lot better.

So did Father Bernard's company. It always did. Fancy the driver thinking he was her father! She could talk to him about so many things she would never be able to talk about with her Pa, who only ever said no good would come of it.

She asked him why there was evil in the world.

Maybe it was so people could tell good from bad and make a choice, he said, but she said when she had run past the graveyard in the night she had known straight off that evil was evil just by itself. She would never choose evil.

'That little white lamb being sacrificed, and the hooded figures chanting Ma-Jes-Tor, and the bell ringing thirteen times, and poor Sidney's death cry.'

The Priest, who had thought she was talking about the events of the morning which were terrible and testing, was overcome with a sudden fit of coughing. It was the apple, he said through his tears.

He had to act naturally, she had encountered the dark forces of evil of the occult. That was one burden she ought not to carry.

'Poor little lamb,' he said.

It must have set her mind at rest he thought when she fell asleep against his shoulder, as suddenly as a little child.

As he put a steadying arm around her he mused on how he had been hurt and allowed to escape, but death had eluded him. Was it God's purpose in his life to look out for this girl, he wondered. Just then he felt cramp in his right arm, a great pain, followed by tingling as the blood was coursing through his useless arm.

God be praised!

When she awoke, she shivered.

'I don't know why, but I feel afraid,' she said, and he gave her his cross.

When she put it around her neck, it was still warm from his body.

Nathan would go mad if he knew about it, but where was Nathan?

Chapter 35

He wondered where he was.

He was moving along, feeling sick and his head hurt, and after a while he thought that he was laying in a cart of some sort. There had been a darkness about him and stars in front of his eyes, but now he saw that it was daylight and that he was laying on top of something warm and soft.

When he twisted his head he saw that he was laying on top of his friend.

The Ranter didn't have his hat on and he was black in the face. He looked surprised, his lips forming a great round 'O', although no sound emerged because he had a gag in his mouth.

He was dead.

Why had the Ranter died and why was he was still alive, he thought, and then it came him that the Ranter was always short of breath, always panting after him, strong fellow that he had been. Maybe something had been amiss with his breathing and not due to his talking like Nathan had assumed.

His feeling of rising panic was due to the gag in his own mouth, he realised. It was a leather gag and it had been used before; there was a foul taste of old sick on it and the gore rose up in him. He tried to fight it, knew that if he didn't he would choke on his own vomit. But ill as he felt, what could he do about it?'

The cart hit a pothole and he caught a blow from the rails. He must have passed out again.

When he came to, a soldier was cutting him loose. The soldier was setting about this task with a knife flashing like a flame, frantic and cursing, looking around him with cruel eyes muttering something about the plague.

For a minute he thought that he was in Heaven. *In my Father's House there are many Mansions,* like it said in the Bible and then he saw that it was an alleyway of tall, narrow, rickety wooden houses with wooden passageways with rails along the first floor.

'Seen any rats?' the soldier asked after he threw the gag away. He was frightened of rats seemingly, and Nathan played along with it.

'Rats, never seen so many of 'em in my born days. Coming out of my boots and in the cooking pots and in the grain.'

The soldier was cursing non-stop now and placed the Ranter against the wall of one of the tall houses. Rickety houses they were. Likely they would have rickety benches inside, rickety for the poor sitting on them.

Fit for the poor, he thought. Fit for the Ranter who was equal with God, would you believe. But it wouldn't happen to him, not if he could help it.

The Ranter's face was black, and what he had called his trouble, the bumps on his face, had burst in his fight for breath. His face was a sorry and evil mess now his beautiful soul had departed.

'We killed a rat the minute you saw us, and rats can't abide the smell of wild orchids,' Nathan said. 'Myself, I can't abide their wriggly tails, worse than worms.'

The soldier said he had thought it was a bee, but that it was the plague for certain as he made off as if all the devils in the world were after him.

Nathan carefully placed his own fur hat on the dead man's head. Hat doffing had never been an issue with him, but the Ranter always reckoned he was equal with anybody and kept his hat on.

Even so, he had taken it off to kill a bee and that had been his undoing; Nathan's own fur hat had been right down to his ears to keep the rain off, and it had cushioned the impact.

Unlovely the Ranter had been in life and unlovely he was in death, to look at any rate, but Nathan had felt a rare friendship for him. Nevertheless, he didn't remove the Ranter's leather gag; it was best to leave the nastiness that had killed him inside.

Nathan left him propped up like a barrel of cider gone frothy with the stop left in, and he sat by his side for a long, long time.

A noise like a strong wind and many footsteps passing, and he thought it best to be gone before questions were asked; when he emerged from the alleyway he was swept away by a crowd.

It was an exited crowd. The excitement of a crowd that went to a hanging, the excitement of a crowd that went with a hanging.

A great shout would go up, they all knew it. They were alive and breathing and the man dancing at the end of the noose, well, now he wasn't. He was as dead as they all would shortly be.

The Ranter had enjoyed his life whilst he was breathing and he, Nathan, intended to do the same.

As for Jenny, she was bad luck for some, just look at the Ranter now. Fond of her and fetching flowers for her.

Nathan would have liked to say his name and bid him a proper good-bye, but he never knew the Ranter's name.

Chapter 36

Jenny knew when they had reached London.

The horses' hooves sounded sharp and alive all of a sudden and she thought of a wood when she looked around her. Many people were abroad, walking amongst many houses as tall as elms but crowded together, they were not able to see where a foot had planted itself.

The Priest and the girl jumped off the cart which came to a halt when it could go no further. It was stopped by a great throng of people and Jenny's heart was beginning to beat very fast. She was deathly afraid now and she was glad she had Father Bernard's quietness about her; and then they were both swept up by the crowd.

There was to be a hanging. She didn't want to go but she didn't fight it. Her dream had become real; there would be a great white bird overhead and there would be screaming.

She didn't know how long it would take to live it, how could you tell the time in a dream? There was only the dreaming and the living and then the dying.

The crowd divided into two in the square which was large, and at the end, facing them, was a tall house.

Beneath the house were two posts. Between the posts, fixed onto the house, was a gallows.

In front was a cart but no horse, just the Militia men about and onlookers clambering about on the wheels of the cart.

A man stood on the cart with the noose around his neck. He wore a plain white gown and he was very handsome, so folks about them said.

They had always said that about Gideon.

Gideon was ready to meet his maker one minute and

the next he had thought of something else to say and the crowd got a bit restive. Only a bit though, the Militia men's presence saw to that.

Jenny heard somebody say the man about to be hanged had robbed a coach and killed a man and took jewels from a lady's neck 'n ears and fingers, and it served her right, flaunting her wealth when they starved and rotted for the want of a crust.

Somebody else thought the man about to be hanged had it coming to him for being so stupid.

'Killing and robbing and thinking he could get away with it. About as safe as a clout by an old woman's fist.

Whilst round about her the crowd fell to laughing, Jenny thought of Mother at the inn. She had loved Gideon to distraction, but she had lost her respect for him when he went against her wishes; he had taken a life and now Gideon was truly on his own for the first time in his.

Look what he had come to, Jenny thought when a hood was placed over Gideon's head, and then she felt a clammy hand on her body.

'Get them paws off me,' she said icily, and one of the louts dressed in brown said Country Cousin was a pretty sort. The sport was always better with a pretty sort and then he peered down the front of her dress.

'Will have us some sport with pretty Country Cousin in a while.'

Nathan was in the crowd listening to the gossip, that the man about to hang had robbed a coach and killed a man and took jewels from a lady, and that only the cash had been recovered but not the jewels worth many pounds.

A lot of money, he thought, like the rest of them, and then he saw that he was facing Jenny and she was not far away from him.

'Jenny!' he was about to shout, and then he saw the

250

Priest. Right behind her, he was, and he thought that it was the Priest who brought him bad luck. How many times had he told Jenny not to have any truck with that Priest?

And what did she do the minute he was gone? How on earth had she got there, at the same time as himself?

Well, he thought, let her stew for a while, serves her right, and then it went very quiet. The men rolled the cart away and then a great shout went up.

Gideon was dancing at the end of the noose.

It was the great white bird of Jenny's dreams.

The men in brown pressed closer to her. When she turned around Father Bernard was setting about him with both arms, and then a knife went into him.

There was blood between both his hands and it came from his body.

The poppies of her dream had turned into blood.

Two of the men carried her by her elbows, bundle and all, and her feet dangled like a rag doll's might.

The men pressed so close that she couldn't scream. She didn't see Nathan who tried to get to her, but by then it was too late.

Chapter 37

The hanging was watched over from the great house by a fair amount of people for reasons of their own, some holding delicate white handkerchiefs at the ready from white lace sleeves.

The Judge who had presided over the trial liked to see a job well done.

A few well-connected people, well-living people, liked to see a bit of poor living and poor dying as long as the sport of it didn't reach their delicate white noses, and, of course, the beautiful lady who had been robbed so cruelly and whose future husband had been so meanly put down by the ruffian below.

What bravery the frail and lovely woman exhibited!

But here she was, attending an event which would tax sensibilities of the strongest, and, it was rumoured, she was still ailing after her great ordeal.

He had not intended to pay his respects; what could you say to someone whose loved one had been killed, who had had his face shot off? However, her Companion had fetched him to her side and introduced her.

'Lady Eloise.'

He bowed.

'My pleasure.'

She fanned herself and then she put her fan down abruptly.

'I do not know where to start exactly. You have heard of my ordeal, have you?'

'Indeed, my Lady. Let me express my most sincere condolences.'

'This is greatly appreciated by me,' she said and then she sighed. 'I have a great favour to ask of you, although I hardly dare to mention it.'

'If it's within my power at all I will grant it.'

'I am greatly afraid of travelling on my own after what has happened.'

'I have heard,' he said.

He could not imagine what it would be like driving a trap with the dead body of a loved one by her side.

'I am, well, terrified to go back on my own today. I wonder if you could ride in my coach with me. It will draw up here after the hanging. It would greatly ease me to have your company on the journey.'

He looked down at her thoughtfully, wondering how in the name of good manners he could get out of it.

'Alas, I am devastated, but I must decline, my lady,' he said with an exaggerated bow, 'urgent business takes me elsewhere.'

He scanned the crowd below. Dull colours, pale faces like raindrops on dirty grass. A bright spot of blue, the morning blue she had worn, and he smiled. Just recalling the clothes she had worn made him smile.

Her blue cloak!

It was Jenny, and it would be just the sort of ruffians she got herself mixed up with, he thought. The girl had innocently wound a thread around his heart which pulled him to her when he had least expected it. She held him as fast as the belt had held them when they riding together. He thought about the young man, Nathan. What was the reason for Nathan's cold eyes? Did he simply not like him, or did he dislike his authority? Was he himself right for the girl? Could he involve her in his uncertainty?

Questions, so many questions!

The hanging was about to start, and the spiritual comfort had departed in his long gown with the drawn-out sounds of bells.

Squire's Daughter watched him covertly. He was a mighty powerful man, was Lord Bennet, with an air of authority about him, just the sort of man she was looking for now her father had lost his senses and Jonathan his life, she thought, hiding her face deep within the outspread fan.

He had concluded his business in London the day before and he had stayed on for the execution.

He had been involved with the girl and he owed her something.

He had led her into that very den of thieves himself. Riding so fast over the sodden dykes of the fens when he had known full well a horse could be buried right up to its neck, and all for the sake of creating an impression!

He had ridden like the devil with the great black dog after him, with her arms around him, and he had been in a foul temper with himself afterwards when he pictured how easily they could have taken a tumble.

Her face was before him at all times.

He wondered what his own future course of action should be now that his father had passed on. Life was a short journey from one dark place to another.

His father had passed away. He was the eighth Earl of Romney now, but how long for?

When he thought of his son, Edgar, his heart bled, and he hadn't been able to believe his father's dying words. 'He desires all, and he desires it now. Test him'.

He had told Edgar that he would have to leave England for the sake of the family, never to return. How eager he had been to assist!

'You are a wanted Royalist, Father,' Edgar had said.

A boat would be ready at Dover with a trusted Captain. Trusted by who, he thought, and he knew his son was lying when he had seen that he was crossing his arms; from a small boy onwards Edgar had always crossed his arms in front of his chest when he had told an untruth, and looking up at him with innocent blue eyes and biting his upper-lip, which he did now.

He had waited in the darkness of the stable, and the wind of his beloved Kent had mingled with the whisperers.

'Kill him, but don't throw him overboard until you're well out,' his son had said, but he had other plans. He and his trusted servants would hang around Dover, seemingly setting sail for Calais.

Instead they would ride onto Folkestone and make for Brittany instead.

Plans had to be made, but plans had to be worked out, and they depended on the tides, but for how much longer would it be safe for him to stay in England? Although Parliament had not yet been suspended, would England be ruled by decree once more?

The very fact that he was here showed that his credentials held good, although he had detected a certain coolness, a certain distance in people of late. The eagerness to lick his boots at the slightest excuse was no longer apparent.

He had ridden to Huntingdon and stayed at the coaching inn waiting for a letter, where he found out more about the girl and the young man, Nathan.

Then he made for London, where his friend had asked him to be on his guard; warrants would be posted for him as he had been in the King's service in Oxford, overseeing the arsenal.

This was no time for thought, but for action.

He bowed to Squire's Daughter and left, and as he did, silence fell on the room with his departure.

'Poor Lady,' they whispered around her, 'poor lady,' not daring to insult her grief with idle chatter, and her fan hid her eyes.

She had been bled before she started out for

London. However much she disliked the small knifes popping out of the container slicing into her flesh and her blood leaving her body, it was better than waiting for the leeches to swell up and fall off.

It had seemed to do some good. How long would it last though, she thought. She had lost all faith that the devil looked after his own.

The departed John Morrow had been a disappointment to her in many ways as well. Letting that girl get away had been one of them.

Getting himself shot had been another, she thought.

She had put her trust in him and she recalled when she had realised how misplaced it was.

'You are my strength, Jonathan,' she had said, and what had he told her? Only that he had nearly wet himself when confronted by a few villagers after taking a small child, and then he had really wet himself when confronted by a pretty boy.

She clicked her fan shut impatiently. Her Companion, always at her side, bent down.

'Go after him. See what he has in mind.'

'How?'

'Do what you think fit,' Squire's Daughter whispered, and that she would have to remember that Sir Richard's father had passed on and that he was now an Earl.

'Of what?'

'Romney. Lord Bennet of Romney, I suppose.'

As the Companion sped after the Lord, Squire's Daughter opened her fan and hid her face. Her anger had added to her weakness, the mere effort of clicking her fan had exhausted her.

Below was a great hue and cry, and the two men put Jenny down in an alleyway unharmed when it became clear that they were pursued. The murder of Father

Bernard had given Lord Bennet time to find her. They fled and pretended to be part of the excited crowd when the bleeding body was discovered. A hanging and a murder at the same time, what more could anybody want?

Lord Bennet wasn't fooled and was after them with the Militia men, and Nathan was not far behind.

The crowd had parted for them as easily as the Red Sea had parted for Moses. The dead body of the Priest had done this for Jenny, although she didn't know it. She didn't know anything.

She was in an alleyway and she wondered about the passageways in the air. Was she dead and could she walk straight up into heaven?

When she looked down, she saw somebody sitting against a house. It was Nathan by the looks of his fur hat.

'What are you doing here?' she said stupidly and she took his hat off.

The body toppled over and then she screamed and she screamed and she screamed.

They found her quite easily just by following the sounds. She was unharmed and she looked up at Nathan.

'You are dead,' she screamed and pointed at his body, but he said that it was the Ranter who was dead. 'You Are Dead,' she screamed again, pointing and insisting that it was him. He looked around him uneasily when he noticed that a lady dressed in white muslin was watching them.

'Hush your hollering,' he whispered, 'leave off screaming. Do I look dead to you? Look, it's me,' he said and he put the fur hat on. He told her not to give way to her fancies, there were folks about, fine folks. 'What must they be thinking?' he asked and when she looked up, there was Sir Richard.

If it wasn't for him she would go crazy, Jenny thought, quite crazy, and she concentrated on what Nathan had to say.

When she looked for him next Sir Richard was gone.

The girl was safe, best to leave her now. She had the young man Nathan by her side. Even if he looked a bit on the mean side for all his handsome looks it was best to leave it, best not to interfere, he thought; but the crowd held him fast, and he was forced to linger.

He turned for a last look.

He saw the young man who was hard and cold as if tenderness was a stranger to him. The girl looked at the young man and her face was that of a sleeping child rudely yanked out of a warm bed.

'Father Bernard is dead,' she said and Nathan said good riddance and Amen to that, and he thought he would be even more pleased if that fine rider of Jenny's took a turn for the worse.

'Look after her,' he had said when they found her. Dishing out his orders, he was, and what's more, Nathan had obeyed him unthinkingly. 'Yes, Sir,' he said, 'I surely will.'

Nathan had told him that they would head back to Jenny's village, Ninewells in the shires of Cambridge and get wed properly.

Get wed properly. It wasn't too late, the watcher thought. He would follow her like he always did, but this time he would follow from the front, he thought, when he heard Jenny say that she thought it was a long way off, the village.

She was leaning close to the wall for support and trying to get hold of her words.

'The village,' she said, and she didn't think she could walk it again.

'Couldn't we get there some other way, Nathan?' she

asked listlessly when a scruffy old man approached them. He looked around him uneasily, but the unknown lady who had given him some money to see to these young people had vanished.

Might as well make the most of it, he thought.

If they had some money to part with he knew of a coach going Cambridge way, he whispered to Nathan. A lady in white had told him of the very coach, and she had given him a guinea to arrange it and keep it to himself, which was of no trouble to him.

Nathan said he had no money, leastways not for riding on coaches. That money in his belt around his body was for his new start; in any case, Jenny knew nothing of it.

All the same, they travelled on a coach. Half as far as Cambridge, and they rode outside, as they had been told to by the old man.

It was Parson's wife's guinea which paid for the journey.

'What a coincidence,' said the old man when Jenny took her boot off and showed him her guinea. 'That's the exact money for the fare.'

To ride inside a coach was more than that, far more, although the fine lady riding inside the coach paid nothing because it was her own coach; that was the way of fine ladies like Squire's Daughter.

It had been a bad sort of a day for many people, but a scruffy old man had made a handsome profit. Most handsome. Two guineas' clear profit but it wasn't dishonest, or a hanging matter. He had seen them on the coach like he had promised. Nothing had been said about the pair of them not paying.

All in all, a good day was had what with the hanging and the murder, and then the profit of course. Life wasn't all that bad at times if you made the most of it.

Chapter 38

As Jenny and Nathan rode away from the town, Nathan too thought they had a good bargain. Tightly wedged by the side of the coachman, they left the stench of London behind and rode into the sweet air of the country.

Jenny leaned this way and that way along with the coachman, although parts of her body seemed to have a life of their very own. She was shaking and shivering as if she had a fever, although the fevered life sprang from a cold well deep inside her.

Would she ever feel warm again?

Her lips were moving as if she was telling some involved tale and her teeth were chattering as if it was a cold, frosty morning and her just out of a warm bed, and her poor hands were fluttering so that she hid them under her cloak.

'I don't feel well, Nathan,' she said after a while, 'I think I'll be sick shortly,' but Nathan would hold no truck with it. How did she think he felt? He had a bump the size of an egg on his head and he had his own worries.

'Did you think of looking for my saddlebag in the fire?'

Jenny admitted unhappily that she had not, and Nathan reminded her that she was not the only person in the whole wide world, but try as she might, she couldn't think of anything else.

The ride was bumpy and the road was full of potholes and sometimes there was no road at all. The horse's sweaty smell filled her nose, and she felt an ominous tickling in her throat. She knew she would be sick very shortly as she tumbled off the coach with Nathan after her.

'I'll find a safe place to be sick, Nathan.'

She tried to talk as clearly as she could, no need to make a fuss, and then she disappeared into the bushes.

Squire's Daughter was getting out of temper with the potholes and the stopping. The memory of being stopped the last time lingered, and the memory of it was humiliation.

Her jewellery had been yanked off her by nothing more than a pretty lad, and it had been the start of a greater humiliation, her weakness.

Until then, she had been fit for anything, but now she was getting weaker by the minute and she longed to be home.

Her Companion had reported that Lord Bennet had taken an interest in a young couple unknown to her, but also that he had installed a young man to ride in front as a guard.

She looked out of the carriage window to see why they had stopped this time. If it was hangers-on once more, her coachman would get a roasting and then she saw a pretty girl in a blue cloak.

There seemed to be something familiar about the sweep of the round cheek and long eyelashes but she couldn't quite put a name to the face.

'I'll find safe place to be sick, Nathan.'

A clear young voice.

'I'll find me a safe place for the night.'

A clear young voice.

Well, well, well, the devil looked after his own after all, she thought.

'You have done very well,' she said to her Companion, 'you have brought me the young girl who overlooked us in our worship.'

What was Lord Bennet's connection with the girl, she wondered. No matter, she thought, if the devil looked after his own, it might be best to give him a helping hand.

She rapped sharply at window. The young man turned round and looked at her. Then he yanked his hat off and grinned.

An unpleasant young man, she thought, but no matter, it was the girl she was after, although he might be the means to an end.

Jenny was still heaving her guts up in the bushes as Nathan talked to the lady.

Squire's Daughter she was, she told him. Wasn't that the child that had gone missing from the village, Jenny, causing such grief to her parents?

'It isn't right that families should be split asunder,' she said.

She gave him a guinea and told him to rest the girl up at the coaching inn in Cambridge, the one over the river crossing, her coachman would know it.

In the morning, there would be one of her carts going to the village which would be empty after the market.

They could catch a lift and she, Squire's Daughter, would see to it that he would be well set up with the girl.

They thought a lot of Jenny in the village, and she seemed to think a lot of him as well, Nathan thought.

He had smiled at her and likely she was no different from other maids and women giving him the eye. She might do him a power of good, he thought, and then he turned to Jenny who had finally stopped being sick.

It had been an awful business this time with her stomach heaving up the apple she had eaten that morning. She didn't bother to straighten up when she came out of the bushes and she saw Nathan through the red and rheumy eyes of an old woman.

Strangely enough, she saw clearly through these old

eyes.

She heard what Squire's Daughter said to Nathan and she thought she might as well have given in that night and gone into the graveyard.

She caught a glimpse of the other lady in the coach and Jenny recalled the bells at midnight.

The Companion!

It was her who had rung the bells. Her hood had fallen from her face when she came out of the church door and joined the hooded figures.

Jenny had fled from them and now her flight had never been and she had been betrayed by the one into whom she had put her trust.

She couldn't run away again, she knew that, and now she would be clear and free to do their bidding.

'Here I am and do your worst,' Jenny should have said, and she would say it now.

Chapter 39

Jenny had started to walk towards Squire's Daughter when a sharp pain in her hand stopped her; she looked down to see what this new pain might be. Drops of blood fell from her hand from the cross Father Bernard had given to her. She had held it tight to her body so it wouldn't get soiled when she was sick.

She had clutched it so hard that it had cut into her hand.

As she straightened up, she heard a soft snorting. When she looked ahead she saw the dark outline of a rider and horse.

Her back was straight now and there was a certainty to her step, although it had been a near thing, she thought.

She stopped her slow advance towards Squire's Daughter and hastily climbed back next to coachman when she saw a white hand beckoning to Nathan.

'Is she chaste?' Squire's Daughter whispered, at least he thought that's what she had asked. And he had nodded. Is she chaste, he thought. As pure as a newborn babe.

'Keep it so!' she commanded.

It was a funny sort of question to ask, he thought as he climbed up next to Jenny.

'Get them paws off me,' she said when Nathan tried to put an arm around her.

'You tell him, my girl,' said the coachman, 'he ought to look after you a bit better, you look right poorly,' but Nathan would hold no truck with it and told him to see to his business which was driving a coach and not interfering in other folks' private affairs which he knew nothing about.

'Nose,' he said, 'business,' tapping the side of his

nose.

How did she think he felt, he asked, turning to her.

He had a bump the size of an egg on his head and he had his own worries.

'As I said, did you think of looking for my saddlebag in the fire,' but Jenny didn't admit unhappily that she had been too late this time, instead she coolly told him to look after his own things better in the future if he didn't want to lose them.

'All those promises already broken,' she sighed, and then all hell was let loose.

The coachman said that it appeared that promises and pie-crusts were likely the same to Nathan, made to be broken.

'I don't have to listen to this idiotic village gibberish,' said Nathan, 'do I?'

'As a matter of fact you don't,' said the coachman, he wouldn't force his company on him, and the coach stopped. Nathan was thrown off, but he wasn't too put out, giving the lady a cheery wave as he ran around and after the coach.

He didn't mind it at all, there was no point in Jenny being sick all over him. Instead he thought about the lady; now there was beauty and wealth, if she wanted to do him some good maybe as head-groom at her stables, he wouldn't go against it, he thought as the coaching inn's comfort beckoned to him in the evening. A few mugs of ale in male company wouldn't get in the way of upstairs.

'Look after her,' said the coachman before they parted company.

'Just who do you think you are, a coachman, telling *me* what to do?'

'What makes you think they can run to a coachman? I am the groom, and this coach is a coach'n'four driven by only two horses.'

So, the lady was a big fish in a small pond, it made no difference to him, Nathan thought, clutching his guinea which would pay for their night and some ale.

Chapter 40

Jenny was in bed. She thought the hour was early, but she had no choice, her legs had finally buckled under her.

She laid in a fine bed with clean linen, and the maid brought her some food up on a tray. Afterwards, she reclined like a fine lady in her white shift.

Like a corpse got ready for the burying, she thought, but when she crept out of bed on unsteady legs to wash and brush her hair she had looked into the looking glass.

She had lived at such an intense rate that she had quite expected Father Time to have taken away what Mother Nature had given to her in the first place.

She had felt so old throwing up in the bushes that she had forgotten youth, but instead of the old crone's reflection she confidently expected to see reflected in the mirror, a lovely young face looked back at her gravely and she had been amazed.

'Have you finished, My Lady?' said the maid.

Her hands were grimy from seeing to the fires and she wore her mobcap to keep her hair clean.

Jenny looked at her own hands like white butterflies and as idle. At first she had thought there was somebody behind her when the maid said My Lady.

Nathan was downstairs talking to the other lads, having some ale and she was glad he was not with her. She felt so well now that he was bound to say she had made too much of it.

She touched the cross that Father Bernard had given to her.

What would she do now if the fair rider didn't turn up, she thought when she remembered the dark outline of horse and rider.

She was glad that she looked lovely, but it wasn't right that she should be abed before nightfall.

After a while she wondered where he was.

After another while she practised her expressions.

She would fake slumber and on waking up she would give him a great big smile, but when she practised it, to her surprise the smile was followed by a great shuddering sob. Smiles and tears were so close there was no telling what would come next.

Later there was a persistent creaking of floorboards outside her room, and finally she shouted to come in whoever it was, not like a lady at all.

The door opened and the rider came in at long last.

He looked about him and his air of authority had vanished with the diminishing light of day.

He had no right to complain about the window left open in this room. He looked at the yawning mouth of the fireplace, there should have been a fire roaring away on a damp night like this. There was only one candle by her bedside throwing out a feeble light, whilst the candles in pairs on the walls were cold and unlit.

He walked over to the window and from the fading yellow light there came a gust of wind setting curtains billowing.

In the yard below puddles laid with straw and floating dirt and he felt like shouting at the grooms who were larking about. He would have liked to bang their heads together like flints until the sparks flew.

It wasn't their fault that horses were looked after well and that one who came in from the road with only a bundle got the bare minimum.

Jenny had been a pretty child out of the rain when he had first seen her by the roadside, but now she was a golden woman with the glow of summer about her.

Finally he perched on her bed.

He took hold of her hand and she stopped practising what she should be or say.

'Thank God you are here. I don't know what I should do without you. Nathan is downstairs with the lads. Just tell me who you are, I don't know what to do next.'

His intentions towards her were honourable, he said, first things first. She was to let him know all about herself, how she came to be on the road.

Even as he said it he cursed himself for a pompous old fool.

His words fell like clods of earth from a grave-digger's spade, but never had he met a maid or a woman who made him feel so inadequate.

'Where to start,' she said.

It didn't take long to tell it, although it had seemed a long time to live it.

The Parson's wife and the flight. The graveyard and Squire's Daughter and Nathan. Mother and Father at the inn. The Diggers and Rose. Father Bernard and the hanging.

He got the picture well enough, he said, and then he went downstairs.

'Free ale,' he said to the landlord.

'Who for?' said the landlord.

'For those who want it,' he said and looked in Nathan's direction.

When the landlord said a wink was as good as a nod to a blind horse, he controlled himself quite well, They had to have enough time to talk, the girl and he, and he thought that some of what he had to say would hurt her.

'Are you wed to Nathan, Jenny?'

She said she didn't know.

She agreed that most folk would know if they were wed or not, sitting up now with her rounded chin held in her hand.

She wasn't like most folks, she said, but she wished

269

she was.

This was not Father Bernard, who was a holy man whatever Nathan's feelings were on the subject. She supposed this man sitting on her bed who made her feel as if she was worth knowing, was what might be called a suitor.

Whatever he was or was not, she felt alive; she always had when he had been about.

The Ranter, it seemed, had performed some sort of a ceremony, but they was not promised in the sight of God and they were not entered on the Parish, Jenny and Nathan.

'I haven't laid with Nathan yet,' she said after a while. 'He was disappointed,' she said but it didn't seem right. The ceremony itself had seemed unreal to her. 'I didn't say 'Aye.'

He knew all about Ranters and Baptists and Anabaptists and Quakers, they flourished like fool's corn and, like fool's corn, their seed would fall to the ground and nothing could grow from it.

He said that the Presbyterians themselves were altogether too familiar with God, he was a Laudian who held the view that God should be worshipped in the beauty of holiness, but Laud, like his King, had been beheaded.

She said that Father Bernard, who had walked in the beauty of holiness, ought not to lay in a pauper's grave, but he said he had talked to the Militia men and they would give him a decent burial, for payment, of course.

'He was good to you and he deserves it,' he said, and a weight fell off her mind.

'He gave me this cross,' she said, 'isn't it amazing?'

So it was. A wonderful shape, encrusted with rubies and diamonds.

'Where did he come from?'

'Spain, I believe he was a Catholic.'

'Somebody high up, who was brought low down. It happens.'

'Tell me something now,' he said and his face was stern and serious, 'why do you cleave to him? Why do you not leave him?'

'Nathan, you mean. He stuck by me and looked after me when I knew he didn't love me like I was. He might love me if I was different, but he won't because I can't. He betrayed me, and now I'm clean out of courage if it wasn't for you.'

She sighed.

'That inn, it must have looked awful and mean to you. You likely have a large house with many rooms and servants. Maybe even two houses.'

He had.

'You might even have servants who open the door for you.'

He said he still recognised a door if he saw one.

'You wouldn't know about the feeling you get when you don't know where you are heading for and can't go back where you came from. There is a lot of shame for being on the road and homeless even if it's not your fault.'

He didn't know about it yet, he thought, but he would shortly.

'My fancies that Nathan hated, they kept me going. The signs from the Bible, weeping for Stray when he was still alive. The dream. When the lads carried me off to rape me and Father Bernard died, well, I couldn't have coped at all if I hadn't lived it before.'

And then it was his turn to tell all, although he said there wasn't much time left to them, Nathan would be up shortly.

'What do you know about the aristocracy?'

'There's them,' said Jenny, 'and there's us,' and he laughed long and loud, and his laughter finally had an excuse. It had bubbled up in him from the minute she had said, oh so gravely, that Nathan had been disappointed that she hadn't laid with him, and finally he turned to his life.

He was a widower, he had one son. His wife had died giving birth to a still-born girl more than ten years ago. His son blamed him, and since then, had done everything to oppose him, including choosing the opposite side in the civil war.

Jenny saw it in her mind's eye; a lovely lady, gracefully ruling a large house and then the birth and the death and the man broken-hearted riding and cursing in the wind.

Not at all. He was sad of course, how could he not be, he said, she had been a good mother and entertained well for him, but that it had been an arranged match to join the estates.

His father was the heir to a title, as he himself was.

Love hadn't entered into the arrangement, he had been twenty, and it hadn't blossomed. She had been spoiled, fond of gambling and card games.

'How about the son, has he come to his senses yet?' Jenny said.

As he had said, they had been on opposing sides in the civil war. He himself had supported Charles Stuart when he had raised his Standard to the Parliamentarian forces. His world had been turned upside down, a King appointed by God could not be put down, but his son defected to the other side.

She pictured it. The battle, the horses, the fighting. A man riding his lance, plunging it in deep and then kneeling by the side of a dead man. Father!

Although it had happened, his son had been too young to fight at the start of the Civil War, and he would never fight in the same battle as his son. Battles had to be organised and planned for well in advance. A suitable place had to be found and opposing armies had to be marched to this place at an arranged time.

'I fought in Burford under Byron but my son didn't,' he said, 'he fought at Marston, whereas I didn't.'

'I was on the losing side but my son wasn't. The estate is secure through him.'

He, not his son, had fought in the second Civil War after Charles I had escaped from Hampton Court. In his opinion, he had been allowed to escape, nobody really quite knew what to do with him when they had got him the first time. It was hoped he would go away, but then he had engaged with the Scots.

'Did you ever meet the king? And what was he like?'

He paused. Yes, he had been in his presence, he said. 'He was a quiet, thoughtful man. He adored his wife and his sons, and there was an aura about him, a certainty of his fate to be King, but bravely born when it was snatched away from him.'

All this was past history finding him out; it was no longer safe for him in this country. It had all changed with the succession. His son had arranged everything for him so nicely. A new identity, a trusty captain, and he would disappear forever. Not by trial and execution, there was honour in its horror, but he would disappear with a slit throat and be chucked overboard like a dead rat.

'If you marry me, you'll marry a plain man,' he said, 'we would go across the water and live a new life together as Mr and Mrs Bennet.'

Fleeing Royalists tended to go to the Netherlands, but he had heard of a place, deeply wooded, called the Alsace-Lorraine, where they would settle down to a simple life.

'A simple life, you wouldn't have a maid but you would have Linda to help you.'

As if she ever had a maid!

'We will have Linda, and also Barnaby, they're with me in this, and they're the best. I could go ahead and send for you when I have made a home fit for you, or you can leave with me on Sunday. We'll catch the early tide at Folkestone on Monday and cross the channel to Brittany.'

He was expected to sail from Dover to Calais on Wednesday.

'To be honest, I aim to take as much money with me as I can muster.'

Leaving England forever he had accepted, but a life of poverty was not for her if he could help it.

The threads all led to the village where her life had unravelled, and back in the village the threads would wind into an entity once more.

She would be able to make her choice then, he said, but by God, he would not go penniless if he could help it, and Jenny thought that nobody had insisted on him being a poor man, although she tried to suppress her rising mirth.

'Being poor is not that wonderful,' she said, distracted. She wanted to give him something for remembrance, but what? And then she remembered Mother's blue comb.

'For me?' he said. He was hard pushed to remember when someone had given him a present.

He took the pin out of his cravat.

'We have exchanged gifts,' she said, 'we are sweethearts now.'

'So we are,' he smiled at her. 'If you decide to ride away with me, would it be fitting for you to sit in front and for me to have my arms around you?'

'Entirely fitting,' she said.

'What makes you so fair?' he asked, leaning forward and she leaned towards him to say that she was not fair enough for him, but instead they kissed. A long, long kiss, and their bodies were connected only by the kiss.

Jenny was floating and she liked it, she loved it, she was normal after all and she knew why it was called sky-larking now, her heart was beating like the little larks in her hand had when she had gleaned after the reapers.

They pulled apart when they heard creaking floorboards.

'Where is it likely you will meet?'

"Well,' she said,' Ma and Pa and Adam and Parson and Parson's wife and Squire's Daughter and her Companion, that'll be in Church. On Sunday.'

'If you decide to come with me now and not join me later, come out when the organ is playing.'

At one time she would have said she couldn't do that because his son's side had ripped the organ out, but now she didn't. She knew that he wanted the moment to be special.

'Come into the church,' she said, 'and sit by my side.'

'My name is Richard, what is yours?'

'Bashiba,' she said, and Nathan burst through the door.

Chapter 41

'Has he been about then, your fine rider?' Nathan asked as he fell into the room.

The night was full of mysteries and he had thought there was a shadow lurking on the stairs; besides that, he had seen that chestnut horse of his, although not stabled. 'He's not staying the night, that's for sure,' he said, 'but he's about, that you may depend on,' and as Jenny airily said that he was full of fancies, she was trying hard not to look at his Lordship's boots sticking out from under the screen.

In the hunt, Lord Bennet was used to becoming part of a tree. With the deer down-wind of his scent, he would remain undetected; the adrenalin caused by panic could not spill into the blood and spoil the meat.

He was part of the screen, down-wind of Nathan and it would be best if it remained so. Their life together might be spoiled before it had even started if he was found with her. They would be forced to ride off together into the night and force had neither a right nor a part to play in their lives.

Could be worse, he thought, but not much. He might be under the bed breathing in the dust of the ages, and it had crossed his mind to take a dive. He hardly dared to take a breath, but he need not have worried, Nathan was overcome by the cross twinkling away on Jenny's chest.

'Wherever did you get that cross from? he said. 'I have never seen the like before,' and then he belched. 'That must be worth a lot of money, it's fairly enc... it's fairly encursted with diamonds.'

'Encrusted,' said Jenny, 'and you will not get your hands on it. Father Bernard gave it to me and it is going to be buried alongside of me.'

She glared at him, trying to keep his attention, although she was in deadly earnest. 'You understand? That cross is going with me to my grave.'

'Let me know where that is,' said Nathan, and when Jenny glanced at the screen, the boots had gone.

The door closed softly and Nathan was maudlin with the ale. He talked about Squire's Daughter a great deal, how beautiful and how good she was.

She had been right, Jenny thought, he was full of fancies, but she was biding her time and biting her tongue. She pretended to be fast asleep when he put out his arms for her.

'Jenny for short,' he said, and she sank her teeth into his hand like an old polecat. A large, red drop of blood welled up on his finger and her anger evaporated as fast as it had come on her.

'That looks like the ring Squire's Daughter lost in the robbery,' she said calmly, hanging onto her cross, and Nathan looked up.

'What robbery?'

'Amazing,' he said after she had told him, 'I wonder what became of the jewels?'

The thought of all that wealth nearly set him dribbling, Jenny thought, although she herself hadn't set much store by it.

In any case, it didn't belong to them. Somebody had already been hanged for taking it.

'Well,' she said, 'Gideon left the jewels on the table when he fled and I put them in my pocket, the one in the skirt Mother gave me at the inn. Only you told me never, ever to mention her again, remember, so I didn't when I found them. I planted the pearls and gold in the forest.'

'Gold?'

'For her hair.'

'Of course,' said Nathan.

'How about the ruby,' he whispered after a while.

'Well, 'she said and she yawned a great yawn of pearly white teeth, 'I looked at the ruby and then a red deer came along and sniffed at it.'

'Of course,' said Nathan, 'and then the deer gobbled it up and said can I have some more, please,' and Jenny gave him a tired look.

'Then you called me and I put the ruby in my pocket. And you said what was I smiling for and I was smiling because of the deer.'

She was beginning to feel exhausted.

'I put it into the pocket of my blue dress this morning.'

Was it only this morning?

'Which dress, is it that one over the screen?'

When he went over to investigate, he mumbled something about boots. He had thought her boots had stuck out from under the screen when he came in, but they weren't there now. Then he fell over them and Jenny enquired sweetly about the amount of ale he had supped.

He said he would take the dress to the window, maybe he could see it better there.

'Moonlight will help me,' he said, 'and why don't you go to sleep? I don't aim to wake you, besides, somebody likes you chaste.'

He hiccupped and said to forget that, and after a long while he came to the bed. He said there was nothing in the pocket, and the ruby must have been lost.

'What you never had you never miss,' said Nathan, and Jenny didn't know if he was talking about the ruby or himself.

Chapter 42

Why aren't there any chairs in this chamber? Nathan grumbled. He left the room and returned with a hard-backed chair, as if he had not spent most of his life sleeping on the ground. He slumped in it, dozing off with his hands in his pockets.

When he awoke, he said he had a crick in the neck, but he never complained about it although he talked about his breakfast.

The man from the village drove home from market in a sunny mood.

He was halfway home and his head was a bit sore from the ale the night before, but it had been a good night all told.

Staying away for a night would need some explaining when he got home, but there was no arguing with Squire's Daughter, everybody knew that. Besides, it had been a good evening full of strong ale and good company.

He didn't think it would be when She had come up to him earlier on, but it was only to tell him that he was to fetch two strangers along with him this morning. There were some that thought her beautiful. There were some that thought snakes were beautiful and she always put him in mind of a snake; poised and ready to strike.

If someone grabbed her around the neck like a snake and tamed her and squeezed the poison clean out t'would be another story but it was not likely to happen now, and him that got himself shot had never been the one to do it

Besides, she was getting a bit long in the tooth and t'was rumoured she was falling low to the dropsy like her mother had.

Like a large piece of furniture her mother had been, not able to get out of her room and pissing and shitting herself like a newborn.

He thought if that happened to Her he wouldn't want to be the one to look after her, she was an evil one to cross.

It was good to have a stranger to talk to now and then, like the young man. Very clean he had looked, the young man. Very handsome, with blue and distant eyes, and then he thought there was something missing from the cart.

He turned his cart around.

Nathan was not best pleased to be kept waiting and Jenny was all for walking. She felt refreshed and full of hope and joy, and they were no strangers to it.

The innkeeper had behaved in an odd way, to say the least.

He had brought their breakfast and when he put the dish of bacon down in front of her he winked, slowly and deliberately as he looked sideways at Nathan, time after time.

Is there something wrong with your eyes, she was about to say, when she recalled the visit she had whilst Nathan was drinking below, and she blushed.

The innkeeper's wife wiped her hands on her apron in the doorway and the maid scuttled in to get the dirty dishes, and an old man carried some logs upstairs. All and sundry stopped their tasks and stared at her and thought she was no better than she ought to be, but finally the cart rumbled up.

Nathan's drinking companion raised his hat to the lady in the blue cloak; he recognised Jenny and so he should. He was Caleb, a close neighbour of her Pa.

He turned to Nathan.

'You best get in the cart with the dog.'

When Nathan pointed out that the dog had four legs over his two as far as walking was concerned and so had the advantage, Caleb said the dog was used to riding home in the empty cart.

'He allus rides, and you best mind your manners with him. He's a bit of a loner, that dog,' and the dog growled in agreement.

'Grrrrr.'

'And Grrrrr bloody Grrrrr to you,' said Nathan.

The dog seemed to recognise a kindred spirit and Nathan wished that the dog had not taken a liking to him. It was a brown dog with big jaws and it slobbered all over him.

'T'is a one-man kind of a dog, it only ever bites me.'

'Ha, ha, ha,' said Nathan whilst Caleb laughed heartily at his own joke.

'Isn't that Stuttering Jim's dog?' Jenny asked and Caleb said it was his own since Jim had passed over.

'What did he die of?' asked Jenny. She was about to ask Caleb who had killed Jim when it occurred to her that it might still be possible for people to die peacefully in their beds.

'He died of living,' said Caleb, and added that he had found Jim in the road, dead as a doornail.

'The beast slobbered all over me, as I fended it off. I said 'k... k... keep... aawway... frommmm... mee,' and I reckon the dog thought I was stuttering like his old master had done and attached hisself to me.'

'A likely tale,' muttered Nathan.

'Aye, maybe, but likely tales help to while away darker hours.'

'I lost my dog, Stray, you may recall him,' Jenny said, and Caleb was not surprised.

'He went a-missing same time as you.'

He whistled sharply and the horse started its slow trot towards Ninewells, and Jenny at last gave in to the luxury of thinking of her kin.

'Your Ma and Pa will be pleased to see you no doubt.'

They were free-holders now, it seemed and Pa was building up his herd.

'Started on a barn, separate like, as well.'

Parson Wilcox, and especially Parsons' wife, had been very good to them.

'Parson's wife has been very good to them?'

'See. You and your fancies,' said the old flea-riddled dog from the back of the cart; any rate Jenny wished it had been him and not Nathan.

Parson's wife had also been good to Sidney and his Ma and Pa.

'Sidney?' she yelled.

Wasn't he dead? she thought.

What reason he possessed had fled overnight, Caleb said, some of it had come back, but not his speech, although he now grasped that boots went on his feet and his hat on his head.

'After a few weeks had gone by,' said Caleb

'Your Aunt Kate returned one day, clean out of her mind, and Parson's wife insisted on looking after her. Quite a trial Kate is, and your Ma would have had her work cut out with that one.'

She thought she would believe in Parson's wife's goodness when she saw it, but there was more; Parsons' wife had become a veritable saint in Jenny's absence. When Joshua's widow died, she had taken the three orphans to her bosom, so to speak.

'A rare treat it is to see 'em all in the Parson's pew on a Sunday, all well-behaved and spruced up, and baby Jessica of course. She's a rare treasure, that one.'

Jenny was speechless. Are we talking about the same Parson's wife, she thought, the one who had chased her off into the night?

'I was hard pushed to believe it myself,' said Caleb. 'I'll be putting you down where the south-meadow's barn used to be. It was burned down by travellers, so they say.'

She knew where it was.

'Good directions they give you,' muttered Nathan, 'how can you tell where something used to be?'

Caleb drove off, safe in the knowledge that Squire's Daughter would sort this one out good and proper. The departing dog whimpered from the back of the cart for Nathan. He was that pleased and flattered but he wouldn't admit to it, of course. In the end they both laughed about it.

The light in Nathan's eyes, the light she had seen that night when they were dancing around the fire, was back. She had read it wrong. It was the light of friendship, not love, and it went out as fast as it had appeared.

Ma and Pa and Adam were out when they reached her cottage. It seemed small, but comfortable. The stairs on the right, to the left the table and chairs against the window, a jar with daisies on the sill, the cooking pot on the fireplace.

After a while, Jenny thought she would go and see how Parson Wilcox fared and find out the truth about the saintly Parson's wife!

Jenny would be able report to the Parson that she had made it in the great big world outside with her mind intact, unlike the great, lumbering lad who had stayed in the village and who now tapped her on her shoulders when they were half-way there.

'Sidney!' she cried. 'My Sidney!'

'Aye,' he said, tearing his hat off and holding it against his chest, grinning.

Jenny,' he said, 'Parson,' and he lumbered off,

clapping his hat back on and holding her hand.

The house looked just the same, the old willow tree as askance, roses rambling and blushing as lush against the porch and the little leaded windows, the path to the door as lined with blue lavender and alive with butterflies and bees.

Nathan sat against the willow as she followed Sidney who was banging against the door.

What if Parson's wife opened the door to her? she thought. It wasn't her but the Parson who tugged at it frantically and shouted for whoever it was not to go away, just as he had always done.

Sidney tore his hat off, grinning, when it finally opened, and pointed at Jenny.

'Look, Parson,' he said proudly, pointing to her. 'Must tell Ma,' and he took off.

'A miracle,' cried the Parson, 'Sidney has spoken and Jenny has returned,' opening his arms wide, 'now I can die happy and in peace.'

She wiped her eyes.

`'I hope you were not thinking of dying.'

'Not just yet,' he cried, 'I have my sermon to prepare afore I do.'

'May I ask you not to write aught special, I would just like to pretend that tomorrow is like any other ordinary Sunday.'

There was something she wanted to ask him.

'I have been fretting about not walking on the straight and narrow road, but now I think it might be like an example,' and he said it was so, a spiritual road, but he never asked her if she had kept to it, it was a miracle that she had come through, he said.

'The miracle is that I have met with so much kindness and help on the road by so many strangers,' she said.

'You have found charity on the road, God be

praised,' he said, 'unlike your Aunt Kate, God help us all.'

'The masterless men in the forest killed James over a pewter mug,' she said, but a kindly man set her on the road to Ninewells.

He took her to the window, and there was the Mistress, looking younger somehow and wearing a white cap, bending over a thin, white-haired woman sitting in a chair, and there was Agnes, Sidney's Ma, and an awful lot of boys running around.

Their little blessings, and Kate was their big cross, the Parson said, but he also had a minor kind of miracle of their own making right here on his patch.

'Come now and see the little miracle upstairs.'

When she did, she saw that a small landing led right to the back bedroom, and that all the bedrooms had doors leading off from it.

'Had to do something,' said the Parson, 'with so many people in the house now,' and the first bedroom - partitioned off now - was barely big enough to hold the four-poster bed and the big, intricately carved wooden chest next to it.

'She's a lively child, is Jessica,' he said proudly, waving at the box, 'so much so that we had to take the rockers off the cradle at three months, less than that.'

The babe was fighting against the confines of its swaddles and the bonnet had slipped in her struggles and covered her face. When Jenny gently put her straight, little Jessica smiled at her. It had been such a wide smile and she had such merry brown eyes the likes of which Jenny had rarely seen before, that sudden unshed tears stung her eyes.

Why do I feel like crying again? she thought.

'There,' he said proudly, 'what do you think? How is it that I have such a wonderful child?'

'I cannot think,' she said dryly.

'Why, Jenny, is that irony? I can see that you are quite grown up now.'

'Not quite yet, but I shall be presently, just as soon as I make up my mind on some matter.'

She walked back to the window.

Below Old Agnes and the Mistress seemed to have locked horns in battle with Kate, staring at her with their hands on their hips, the Mistress's face puckered in bewilderment.

'Kate was in a dreadful state, terribly afraid of men, understandable now you have told me,' said the Parson, 'tearing her clothes off at the slightest excuse and howling at the sky. When we finally got her out of it she started swearing, cursing, such language, and we have the boys to consider now, but the worst of it is that she has taken such a liking to Jessica. I shudder to think what that child's first words will be.'

More than likely Jessica would sit up in her cradle and tell her father to sod off and call him a misbegotten black-hearted bastard, Parson said and laughed, but what they were doing below was giving Kate lessons in speech, 'Thank you kindly', 'not just at present', that sort of thing.

'We can cope, and we will cope gladly, we have a lot to atone for, the Mistress and I,' he said mysteriously, for Jenny thought that the Mistress had to but not he, and she resisted the invitation to meet her; the turn-about was too much to take in.

'I'm not ready to face her yet,' she said, 'thank you kindly, not just at present,' and they both laughed again.

Nathan waited for Jenny under the willow, wondering, as always, what sort of folks Jenny had got herself mixed up with.

They were some way off Emily's cottage when Jenny saw a figure emerge, carrying a basket and swinging an empty milk jug. The figure walked quickly ahead of them and Jenny just walked on and looked at her Ma.

'This is my Ma,' she thought, 'this is my Ma,' and she savoured the moment which she had thought would never come again.

'How's your Aunt?' said her Pa.

How was her Aunt?

Who was her Aunt?

'Ma's sister in Southwark.'

Jenny was amazed to find how fast old events had been wiped out by new happenings and her Pa realised she had never got there. It had been a sort of fantasy that Jenny had got safely to her aunt, and gradually the fantasy had become reality, so the whole village believed it now.

Brother Adam had grown. He was overcome with joy when he saw her. Would you believe it, Jenny had brought his best reed back! It nearly got burned, Jenny told him, and nearly got itself stolen as well.

Adam thought of the night when he was told to make a nuisance of himself when the figures of menace had looked everywhere for Jenny. He was going to say he was mighty glad they hadn't found her when it dawned on him that he was in great danger of being hugged to death by a girl of all things, and he couldn't live with that.

'Fancy being kissed by nothing but a maid,' he shuddered.

'Fancy,' said Nathan, ruffling Adams' hair, and for some reason, everybody laughed.

Pa was pleased with what he thought of as Jenny's young man.

He was getting settled in the village with Jenny, Nathan said, and he had got some money in a belt around his body.

'Yesterday you told me you had no money, Nathan,' Jenny said teasingly, and her Pa tapped his nose and winked at Nathan and said it didn't do to let women know too much.

No good would come of it.

It was dark outside when she talked with her Ma. Pa and Nathan were talking with the conspiratorial air men have about them, even if they only discuss a sick pig.

The Bible was once more in its place on the table and Jenny recalled the Sheriff's man commenting on Pa's fine hand. Ma said that the Parson afore this one had been a saintly man who had taken her Pa's learning in hand. He had been a sickly child, it didn't surprise Jenny, but something else needed an explanation, something that had struck her the minute she had walked into the door. Not the alterations and the comfort, but her Ma.

She didn't seem so bent now and she didn't peer at things as closely as she used to. Her eyes must be better and her Ma said that they were.

'An awful lot better. I cried so many nights after you left, Jenny, I reckon I cried something clean away from my eyes.'

The business with Parson's wife had been a bit of luck. Well, they had made their own luck and some would call it sin money, and Jenny thought of Mother at the inn. If a body aimed to breathe in after breathing out, did honesty figure in it?

Whatever you might call it, they aimed to repay Parson for every penny. With no rent to pay and fresh livestock, it wouldn't take that long either.

'I heard about that, you're building up a herd.'

'Let us call it one more cow,' Ma said, but that was village gossip for you.

.What it meant first off, her Ma said after she had

told Jenny how they had got hold of Parson's confessional, was that Aggy was buried outside of God's grace, only it was nearly impossible to know where exactly outside God's grace was.

'She was buried in a hurry. Somewhere in one of the meadows, and you know the size of 'em.'

Only the Parson and the Parsons' wife thought they had found it and buried a crucifix and he said a prayer.

'Which is as good as.'

The past was the past, and her Ma said they would do something to put things right just as soon as Pa thought it was his own idea like.

'Right under Parson's wife's nose the papers are, where she grows her herbs. We're not asking for more money, the freehold is just wonderful and we can use the rent money as we please when the tax is paid, it's just in case.'

Parson's goodness to them had to be explained somehow and so Pa had taken to helping in the stable and the fields. Never went into the fields, Parson's wife didn't, she saw the wall only from above.

'He's right handsome, your Nathan,' Ma said after a while, 'I'm not saying any different, and I could get fond of him, but likely he'll need handling and I don't think you are the one to do it.'

And what about the business with Squire then?

Cook had said that night, when Jenny had left, Squire was brought back insensible. Covered in dirt he was. There was blood on his hands and the graveyard had been disturbed in the night.

'Cook had heard ghostly bells, same as me, and it makes you think, Cook had said and then she didn't think any more or talk any more or cook any more. Right as rain one minute and dead the next, choked on a bone.'

Jenny said some evil ceremony was taking place by

the church and she had witnessed it, but no more. Why should she burden her Ma with the memory of that awful night?

The shock of Squire's seizure that night had brought on her mother's illness in Squire's Daughter. Likely it was not helped by the shooting of her intended and losing her jewels.

Awful as it was, nobody shed a tear for either her or young Morrow.

'That illness of hers, that's just like her wickedness is. Always about her, not here one day and gone the next. And what I say is that no amount of conjuring up the devil will make her illness go away.'

Ma did know about it.

Jenny might not know about the robbery and not believe it either, but t'was nothing but the plain truth. John Morrow, her intended like, him that the children called Silk-breeches, had been murdered and Squire's Daughter had her jewellery taken right from her neck 'n ears.

'And her ring, the ruby, that ring she flaunted.'

'The ruby is in my pocket,' said Jenny, and she told her Ma how it ended up in there.

It seemed to be nothing but a story, just a tale told to her Ma, and it made her feel so comfortable and so safe to be in her own home with her own village all about her, but all the same she recalled the thin voice of the bells urging her on.

It was an illusion of safety and it all depended on that one in the mansion her Ma said, recounting events, and Jenny sifted the gold from the dross.

Father Morrow was elderly and his daughter had married and moved away, and the death of his son had brought on a low spirit. Squire was wanting, her Ma said, so that left only the Companion and the Daughter. Likely she would rear up one more time. Either involve

Jenny in their unholy goings-on, or - was it more likely? - silence her for good.

John was itching with uneasiness, recalling that Nathan had thought Squire's Daughter was good and that she would help him and Jenny to get on in the world.

'That one, help?' he had asked. 'Likely you don't know what happened to Jenny. Riding after her and turning the cottage upside down.'

At that the young man merely shrugged his shoulders; some young girls were like that, full of notions and fancies.

Full of notions indeed! Jenny was no safer now than she had been, Squire's Daughter's interest told him that, but he didn't want to worry Margret. Not today of all days, not now that Jenny was home once more, but he had to warn her in some way. He waited until he thought the youngsters were asleep.

He nudged Margret.

'That young man she brought back with her. No good will come of it.'

And she agreed with him, that was the wonder of it, but what she told him was even more wonderful.

'A Lord? A fleeing Royalist? Across the water. My God, she'll have to speak foreign like that companion Emily looked after.'

He couldn't take it in.

'Across the water? In a boat? On the sea? Isn't that dangerous?'

'So Jenny said. They have exchanged love tokens. He'll come for her tomorrow. She has to make up her mind whether to go with him or stay here until he sends for her.'

She paused.

'She says if she goes with him she'll send us a letter by messenger to let us know where she is.

A letter from across the water.
When had the world grown so small?

Chapter 43

Jenny for short had become a lonely traveller in a fog-ridden night.

She returned as Bashiba. She was eighteen, a grown woman and she returned in the golden glow of a mellowing September day. It was a fine morning and it would be hot. Not as hot as in Aggy's summer, the villagers said; Aggy was remembered as if all the summers belonged to her.

Church bells were ringing in merry competition with the singing birds, insects were buzzing over meadows as fragrant as newly baked bread.

Jenny had measured herself against the village's long meadow grass when she was little, against the bull-rushes of the fen-bogs and the wild cow parsley growing next to the pathless woods, and she had been in London with defeated city dwellers who had nothing of nature to measure themselves against.

There was the step to the cottage, and she remembered falling over it many a time.

She had been little then and quick, but now she walked slowly and upright like the others about to worship, and gradually joined the procession winding its way to the church.

Parson Wilcox was in front, black-gartered, his hands under the tails of his coat performing a merry dance. His wife kept her eyes on her child, and Old Agnes kept a watch on the three little orphaned boys, whilst the villagers looked silently and sideways at Jenny and the young man at her side.

Going to Church was a solemn business. Looking around and seeing what was going on was kept to before the service. Gossiping was kept for after, and everyone looked out for Emily. As Margaret's friend, she was sure to know all.

Jenny composed herself as befitted the entertainment of the day which would have to last for many an evening's fireside talk.

They reached the pond which lay green and still as if nothing had ever disturbed its cover of chickweed. The old elm brought down by lightning had been put to good use, it had made many a solid coffin; Jenny looked at its stump where she had been hiding, with half of her sticking out of it and her face covered in ashes.

That had been in the night and the church had looked dark and threatening. But now the doors were wide open welcoming God's good sunlight.

Ma and Pa, Nathan and Adam and Jenny walked slowly. It was fine to be a together as a family amongst families.

Pa said they would be in for a dose of the Prodigal Son for certain. He said jokingly that the last would be last if they didn't look out and hurried to church, but Nathan insisted that this wasn't right, the last would be first, it said so in the Bible.

Squire's Daughter was dressed all in green silk. She was sitting in the front pew next to her Companion.

Jenny and her family sat in the back pew as befitted the last of the cottagers joining the procession. The last were indeed the last and Nathan was trying to work it all out.

He had been mildly surprised when they had been dumped at the meadow, but then he could see that a cart was not fitting to turn up at the Manor.

He had thought that their place would be in front seeing he had brought Jenny home as the Lady Eloise had wished.

A hush fell on the congregation as Squire's Daughter turned round in her pew, and Jenny clutched Father

Bernard's cross in her anguish.

The Lady Eloise looked beautiful, from her hair curled and tied like bunches of grapes to her draped green sleeves, although her white hand bore no ruby as it rested lightly on the rail as she looked and looked at Jenny and Nathan with her shining eyes.

It was hypnotic, that green gaze, and Jenny's hand fell helplessly from her breast. The sun's rays struck Father Bernard's cross, its white reflected light mesmerising the lady.

As the sun moved onwards, it briefly illuminated the stained-glass window and bathed Jenny in St. Agnes's light, like it had when she had been little.

Squire's Daughter seemed to shrink in her pew. Her black eyes sank into a white face which had the look of a dough which was about to rise, and Nathan went to her, with never a look at Jenny.

She felt only pain for him. She had tested him that night at the inn with the ruby, and he had been found wanting. He had denied it, and with it herself.

She had owed him, but his lies had set her free.

He moved carefully towards Squire's Daughter, and he looked like an old man dancing to a long-forgotten tune, but nevertheless he went to the front with shining eyes like a bridegroom to his bride.

When she motioned him to go and sit with her servants he needed no prompting, he would always do her bidding

The villagers saw it all then and they understood. The young man was in Lady Eloise's service. He had been bidden to bring Jenny home and he had forgotten his place in life and in Church, which amounted to the same thing.

It was getting interesting.

The Parson in the pulpit cleared his throat.

'In his letter to the Corinthians,' he started, his

thumbs tucked in below the shoulders in his gown. He beamed at Jenny as he loomed confidently over his congregation and over the second pew where his wife sat with their child, never taking her eyes of it and their orphaned brood, and neither did Old Agnes.

'When I was a child, I thought as a child and understood as a child.'

He had an air of authority about him, and he was tall and he had oh, so manly a bearing and such looks with his fair hair and fine clothes, did the stranger, as he entered the Church. He looked about him, adjusting to the light, and then he sat down in the pew still warm from the young man.

Jenny looked at him and nodded. How could she bear to have that water, that single channel, between him and her, between their happiness?

He took off his hat. He looked past the girl and he bestowed a little bow on her Ma and then on her Pa.

They had to strain their necks a bit, did the villagers, but then they saw that Jenny and the stranger were holding hands and looking at each other.

'Now abide Faith, Hope and Charity, but the greatest of these is Charity.'

Jenny had sat by the beeches and looked in the Bible for a sign. She hadn't been able to trust in charity because she hadn't known its whereabouts, but now she knew charity had kept her safe, charity was in people's heart.

Through charity she was able to trust her love to the man by her side. They had found their sanctuary; it could be any place, just as long as they were together.

They left the church and he helped her up on his horse.

They rode to Jenny's home for her belongings, where Jenny spotted somebody waiting by her cottage.

It couldn't be, but it was.

'Rose,' she cried. 'How did you get here?'

'I took a coach to Cambridge and I walked here,' said Rose, 'and a great soft man took me here when I asked for you.'

Sidney.

'Are you ever getting off that horse?' Rose asked.

'I'd better, I've come for my things. This is Richard Bennet,' she said, pointing up to the rider who had helped her dismount. 'We're going across the water for a new life.'

'Most certainly,' said the rider.

When Rose said it was a pity there was no room on that horse for Jenny's best friend, he said they would send for her once they were settled.

'Stay here in the village,' said Jenny, 'my Ma will love you.'

That was what she had said about that weird couple at the inn, said Rose. Eli and the boys were welcomed with open arms but all she got was funny looks.

'And the last straw, I was sitting down, and the old man said, 'Get thee up and help Mother,' and he looked upon me with his mean eyes like my Pa did before I got a beating, so I took off.'

They went into the house together, where Jenny found her belongings bundled up; her Ma had known she would leave.

'My God, Jenny,' Rose cried, 'and where did you find him with the horse?'

He had found *her*, said Jenny, and she agreed that he was indeed the very model of a man to go across the water with.

'Nathan is here,' Jenny added, 'and he will need handling. He has a disappointment coming to him.'

'Of course.'

'Now I must go. Stay here, promise me, and we will

send for you.'

Rose promised. She watched them as they rode off together, the rider taking away her best friend, but it wouldn't be forever.

Epilogue

Nathan sat in the pew next to the de Brevilles' servants.

He had thought that Jenny and he would have a good place in the Manor, but that woman, Squire's Daughter, now she had turned out to be ugly and foul smelling close to.

He thought it likely that Jenny had been in danger from her. He would tell her so just as soon as they were on the road again, he knew all about the power of the rich.

He was rich himself now what with his money and that ruby, but was there any danger attached to it? But someone had already been hanged for it, like Jenny had said. How was a jewel like that disposed of, he thought, and then it came to him. He and Jenny could open an inn, you get all sorts in an inn, as he knew full well from his time spent as a groom.

The size of that ruby, and it had been in Jenny's pocket all of that time! It was in his pocket now, but he would tell her all that later, they had all the time in the world together. He had hardly believed it that night when his fingers had felt the lump in the material. He felt for the stone's reassuring presence, but when he brought it out and looked at it, it was indeed a stone, a large pebble.

He looked in Jenny's direction and he knew that he would never tell her anything again, she had eyes only for the man who was holding her hand.

He had come in last, and the last had been the first after all, like it said in the Bible.

They were singing away now, the folks standing up in their pews and he stood up and joined them. When he looked for Jenny, there was only an empty space next to her Ma, an empty space in his heart.

He couldn't imagine coming out of church without Jenny by his side, but he could imagine her with the fair rider on that chestnut horse, Blaze.

He imagined his future. An old man walking in the shadows, bent over, dying somewhere in the green wilderness, unknown, unloved and not mourned, but when he looked up, he looked at Jenny's Ma. She looked at him kindly and with compassion, so it needn't be like that. He would get it out of her where Jenny had gone and he would fetch her back. It was only right after all he had done for her.

When he emerged into the bright sun-light, all hell had broken loose, a hell which centred around the Lady Eloise and Parson's wife. Eloise was very agitated. Her Companion had sewn her into her dress that morning and the side-seams had started to split, showing bulging white flesh, her hair had began to uncurl and laid about her head like rats' tails, and worst of all, she had messed herself.

'You must have seen him,' she screamed at Parson's wife and then at her Companion.

'Lord Bennet came for me, he was in church, but he rode off with that girl instead.'

'Hush, Eloise, I haven't seen him since London,' said her Companion, who had had her doubts about allowing her charge into church that morning the state that she was in, and the Mistress had enough.

'Jenny has left the village some time ago,' she said to the Companion, 'ask Mistress Cooper, her Ma.'

Squire's Daughter saw Nathan lurking in the porch.

'There he is,' she screamed, 'ask him, look, in the porch.'

'Hush now, that isn't Lord Bennet, that's the young man riding guard on the coach,' her Companion said. When her charge started to scream that she knew that he wasn't Bennet, the Mistress told her to keep the

Lady Eloise confined to the Manor in future.

'She is a disturbed woman. She is no longer fit to be let out, look what she's doing to the babe, screaming fit to burst, and terrifying these little boys,' who were trying to hide behind and under her and Agnes's skirts.

'Is all well?' asked the Parson, coming to fetch his wife on the pony and trap. She assured him that it was.

'One mad-woman is quite enough for us to deal with, Matthew, let us hope Kate hasn't burned the house down in our absence.'

'Let us go home, my love,' he said.

'You preached a fine sermon this morning. I was surprised, I expected a sermon on the return of the Prodigal,' she said.

'I hoped to please Jenny, she said she found charity on the road.'

'Do you think now is the time to tell Mistress Cooper that little Joshua found the black box hidden in the wall? And that a leak in the box destroyed the ink on the papers?'

He thought about it.

'Maybe later,' he said, 'perhaps if they want something else from us, which isn't likely, or if they want to tell us where it is.'

He waved to the Coopers as the pony trotted past them.

Margaret listened as Nathan talked to Adam, passing on words of wisdom.

'Never love a maid; the things and the walking I have done for Jenny isn't to be believed.'

'Isn't it? Come along everybody,' Margret said, 'let us have ourselves a good dinner and wish Jenny well in her absence.'

'And who might that be?' asked Pa, pointing to a tall

and thin girl like a streak of lightning, waiting outside their cottage.

'Rose,' cried Nathan.

'Another of your sweethearts?' asked Adam.

'Not likely,' she cried.

'Perhaps he'll grow on you,' Pa suggested.

'Like a wart, I don't think,' she cried, while Nathan looked at her with a new appreciation.

She had backbone, had Rose, she wouldn't holler like Jenny when meeting a bit of bother, and, he stopped overcome with the truth of it, she harboured absolutely no fancies whatsoever.

'You can stop looking upon me like a moonstruck calf, Nathan Mason,' Rose said, but she smiled.

Moonstruck calf? thought Nathan. Me and Rose? With her so thin and pale and long like a stream of piss? Was it likely after Jenny?

'We know each other, me and Rose,' he said. If he waited long enough she would tell him where Jenny and the rider had gone. He would follow and find him, people did have accidents, fatal accidents, didn't they? He had to fight for what was his.

'I am here to help Mistress Cooper, if she wants me,' said Rose.

'Likely I do. Oh, Adam,' said Margret, 'can you run to the Parsonage and tell the Parson's wife what she is looking for is in the wall of the herb garden. And no sulking Pa, the time is right.'

Whilst Adam ran to the Parsonage, the Companion and Squire's Daughter wound their way towards the Manor on the trap.

The Lady Eloise went wearily into the hall.

Before she went upstairs, she paused in front of her mother's picture. Her mother had been like a large piece of furniture, not able to get out of her room, not able to even look at the painting of a slender girl in white pointing to a white rose, her beauty the varnished memory of a painting in a hall.

Eloise had fought against her fate as best she knew, but she had lost.

'Hang my portrait next to hers, will you,' she said ascending the stairs, 'I shan't come downstairs again.'

Ends.

Premise and some dates. Any mistakes are my own

The poor rely on the harvest for ale and bread, meat is salted down.

Time is measured by the sun and seasons. Candles and rush lights are used.

A renewed outburst of witch persecution in 1640s. Last witch executed in England in 1685.

Class apparent in clothes - Parsons, Lawyers.

Travel: Horseback and coaches for rich, walking for poor. Omens looked for.

Confessional diaries: Common, thought to take place of previous Catholic confessions.

1642: Charles I raises Standard to Parliamentarians.

1648: Second Civil War. Engagement between Charles and the Scots.

1649: Commonwealth. Execution of Charles I (January). House of Lords abolished (March).

1650:Digger Colony suppressed. Of the many sects flourishing in Cromwell's New Model Army, Levellers, Quakers, Ranters and Diggers, the Diggers proposed communal living and sharing property.

(Summer).Cromwell returns from Ireland (August). Fairfax resigns. Cromwell created Commander-in-Chief.

See Google:Charles I
Interregnum
Sects